ALSO AVAILABLE
FROM TITAN BOOKS

Conan: Blood of the Serpent

*Conan the Barbarian: The Official
Motion Picture Adaptation*

Conan: City of the Dead

Conan: Cult of the Obsidian Moon

SONGS OF THE SLAIN

Illustrated by Juan Alberto Hernández

TIM LEBBON

Titan BOOKS

CONAN: SONGS OF THE SLAIN
Hardback edition ISBN: 9781803365015
E-book edition ISBN: 9781803365022

Published by Titan Books
A division of Titan Publishing Group Ltd
144 Southwark St, London SE1 0UP

First edition: July 2025
10 9 8 7 6 5 4 3 2 1

This is a work of fiction. All of the characters, organizations, and events portrayed in this novel are either products of the author's imagination or are used fictitiously. Any resemblance to actual persons, living or dead (except for satirical purposes), is entirely coincidental.

© 2025 Conan Properties International ("CPI"). CONAN, CONAN THE BARBARIAN, CONAN THE CIMMERIAN, HYBORIA, THE SAVAGE SWORD OF CONAN and related logos, names and character likenesses thereof are trademarks or registered trademarks of CPI. ROBERT E. HOWARD is a trademark or registered trademark of Robert E. Howard Properties LLC. Heroic Signatures is a trademark of Cabinet Licensing LLC.

Interior illustrations by Juan Alberto Hernández.

Tim Lebbon asserts the moral right to be identified as the author of this work.

No part of this publication may be reproduced, stored in a retrieval system, or transmitted, in any form or by any means without the prior written permission of the publisher, nor be otherwise circulated in any form of binding or cover other than that in which it is published and without a similar condition being imposed on the subsequent purchaser.

A CIP catalogue record for this title is available from the British Library.

EU RP (for authorities only)
eucomply OÜ, Pärnu mnt. 139b-14, 11317 Tallinn, Estonia
hello@eucompliancepartner.com, +3375690241

Printed and bound by CPI Group (UK) Ltd, Croydon CR0 4YY.

A Promise in Death

Conan knew that he was about to die. As his breath stuttered and weakened and his body spasmed, he observed the approach of his enemies and prepared for his final act of furious defiance.

He squinted through the agonies wracking his body and skeins of bloody mist that still drifted across the battlefield, even though this battle was lost. Past the pain, beyond the mists, he glimpsed the victories, triumphs, and accolades he had once imagined his future might bring, and saw them fading away into stories untold. Barely twenty years old, he was not sad, but he did feel anger and frustration at himself for the mistakes that had brought him to here and now, readying to die in the blood-thickened slurry of a battlefield that few would ever remember.

Even as he'd marched on the wicked city of Shadizar with four thousand other sellswords, he'd harbored doubts about those who commanded the force and drove their plans. He should have listened to his instincts and done whatever he could to change their foolish tactics. Once engaged in battle, a slip here and a clumsy parry there had brought him his first injury, and he should have treated and bound the gash in his shoulder before continuing the fight. More wounds came, until the one that put him down.

His own foolish mistakes had allowed the blades and pikes of the enemy to make him just another dead man waiting to greet whatever the afterlife might bring.

I had so much more to do, Conan thought, berating himself even as his end stalked closer. The stench of death smothered him. The wretched cries of the wounded being finished by a Zamoran pike to the chest or an ax to the head proved a sad final song to sing him away from this world. *Should have been wiser, should have been stronger. And by Crom, if I'm granted one last chance, I'll strive for more wisdom and strength!*

But he felt no benevolent gaze upon him from any gods, known or unknown. They had passed him by, leaving him to a lonely death at the hands of the two Zamoran soldiers coming to a halt beside him.

"What about him?" one of them asked. He was a small bald man, but broad and strong—a familiar Zamoran trait. He held a barbed pike whose shaft was darkened with gore.

"He's almost dead already," the other soldier said through a beard clotted with blood. Was it his own, or did it belong to those he had killed? A tall man, he bore a cruel battle-ax propped on one shoulder, and his chest armor was scratched and dented from the battle. "One more head will give my ax a nice round count of twenty today."

"But he's strong," Bald Man said with a note of admiration. "And big, even lying down in the shite and blood. Take a look at those muscles."

"And take a look at the wounds venting his life-blood into the mud," Beard said. "I'll help him on his way. Twenty." He shrugged a shoulder and grabbed the ax shaft in both hands.

"He's got countless old scars beneath those new cuts," Bald Man said. "Got stories to tell, eh, you Cimmerian dog?"

Conan tried to growl, but it turned into a cough. He spat blood. Gripped his sword in one hand. He'd not be put down like a hobbled beast. This might be his time to die, but he'd do his best to take at least one of these gloating bastards with him. He tensed, but his muscles did not comply. His hand holding the sword scraped barely six inches across the wet ground.

"We can sell a big one like him to the salt mines," Bald Man continued. "If he dies, he dies. But let's drag him to one of the carts and send him there, at least."

Beard chuckled. He had other ideas. He hefted the ax and swung it out and to the right, bringing it up over his head for a furious killing blow.

Conan struggled and strained but his body was weak, his wounds draining his energy and strength, now soaking into ground already saturated with blood.

He growled and stared at Beard, refusing to look away or close his eyes in his final moment.

Beard grunted in surprise as the metal ax head snapped away from the splintered handle and struck his shoulder. It scraped a shallow cut as it tumbled to the ground.

Bald Man laughed, and it was a strange sound, high and unfettered.

"You see?" he said. "Cool fate and Zath have decided. It's the salt mines for this one. You grab one leg, I'll get the other."

"That was a good ax," Beard muttered, rubbing blood from the fresh injury on his shoulder.

"You can buy yourself another," Bald Man said. "There'll be loot from all these dead invaders. Now, one, two, three, pull!"

Conan gritted his teeth and squirmed, but his body gave him nothing back. The sword slipped from his hand, and he could do nothing to prevent himself from being dragged through the guts and gore of his defeated brethren toward whatever wretched future awaited him.

The sword sliced across his upper stomach and chest again and again, and pain surged in waves, striking deep into his core and climbing his spine to explode in his brain. He was shaking so much that his body rose and slammed into the ground, once, twice, a dozen times. His head thudded down and he expected his skull to crack and his tortured brains to leak out and seep into the death-soaked soils of Zamora forever.

At least then this damned pain would end, Conan thought, and he opened his eyes to glaring sun. A shadow was crouched over him, and at first he thought it was the soldier who had sliced him, repeating the execution of that injury forever like some awful purgatory. Conan had often thought about what came after life had ended. Death was his trade, so such thoughts were common. He supposed that this torture might be his eternal fate. If so, he would accept it, and fight it as hard as he could forever.

Then the shadow leaned in closer, and a face appeared.

"Try and be still," the man said, his voice strangely distorted. "I'm stuffing your wounds." He took something from his mouth and pressed it into the injury across Conan's torso, and Conan flinched back. "I said still! I'm trying to make it better, not worse."

Conan turned his head to the side and looked around. They were on the back of a large cart with several other captured sellswords, all of them injured in one way or another. One woman glared at Conan through her good eye, the other a bloody wet hole buzzed by flies. A man sat against the low side of the cart with his eyes closed and arms resting on his crossed legs, one hand and forearm crushed and smashed to a gory pulp. Conan looked back to the man aiding him.

"What's your name? Why are you doing this?" he asked.

"My name is Baht Tann," the man said. "Pleased to make your acquaintance. And I'm doing this because of all the injured fighters in this cursed cart, you appear to be the biggest and strongest. And where we're going, I fear I'm going to need a big, strong friend."

"You're trying to save me for your own benefit."

Baht Tann shrugged, pulled more stuff from his mouth, and pressed it into Conan's wound.

"Fair and honest," Conan said. "My gratitude."

"Thank me later," Tann said. "For now, try and stay still. Almost done."

Conan lay back and let Tann do his work. Already the pain from his wound was fading from agony to an uncomfortable numbness. He smelled horses and blood and shit, heard the cheerful banter from Zamoran warriors as they walked beside the cart and the buzzing of filthy flies around the wounded, and at last he remembered what Bald Man had said before Beard tried to part his head from his body.

"Salt mines," Conan said, looking up at Tann.

"Aye, the worst. They say a person's lucky if they survive one moon digging the salt." Tann finished his work and eased himself down beside Conan, and Conan had a chance to look him over. Another sellsword for sure, though he didn't recognize him. He had the look of someone from the west, Zingara perhaps, and at first he saw no obvious injuries. Then Tann tilted his head forward and gingerly pressed his hand to the back of his neck, and it came away clotted with blood and hair.

"I will survive," Conan said. "I dreamed I was dying again and again. When I woke, you were there. My ghostly guardian."

Tann laughed, loud and heartfelt, and in return one of the

Zamoran guards threatened him with a pike to the gut. He quietened but remained smiling.

"Maybe fate brought us together, friend," Tann said. "Though I am no ghost. So what's your name? You know, just in case I have to save you again."

"Conan."

"Conan. A strong name."

"It will be known across these lands," Conan said.

"It's a name that will be swallowed and melted by the salt mines of Tangara until it's forgotten even by its mother," Tann said. "Meanwhile, it's two days' hard travel to get there, and I doubt these bastards will spare us any food or water."

Conan struggled to sit up, shrugging Tann's restraining hand from his shoulder. He looked down at the ugly wound across his midriff, now stuffed with a wet, chewed mixture of capot leaves and spit. The edges of the wound pouted, and Conan knew it needed stitches to draw it closed, but the hardening capot held its edges together.

The two men leaned against the side of the shaking cart. The sun blazed down on them, dust from the road coated their skin and entered their mouths, and the four huge horses pulling the wagon filled the air with their rancid farts.

"I will survive," Conan said again.

"You do sound determined. In that case, I'll do best to stay by your side." Tann looked him up and down. "You're even bigger than you looked lying down."

The Tangara salt mine sat at the foot of a high hill on the edge of the great desert, a giant hole in the ground two miles across and a thousand feet deep. A rough road spiraled down around the hole's sloping outer edge, hacked into the ground and retained by huge cages of rocks and massive timbers hauled down from the surrounding hillsides. Lines of slaves trudged up this road bearing heavy hessian bags of salt. They were pushed and whipped close to the road's inner edge so that they did not fall from the edge and spill their precious load. Once they reached the surface and disgorged their cargo into vast wooden storage tanks built on the surface, they slung the sacks across their shoulders and heads—the only precious respite they had from the cruel and relentless sun—and started back down.

Their return journey was close to the precarious road's edge, keeping out of the way of fellow workers on their loaded upward journey. Some slipped on the loose gravelly edge and fell. The lucky ones were able to scurry or slide down the slope to the next road level. The less fortunate plummeted over a steeper section, and their fall could result in a broken limb or worse. Some died on impact. Those badly injured by their fall but still alive were usually dispatched by the guards, because the Zamorans running the mine had no use for a slave with a broken arm or leg. Most of the guards saw this as a necessary duty and expended as little energy as possible in doing so—a simple pike stab to the face or a slit throat would finish the wounded slave—but there were a few guards who enjoyed the sadistic distraction from the long, hot day.

The strongest slaves were all kept down below at the terrible quarry's base, working on the three current salt pits being mined, and they were never given the opportunity to climb back up to the surface. They worked and slept down there, and occasionally were offered rank water and stale or rotten food. Yet even these strongest of the prisoners fell in their dozens. Those who collapsed at the salt face, exhausted or dead, were carried to a redundant pit and thrown in, the dead and the barely living lying in the humid shadows and merging together in rot. The stench of decay from this pit was sickening. The clouds of flies, scampering rats, and carrion lizards made the rank hole appear alive, and from a distance it might have been a giant living thing squirming and pulsing, moist and writhing, as if yearning escape.

The heavily armed Zamoran guards across the mine's floor were also the strongest. They wore loose silk clothing to keep cool and masks soaked in honeyspit to keep the endless stink at bay. Sometimes even they succumbed to the terrible conditions, and there was no ceremony in death—it was the pit for them, too.

Even bearing his injury, Conan was judged one of the strongest slaves, and he worked in one of the salt pits alongside his new friend Baht Tann. Tann was an enigma to him. Older than Conan, with the lean, powerful body of a farmer rather than a muscled warrior, still he carried scars and stories from a lifetime of selling his sword. He was convinced that they would never escape the salt mine and their Zamoran guards, yet he did not show despair. I live for now, and now, and now, Tann said, and a minute from now can go eat itself. That's how I stay strong. Conan asked if he had learned this measured and calm outlook from the mythical Red Monks of Vendhya, who followed Asura and took the scorpion's sting to spend years in contemplative and silent meditation at the top of the highest mountains. Baht Tann replied, No, my grandmother.

They had been in the quarry for ten days now, maybe even twelve, and despite the conditions Conan's wound was healing well. In the brief reprieve the slaves were granted when the night was at its darkest—three hours, four if they were lucky—Tann tended the wound and used maggots harvested from the grave pit at great risk to eat away at any infection. One evening while he was doing this, Tann said, "I saw you fighting, you know. Across the battlefield of thousands, you stood out with your strength and cunning. You're a good warrior. It's a shame you won't live to become great."

"I will find a way to escape," Conan said.

Night after night, Tann dropped more maggots, cleaning Conan's wound and allowing his body to heal itself. The intimate feel of the maggots squirming in his bad flesh kept Conan awake, even during those precious few hours when they were afforded time to sleep.

But he did not waste that time simply lying awake while his fellow slaves slept, snored, and nightmared themselves toward another long, dreadful day digging salt. Instead, he watched the guards and came to know them all, the strong ones and the weaker. He started to observe a pattern in how they changed shifts while the slaves slept, groups of guards marching up the curving road after others had come down. He spotted some that might perhaps be bribed, if he had the means to do so. He also picked out those he knew he could kill with one hand while fighting with the other—again, if he had the means to do so.

Conan's mind was most at peace when he was digging and packing salt, and enjoying brief moments of rest while one filled bag was carried away by a wretched slave and an empty one dropped by another. This was when he assessed his nightly observations, creating schemes and plans and readying his escape.

But after another dozen days in the horrendous quarry, even Conan was beginning to fear that his only chance at leaving that place would be death. He never saw a good escape opportunity. The guards were many, most of them experienced warriors, and Conan was still suffering from his injury. The slaves were never given enough food or water. He felt his strength failing day after day, his body giving what energy it could spare to heal his wounds.

And so came the day when Conan knew he had to make his move or take his place in the pit of the dead.

It was the hottest day yet. Though deep, the quarry was also wide, and the blazing sun scorched its way across the quarry's base well into the afternoon. There was no breeze. Humidity hung heavy, and the stink of the pit of the dead was like a viscous grease in the dank air.

Conan had seen five captives tumbling from the road and being put out of their misery already that morning, and he himself had been forced to throw three dead salt-diggers into the pit. The resultant cloud of a billion flies sweeping up and around him in endless waves had been grotesque, and yet almost beautiful in the way they weaved and waved through the air before landing once again in their stew of death.

After his last visit to the death pit, when he was back at the salt seam with Tann, Conan said, "I will make my move today."

"Then you'll die today."

"Don't you want to go with me?"

"Of course."

"Then follow my lead."

They worked through the day, sweating, vision blurring, while the Zamoran guards drank water brought down by other guards from above. The few drops they spared were poured into a large clay urn to share among the slaves when they paused for a short midday break. It was just enough to keep them alive and digging, not enough to maintain their health and lust for life.

There were always more slaves.

When evening came and the slaves sat in rows so that the guards could dish out their meager food rations, Conan leaned in close to Tann.

"I need your food and water," he said. "I'm weaker than I should be. If we're to have even the slightest chance, I need my strength. A scrape of dried meat and half a cup of dirty water aren't enough."

Tann chuckled, but not too loud. If slaves were found

conversing during this short break, the guards would kick or whip them into silence.

"Conan, my friend, we're not getting out of here. Death stalks us, closer and closer. Last night I dreamed I was in the pit, looking up at the indifferent stars and sinking down into that mess of death."

"Then you won't mind giving me your rations."

"Huh." Tann fell silent as a guard came by and dropped a twist of dried meat into his outstretched hands, and poured brown water into his mug. When the guard moved on he said to Conan, "It's all I have for today. I'm thirsty. And hungry. And I've helped you so much already."

"Because you know I'm your only chance," Conan said.

"Partly that, yes," Tann admitted. "But I've also helped because I think we're friends. And besides, you know there is no chance."

"There's always a chance. I'm taking mine today."

They sat in silence for a while. Conan chewed on his own scant rations, trying to draw as much flavor from the tough meat as he could. He drank his dirty water. When he glanced sidelong at Tann, his friend had not started eating or drinking.

"Very well, Conan. But you'll owe me. If we get out of here, you'll owe me..." He looked up at the dusky sky above, eyes squinted almost shut. "A favor. Anything I ask, whenever I ask it of you. A favor for the friend you'll die with soon."

"Agreed," Conan said. It was small price to pay, to help a friend. And in truth he had no real confidence that his scheme to escape would work.

Checking that no guards were watching, Tann handed over his rations. Conan ate the meat, drank the water. Then they stood to work again.

An hour later, Conan clutched at his wound, staggered away from the vein of salt he had been excavating, and dropped down dead.

Eyes closed, body loose and slack, breath as shallow and slow as he could make it, Conan tried not to flinch as he was half carried, half dragged across the floor of the mine. He knew what was coming, yet he could not truly be prepared.

The stink grew. The buzz of flies first tickled at his ears then rose into a roar, and he could already feel them skittering across his body as they explored this fresh new meat in which to lay their eggs.

"Damn flies!" someone said, and Conan's left leg was dropped to the ground. He did not make a sound.

"Pick him up!" Baht Tann said. He was holding Conan's right arm. "Give him some dignity. He deserves that, at least."

Spitting flies away from their mouths, even four men struggled to carry Conan to the edge of the pit. Though his eyes were still closed as he feigned death, he could smell and hear where he was. His skin felt dirty and slimy with the anticipation of what was about to happen.

"Rest easy," someone said.

"Go to Crom, Conan, and may your god guide your way," Tann said. "One, two, three…"

They heaved him into the pit.

For a couple of heartbeats, Conan was weightless and he allowed his limbs and body to relax, enjoying the most comfort and respite he'd had since being injured, captured, and dragged here to work himself to death. *I live for now, and now, and now,* Tann had said, and for an instant Conan too embraced that way.

And then death welcomed him down.

He struck the surface layer of corpses, and they were soft, almost fluid. The stink was more rancid and overwhelming than he could have possibly imagined, and as he came to rest it took every ounce of self-control to prevent himself from turning onto his side and puking.

Just a few moments more, he thought, because a guard always accompanied those carrying corpses to the pit, and he or she might still be looking down. Just a few moments...

Something gave way beneath him, a swollen body bursting from his weight, and his lower torso and legs sank deeper. The buzz of flies filled his ears, and he felt carrion lizards scampering across his chest. When he could no longer hold still, he opened his eyes a crack, and through a haze of busy flies he saw only the pit's edge and the first stars appearing in the evening sky above.

Conan knocked the lizards from his torso and rolled onto his side, somehow avoiding puking. He looked around, trying to make out the thing he sought across this lake of rotting flesh, stiffened limbs, and bird-pecked eye sockets. At last he saw it, and slowly, slowly, he made his way toward it, keeping himself as low and flat as possible so as to spread his weight across a wider surface area. If he propped himself on hands and knees, he might break through bloated skin and softening flesh.

It was disgusting. Conan had seen and done many things, wallowed in blood and death many times, yet this was beyond nightmare. But he kept going, knowing that there was no way back now. If he failed, if he was caught, if his scheme did not succeed, he would be back in this pit of the dead by dawn, this time with his throat cut. He could brave it now because he had no wish to add to it. His utter determination to escape kept him moving forward, and the thought of all the stories he had yet to tell shoved the prospect of failure far from his mind.

That, and the sight of the dead guard propped at the pit's far end.

The dead guard's dirty silken robe was tight around Conan's big body, but it still covered him well enough. The mask, though

now smelling of the death-stew instead of honeyspit, concealed his features. Best of all, the man had been heaved into the pit with a curved blade still strapped to his thigh beneath his robes. Conan now bore the knife up his sleeve, and holding a weapon gave him a sense of confidence that his situation in truth did not warrant.

It was growing dark, and he knew that the slaves would soon be allowed to rest for two or three hours. This was a time when the guards were sleepy, more at ease, and also when they changed shifts. It would give him a short time to act before his escape window slammed shut in his face.

He stalked across the quarry floor as if he owned the place, exuding arrogance, trying not to wave too much at the flies that still bothered him. They'd followed him from the pit as if angry that he was trying to leave them behind, and he knew that they, and the stinking filth upon him, would soon give him away. But he didn't need to fool the Zamoran guards for long. Just long enough.

The slaves were brought up out of the salt pits and made to settle in lines, the guards ensuring that there was space between them. They allowed no fraternizing and no physical contact. Any muttered conversation was soon put down by a guard's boot or the threat of a blade. Conan watched, waited, and focused. He knew which guard he sought; the man rarely stayed for long, needing to slink away to drain his bladder. Perhaps he drank too much water meant for the slaves. If so, his greed would be his downfall.

Conan moved close to the edges of the mine, silent and swift as a panther despite his size. He felt nowhere near as strong as he was used to, and his injury still niggled, but thanks to Baht Tann's rations as well as his own that day, he thought he was strong enough.

The sound of pissing guided him in behind the shelter of a

pile of tumbled rocks, and when the urinating guard smelled him he turned and his eyes opened wide.

"By the great spider-god Zath! Khartaggan, back from the dead!" the guard croaked.

"And I come bearing you a gift," Conan said. He flicked the blade down into his hand and swept it around in an arc, burying it to the haft in the Zamoran's left ear. He grabbed the man as he slumped and held him upright, twisting and turning the knife to mangle his brains. Life left his eyes, and Conan eased him to the ground and stripped him.

He left the silken robes wrapped around the man's weapons in the shadow of a pile of salt bags, then hefted the corpse and wedged it out of sight between two rocks. He was sweating now, and his own unwashed body odor merged with the deathly aroma that hung around him.

Some of the flies left him for the fresh corpse, at least.

With the blade returned up his sleeve, he marched out toward the resting slaves. This was when he would be taking the greatest risk. He could easily walk from the quarry on his own, up the curving track that climbed the walls toward freedom above, and if he encountered any troublesome guards he could kill them and run.

But he had promised Baht Tann his freedom, and Tann had given his rations willingly. Conan could not countenance fleeing without his friend. Besides, stripped down to his bare bones, hacked with a blade, and put to work for a bunch of brutal slavers, revenge was all he had left.

That, and the hunger to find the great and grand tales of his future.

A few guards glanced his way, but they were resting as well, and in the darkness they missed the dried, bloodied filth caked on his robes. Maybe if he approached closer they'd have smelled him, but most of the slaves stank of death anyway.

Without hesitating, Conan approached the first line of slaves.

"You. With me." He kicked Tann hard, eliciting an angry rebuke. "Keep your mouth shut!" He grabbed Tann and hauled him upright, dragging him back toward the shadows.

There were a few mutters among the other slaves, and some glowering looks that said, Rather him than me. Some guards took slaves away in the night, men or women, and if they ever returned few spoke of the degradations to which they had been subjected.

As they came to the place where Conan had killed the guard, he let Tann go.

"You didn't have to kick quite so hard," Tann whispered, rubbing his leg. "And by the way, you stink."

"You're no perfumed delight either," Conan said. "And 'thank you' would be good."

"I'll reserve that for when we're away."

Conan plucked out the robes and weapon and threw them at Tann. He dressed quickly, then paused, offering the sword to Conan.

"I have a blade," Conan said. "You keep that. If we need to fight, our chances are slimmer than none."

"Then let's go," Tann said. "We've already gotten further toward freedom than I believed possible."

They crept through the shadows behind the fallen rocks and then emerged into moonlight, walking with confidence and an air of entitlement as they headed for the wide area where the road up out of the deep quarry began. They started up, and soon the exertion began to tell. The climb was steep and long, and Conan felt thirst burning his throat and shriveling his muscles. But the higher they went, the more moonlight touched them, the fresher the air became, and the closer he tasted freedom.

A group of four guards approached, coming downhill, and

Conan tensed his arm with the blade hidden up his sleeve. They passed them by, and a woman raised a hand and muttered something he did not hear. Conan grunted and made eye contact from behind his mask. She looked away and continued downward with her companions.

When they finally reached the surface, where huge storage compounds of salt awaited loading and transporting back across Zamora and beyond, they heard the first shouts from the guards below as the slaves were sent back to work. They had walked this far in silence, and Conan knew what Tann was going to say even as he paused to speak.

"I wish we could do something for them."

"We can," Conan said. "Look, over there."

"What is it?"

"A well, where guards draw water for themselves." Conan approached the well, stripping off his silken robes as he went. At last, wearing only the dirty loincloth that had been the sum of his clothing for the many days since he had been injured and caught, he stood beside the well.

"I brought them some treats from the pit of death," he said. Tucked into the robe's inner folds were handfuls of rancid, rotting flesh, a-crawl with corruption and sure to sicken.

He dropped it all into the well.

"Tomorrow, they drink. The next day, they puke and shit and fall."

"Our friends will take their chance," Tann said. "By Ishtar, I hope they make every bastard slaver suffer!"

Conan and Baht Tann left together, heading west back across Zamora. Just before dawn they encountered a group of six warriors riding east to replace some of the guards. They ambushed them, relishing the fight, and Conan enjoyed every moment of slicing, stabbing, and goring. It was a weak reprisal for all that he'd been subjected to, but in the desperate eyes of each Zamoran he killed he saw the faces of those brutal guards. As revenge, it would have to do.

They set four horses free and took the other two for themselves.

That night, they ate proper food and drank clean fresh water, and Conan, once little more than a dead man in a pit of corruption, felt the wide-open landscape of a mighty future laid out before him. He was eager to ride hard and fast toward whatever stories and legends his future held.

A Mistaken Face

"Why is it always the most dangerous places that offer the greatest chance at wealth?" he said as he tested the rope and leaned out over the edge of the cliff.

"Anything worth finding in easy places has likely already been found," his dear wife, Larria, said. Then, from behind her, he heard the voices of their young twin sons, Davin and Korum.

"We're only young but we've seen enough to know…" Davin said.

"…that the world is too large to ever be known," Korum finished.

Just where do they get their wise minds from? he wondered for the hundredth time. And for the hundredth time, a small voice spoke in his brain and said, Larria. He knew that was true. Baht Tann had spent the first half of his life as a sellsword, and countless deaths were carried as scars on his imagination. Sometimes he dreamed of the warriors he had killed, and their faces mocked him silently, but he lived for the moment and harbored no regrets. He was happy with the life he had grown into and the man he had become, and Larria was the main source of that happiness. Meeting her later in life had been a blessing, and her persuading him to leave violence behind continued to be a balm for his soul.

"Ease out a bit more," Larria called from above.

"I am easing," he said. "You know I don't like heights."

"That's because they're there to kill you," she said with a chuckle.

He glanced up, his feet braced against the cliff, into her smiling face. "Thank you," he said.

"Anyway, there's a river down there! All you'll get if you fall is wet."

"It's a five-hundred-foot drop! And even if I survive it, the river's fast and violent, and it'll carry me all the way south to the Styx."

Tann concentrated on what he was doing, edging further and further down, keeping a good grip of the rope passing through the hoop on his belt while also looking for the telltale gleam of the heartgems they had all come here to seek. *Perhaps it's being so rare and inaccessible that gives them their value*, he thought. But there was more to it. Heartgems were more than just shiny, glittery stones harder than anything else in the land. They were filled with depths that could hypnotize a person if they looked into one for too long. Tann had heard it said that if you stared into a heartgem for hours, you could see your own future. If you looked for days, you might perceive the route to your own death. There was a story of a monk in Stygia who had been looking into a gem for his whole life since he had turned seven, and he had the haunted countenance of a man who had seen the end of time.

The problem was, no one knew where they came from, only where they were taken to. Many had set out to seek the source of the precious stones, heading north or south, east or west, or sometimes down, down into the darkest depths of the land. None were ever seen again.

Scarhawks knew. The birds were prevalent all across the land, and they harvested these mysterious gems from wherever they grew or were formed and brought them to their nests.

A scarhawk knew to build its nest in the most inaccessible, remote places there were. Mountaintops on the western shores of the Vilayet Sea. Deep caves on the Baracha Islands off the coast of Zingara. On the swaying tops of the highest trees in the forests of the border kingdoms. And here, on the sheer cliffs of Khoraja that dropped eventually into the Great Eastern Desert.

Tann looked left and right at his fellow prospectors. There were forty in this camp, parents and children, all of them experienced gem hunters. They had worked together as a group for over four years, some family units leaving, others joining. In that time they'd found at least a few gems each, and what they searched for as a group they all benefited from. Finds were gathered together, and once every couple of months several members made the long trip to the markets of Khemi or the coastal ports of Argos to sell them. It made trust one of the prime factors in the hard life they led, and that trust bound them together like family.

He nodded to three others hanging on ropes from the face of the sheer cliff. They nodded back, then focused on their own situations. This was serious business, and dangerous. It required concentration and confidence, and Tann liked to think he had both.

He eased himself down the rope, aware of Larria still up above watching him go. The rope was secured around a big rock on the clifftop, but she kept an eye on him all the same, ready to scamper down if he hurt himself or encountered any difficulties. They took turns—sometimes it was her on the cliff, sometimes him.

Today it was him. And thus Baht Tann's fate was sealed.

As he slowly lowered himself down, he searched for telltale signs of a scarhawk nest. They usually took up residence in deep cracks in the rock face, and these cliffs were full of them. In his right hand was a small, narrow blade, the handle strapped around his palm so that he could hold on to both it and the rope at the same time. He used the blade to push overhanging plants aside and peer into cavities in the rock, and it was also there for defense. Despite their fearsome appearance, nine times out of ten a startled scarhawk would fly away, but that one time it might attack—especially if disturbed while brooding on an egg—could prove fatal. Tann was a man made of older scars, but one of his more recent was a cut across the bridge of his nose put there by an angry scarhawk's beak.

He heard a commotion to the right, and across the cliff a woman kicked back on her rope as something burst from the rock face. She landed back on braced feet, her own blade ready, but it was merely a couple of pigeons. They flapped away, leaving her wiping spattered pigeon excrement from her forearm.

Tann laughed and eased himself down another few feet. He braced, then frowned, and something—a feeling, a change, a silence—made him look up.

Larria was gone. He looked back and forth along the cliff edge thirty feet above, and he couldn't see any of the other prospectors' partners. That was strange. He listened, head tilted, but the warm desert breeze blowing dust in from the east hushed against the cliff face, and he could hear nothing else.

"Larria?" he called, and the alarm in his voice caused the others to look up as well.

"Where are they?" the pigeon-spattered woman asked, and then her rope went slack and she fell away from the cliff.

"No!" Tann gasped, vainly reaching for her, as if that could do any good. The untethered rope flicked and twisted in the air like a snake as she fell and hauled it down with her, her arms and legs grasping at the air. Her right foot struck a protruding ledge and she spun out into space, the trailing rope twisting around her.

The river, Tann thought. She'll hit the water and—

The woman slammed down onto the river's rocky bank far below, the impact throwing up dust and blood.

After a moment of stunned shock, Tann started climbing. To his left another rope let go, and the man screamed as he fell. Tann did not watch. He concentrated on pulling himself up his rope, alert for any change in its tension, more aware of the blade strapped to his hand than usual. One snapped rope was a terrible accident.

Two was intentional.

Larria, Davin, Korum! he thought, and as he climbed he felt himself changing. He'd spent decades putting his violent past behind him, settling his rage and trauma in Larria's gentle hands, but it sprang back to him now. When he blinked, he saw visions of blood, and all of it was flowing across images of his dear, beautiful family. Each handhold he took to haul himself up the rope, he felt his muscles tensing, his awareness expanding, senses opening up in readiness for a fight.

Climbing that cliff, he left Baht Tann the prospector behind.

"No no no no no!" he heard from his right, and another rope-end fell out into space. The woman scrabbled at the cliff face, and for a moment Tann thought she had a grip. Then the falling coiled rope struck her and she fell.

He had moments to act.

Gripping a handhold, feeling for a small ridge with his toe, he unhooked the rope from his belt hoop and stepped to one side. Seconds later, his own rope slackened and fell, and he held on tightly to the cliff, looking up to see if anyone was checking to see if he was gone.

It was silent up there, and no one was in sight.

He checked to his left and right. He was alone. They were all gone. He did not look down, because they were likely all spattered and broken and dead, and all that mattered to him was up there above: his wife, his children, his whole world.

Tann started to climb. Even when he was a sellsword he'd been thin and wiry rather than bulked out with muscle and mass, and he'd only become stronger in his time as a gem prospector. Using fingertip holds and feeling with his booted feet, he scaled the sheer cliff like a spider, focused but fast. In moments, he was close to the clifftop and could see where his rope had rubbed away at the soil and grass growing right to the edge.

He was terrified at what he might see when he raised himself up to look, so he paused for a moment, and that was when he heard the sounds that haunted his nightmares of the past.

The clash of metal on metal, the *schwick!* of blades slicing flesh, the screams of the dying, and the wretched begging of those about to die.

The cruel laughter of brutal people.

Baht Tann changed then, from a mild family man into a demon filled with potential rage, and as he hauled himself up over cliff edge he flipped his hand so that the blade's handle lay flat and gripped in his palm.

He crouched there panting, trying to process the scene quickly so that he did not waste the precious time he had. No one was looking his way, because they thought that everyone working the cliff was dead. Tann used his advantage wisely to assess the situation.

Fifteen heavily armed men and women, maybe more, brutal brigands and cutthroats standing in a wide circle around their temporary encampment. Nine bodies rent asunder and awash with blood and gore—friends he'd valued, people he'd traveled and worked with, and though not fighters, they had done their best and fought back. He could do nothing for them.

Hunkered down close to the central firepit of their temporary encampment were the survivors—twenty or more men and women and children, terrified and wide-eyed. Some of them were pleading, hands held up in supplication. A few still appeared ready to fight.

Among the latter were Larria and their two sons. Even as he watched, he saw her hand creeping toward the previous evening's fire for a heavy stick that still glowed hot at one end.

It was Larria who saw him first, and Tann shook his head. No, don't fight them, and don't give me away. But she had thought him fallen from the cliff and dead, and her eyes went wide. Three of the cutthroats turned to see what she had seen. One of them—the biggest, the brashest, and obviously their leader—laughed out loud.

And Tann caught his breath as shock hammered in his chest.

"Conan!" he said. "Conan, my old friend!" He was even bigger than Tann remembered him, broader across the shoulders, his huge leather jerkin tied with metal clasps, his long black hair hanging in braids. His intelligent eyes sparkled with cruel humor, and his heavily muscled arms and legs were crisscrossed with the scars of a long life of combat and killing.

Conan's laughter faded and he tilted his head to one side. He nodded at two of his bandits, and they came toward Tann.

Tann crouched, brandishing the blade. It looked pitiful against the heavy broadsword the man carried and the multi-bladed whip wielded by the woman. Their weapons glittered with blood, like the alluring red glimmer of heartgems.

"Conan," the big man said, as if tasting the name, and then his voice broke high and loud with the name. "Ah, Conan! You recognize me, stranger."

"I'm no stranger!" Tann said. He eyed the approaching barbarians, and perhaps they saw an echo of his past life in his eyes because their easy smiles dropped and they paused a dozen feet from him. The man glanced down at the blade in his hand. The woman lifted her whip in readiness to strike.

"Hold," Conan said.

"You remember me!" Tann said. "The salt mines of Tangara? The promise you made me?"

"A promise," Conan said. He seemed intrigued, and Tann hoped against hope that whatever long life of fighting and butchery he had fallen into had not slashed away his sense of loyalty.

"I gave you my rations for the day, and you promised to grant me a favor, wherever and whenever I called it in."

Conan frowned, and then laughed. And as he turned his head to look at the captured prospectors, Tann thought, Oh, by all the gods that are and ever were, I think my old man's eyesight has betrayed me. Because this man was not Conan—he saw that now. The huge barbarian was far too young for a start, and the way he eyed his captives, the brutality and relish in what he had done, the murder of innocents... No, Tann did not think anything would have reduced Conan to this.

Among the corpses on the ground were women and children.

Tann closed his eyes and readied himself, because he knew that whatever he did next—however hard he fought for the freedom of Larria and their boys, and however determinedly they battled with him—he was about to die.

"A promise," the barbarian said. "A favor. You know Conan."

Tann did not reply.

"I said, you know Conan!" the man shouted, and the transformation from casual laughter to furious roar was shocking. He was a beast now, hulking and glaring, veins protruding from his forehead and across his wide, muscled neck.

Rusty though he was in the ways of combat, Tann knew that one of the best weapons was surprise. He went for the bandit to his left, jabbing with the blade, feinting, ducking down beneath the answering whip-swing that whistled above his head, and then slashed the woman's thigh. She cried out as blood spurted from her severed artery, and Tann rolled to his left as the other man's broadsword shaved the hairs from his leg and stuck in the ground.

Tann stood, wiping sprayed blood from his face, and he and Larria locked eyes.

The man's great arms slammed around Tann from behind, crushing his own arms to his side. He tried to lift his knife, but another sword hummed through the air and took his hand.

"Noooo!" Larria shouted.

"Kill the next woman, man, or child who moves!" the furious barbarian leader shouted. "But only if they move. We can't kill too many of these mangy mutts because we need them to slave for us. I've heard of these heartgems they've been gathering. They're worth a fortune."

"What about this one, Grake?" the man holding Tann said.

Grake glared at Tann. "Him? I think he'd be trouble."

Tann knew then that he was beaten, and he glanced down with a strange detachment at his severed hand with the blade strapped to it. That's part of me forever here, he thought. Perhaps it was having Conan's name in his mind and on his tongue for the first time in forever, but he decided he would not go down without a furious fight.

He slammed his boot-heel down against the shin of the man holding him, snaked away as his grip loosened, and snatched up his severed hand and knife. Ducking even lower, he twisted and thrust the knife up into the man's stomach.

As the warrior cried out, he grabbed Tann's throat and staggered backward, toward the cliff.

No! Tann thought. If he went over there, that was it, this feeble attempt to rescue his wife and children over and done in an instant. He twisted the knife back and forth in the man's gut, smelling his rank insides, feeling warm blood and fluids gushing out across his hands—the one still attached, and the severed one he clasped—and his senses dropped him back decades to the times when he had fought for lust or money. He twisted, pushed, struggled, but the dying man's fingers dug even tighter into his throat, and then he tripped over the dying woman whose thigh Tann had slashed open.

The bandit's staggering momentum took them both over the cliff edge, and at the last second Tann pushed as hard as he could with his feet.

The man finally let go as they plummeted. Falling free, Tann saw the broken remains of his friends down below, waiting to welcome him into oblivion.

Grake reached the edge of the cliff in time to see the splash far, far below. He squinted and searched the raging river, then saw the dark speck of a head breaking the surface and frantic limbs splashing as the fallen man tried to swim.

"He thought you were Conan!" a man beside him said, and he burst out laughing. "Conan!"

Grake grasped his warrior's arm and clenched, his strong gnarly fingers squeezing so tightly that blood oozed out through the pores of his skin. The warrior cringed and gritted his teeth but did not cry out.

"And that is funny why?" Grake asked quietly.

"It's... not funny," the warrior said.

"No. Not funny." But Grake's grin widened, because he had not ceased smiling since the man had mistaken him for Aquilonia's famed, aging king. Conan had always been little more than a name to Grake, a figure to aspire to and admire from afar, a myth of a man whose exploits were known across this land and many others.

Now, he had just met a man who knew him. A man who claimed to be Conan's friend.

"Shall I chase him down?" the warrior asked, holding his injured arm and eager now to please Grake after offending him. "I'll have to climb down the cliff, but once on the river I can—"

"Let him go," Grake said. "I saw him looking at the prisoners. We have his wife and children. We have his friends. And if what he says is true, King Conan owes him a favor."

"You don't really think Conan would come here?" the warrior said, a hint of fear in his voice.

"Maybe," Grake said. He could still just make out the man far below being carried along the river, floating with the current now and allowing it to carry him away. South, this tributary fed eventually into the Styx, and from there Khemi and the sea. "Maybe," Grake said again. "I hope he will." He dipped two fingers into the pouch on a cord around his neck and took out a pinch of quesh, the gritty Khitain drug that gave him strength and so much more. He dabbed it on his tongue, then closed his mouth and eyes as it surged around his body, setting his veins aflame and pulsing through his bones like pure sunlight, starlight, the blaze of life.

Grake had spent his life striving to build his name and legend as the greatest warrior in all the land. What better way to ensure that title than to kill the most powerful warrior that ever was?

A Ghost From The Past

"The Shirki River ensures that the land in that vast, wide valley is rich and fertile and an abundance of crops can grow there, and indeed sometimes the fields even provide two yields in a good year. Land does not need to be left fallow as the soils and sediments are heavy in goodness, and even if the river floods—and such an occasion is rare, only usually happening when there is unusually heavy rainfall in the mountainous regions around Tanasul—the crops recover, and the flood feeds rather than damages the fields. These farms almost always provide bountiful yields of wheat, corn, oats, and barley, and the vineyards on the upper slopes are renowned for producing some of the finest wines in the land—which I know you are fond of partaking in, my lord. On the other hand..."

Councilor Ortan paused and took in a deep breath, and King Conan held in a smile.

"...on the other hand, some of the farming land on the steppes west of Poitan has been affected over the decades by deforestation due to ongoing building projects to increase the size of settlements in the surrounding areas, and thus soil erosion from wind, rain, and even excessive sunlight sucks the goodness from the ground. This means that fertilizers have to be bought and imported from Ophir at great cost, vast areas of land have to be treated and left fallow every second year so that goodness can return to the subsoils, and even then the crops that grow are not as lush as those in and around the Shirki Valley. Therefore, a representation from the Poitan steppes has requested a new law be written and codified that protects their interests."

"Protects them how?" Conan asked.

"By allowing them to charge higher rates for their crops when taken to market," Ortan said.

Conan frowned, then stood from his throne and stretched. He felt his back creak, shrugged his shoulders, and his first steps caused pains to shimmer through his heavy, stiff legs. Entering his sixth decade, he often felt the effects of his adventurous and violent life settling in his bones, muscles, and sinews, especially when he spent so much time sedentary.

Councilor Ortan stopped speaking and gasped. Conan knew why, so he ignored him. Instead, he walked in a wide circle around the great Aquilonian throne.

It was a huge stone seat coated in a thick layer of gold, augmented with expensive gems and decorated in four corners with weapons from across the kingdom—a broadsword, a battle-ax, a fine bow, and a heavily tipped pike. Above it hung the lion banner of Aquilonia.

Conan hardly noticed the design of the throne anymore, so used was he to sitting within its embrace. The seat was cushioned, though far from comfortable, and he wondered whether it was more molded to his body than it ever had been to any other. He'd certainly been king for longer than many who had held that position, especially the tyrannical King Numedides, whom Conan had strangled to death on these very steps.

"My lord," Councilor Ortan said. The other five councilors sitting with them to hear these points of law shifted uncomfortably in their oaken seats. One of them snorted and sat upright, startled awake by the sudden silence. Ortan was known to run off at the mouth, and he was also not afraid sometimes to question Conan's judgments. That was fine. Conan saw the advantage of having men and women advisors wiser than he in certain subjects.

He stopped pacing and faced Ortan where he stood before his own seat. It was customary for any speaker in the chamber to stand when presenting their argument.

Any but King Conan, it seemed.

"My lord, ancient law dictates that these points of contention are heard by you, and your decrees are made, whilst you are seated on the throne. The throne…" He pointed at the great seat, as if no one else in the room knew where or what it was. "…is rooted deep in the land, perhaps reaching right to the very heart of our world, and it connects you and your proclamations to history by—"

"Here is a new law," Conan said, stretching out and touching the throne's high stone back with his fingertips. "The king might make minor decisions of state whilst in sight and touching distance of the throne." He turned his back and walked around the high pedestal once more. Ortan breathed heavily, as if priming himself to profess his outrage, but Conan heard soft laughter from one of the other councilors—Magdella, he thought. She was the oldest of them, and he liked her because she was practical and logical, and used the trappings of office as a tool rather than as something with which to bind them all.

"Higher rates for substandard crops," Conan muttered. He walked another circle of the throne, in touching distance but never quite touching. His muscles felt better now, eased awake. He was not a man built for sitting still. He was not a king crowned to do nothing.

"I wouldn't choose to phrase it that way," Ortan said.

"I'm stronger than you, Councilor Ortan. If we dueled with blunted blades, would a strike from you score three times more than a strike from me?"

"No, my lord, of course not. But I do not understand why you bring up swordplay when the discussion at hand concerns farming and the fair—"

Councilor Magdella interrupted him. "I think what the king is saying is, the farmers of Poitan will think around their problem and discover other ways to make money, but their produce is worth the same."

"Either that or kill them all and feed them to their fields," Conan said.

He saw Ortan's look of shock and Magdella rolling her eyes. They all knew of Conan's past, and when he grew impatient he liked to tease them with reminders of the wild man who still lived beneath the crown.

Conan heard the soft scratch of Councilor Sugge striking through the crop-price proposal on that day's paper agenda. The matter closed, he leaned against the throne while the councilors went through the usual ritual of closing their meeting, and when they fell silent again Conan nodded his thanks and left the throne room.

Farmers and crop prices and angry councilors, he thought as he walked through wide, bright hallways toward his private chambers. *I used to be a barbarian in the cold north, a pirate raiding the coast of Kush and stealing precious spices and treasures, a mercenary riding with armies along the Zaporoska River, a thief stealing my fortune in Zamora, and a warrior—a scarred man of blood. And now I am a politician.*

As he walked, he tried to shake off the sense of dissatisfaction that had been settling over him for some time now. True, under his rule Aquilonia had enjoyed a period of relative peace and stability unknown in its history, and while he attributed that to the strength of its king—and, if needed, his willingness and even eagerness to fight—it also sometimes made him look back on his past with a sense of sadness. Aging, comfortable, and cosseted, he feared that he was also growing a little soft in soul as well as body.

King Conan of Cimmeria was a barbarian at heart, though it had come to pass that he was also an excellent and just king.

The hallway led him past beautiful paintings and marble busts of former kings and queens, all dead and gone now, their reigns fading into the gilded past or the mists of troubled history. Some of the paintings were smeared, some of the busts broken. Not every ruler held a coveted place in the heart of the land. Conan rarely thought about his own legacy, preferring instead to live in the here and now. An old friend had taught him that.

I need to swing my broadsword more often, he thought with a sigh. As he neared the entrance to his quarters, he promised himself that tomorrow he would train with the Black Dragons.

Conan pushed the heavy wooden door open and took a deep breath. Even softened as he was, he was always on alert for unexpected visitors or dangers, and he'd learned that smell could often be the first indicator of something amiss.

His chambers were as he expected to find them. A fire burned cheerily in the great hearth, casting dancing shadows across the large main room, where smaller fires burned in braziers around the walls. Hanging tapestries gave the place color and real warmth while a dozen overlapping rugs from all corners of Aquilonia hid the floor from view. Like anywhere in the royal palace, its stone structure was worn by a million steps that had come before him.

A large table was set with three candelabras, and several plates of food—meats, fresh bread, and an array of fruit—were covered with a fine, clear cloth to protect them from flies. There was enough for him and his queen, and no more. Conan hated wastefulness.

He could sense that Zenobia was not present, so he closed the heavy door behind him and stripped off his ceremonial cloak, throwing it casually across one of the chairs close to the fire. He shrugged his shoulders, squatted to stretch his legs, and then stared at the weapons hung on the display wall beside the fireplace—his broadsword, notched and dented from a hundred battles, every one of which he could still recall; his knife in its leather sheath that had been gifted to him by the witch Zelata thirty years ago. She'd told him that it was forever wedded to his hand, and he always felt a slight tug of attraction whenever he laid eyes on it. He still could not tell which way that attraction flowed. Probably both.

Conan heard bootsteps from somewhere far away drawing closer, and he went to the table and uncovered the food.

The door opened and Queen Zenobia breezed into the large room, bringing the whole place to life. She had been horse riding with their young son, Conn—who was probably now off hunting in the Wyve Woods with his two best friends and a retinue of the Black Dragons—and she was still energized from her efforts. Sweating, dirty with trail dust, her long dark hair tied in a scruffy bun to keep it out of the way while riding, she looked Conan up and down and smiled.

"I see you've had an enjoyable day," she said, laughing.

"One of us has, it seems."

She walked by him, plucked up a carafe of wine, and poured two glasses, handing one to Conan. She clinked glasses with him. In private they were husband and wife, parents of Conn, and they dispensed with the trappings of formality, which they both secretly despised.

"May all your demons wither..." Zenobia said.

"...and burn in the fires of your heart," Conan replied. It

was an old Stygian toast, and Conan always chuckled when he imagined Ortan's reaction were he ever to hear it uttered in the royal palace.

They drank. It was good wine. Of course it was. Conan closed his eyes and thought of the rough wines of Shem, as likely to strip the lining from your tongue as get you drunk. He'd spent many a night around campfires drinking that stuff and listening to his companions tell tales of far-off places. Conan had rarely relayed stories of his own, because he much preferred to listen.

"Conn is quite a rider," she said. "Better than you, even."

Conan grunted.

"So, what of your day?"

"Councilor Ortan made my ears bleed."

"Oh? Again? What was it this time?"

"You smell," he said, and Zenobia raised her eyebrows.

"Such a greeting for your wife and queen!" She came in close and sniffed at Conan. "You stink of comfort and an easy life."

"Don't mock."

"I'd never mock."

"Sometimes I think…" Conan shrugged, and she saw his eyes flick toward the display wall bearing his weapons.

"Sometimes you think you want to go off adventuring again, raiding here, conquering there, righting wrongs, stealing treasures and vanquishing beasts, and sailing the dangerous seas. But a peaceful life is the curse of providing the land with strong leadership and a period of tranquility." She sighed. "The wild calls you. It always has and always will. You dream of it at night."

"How do you know?"

"You talk in your sleep sometimes." She finished her wine and sat back on the edge of the table, picking up a chicken leg and taking a hefty bite. "But I'd rather have you safe and alive."

"Than wandering and happy?"

"You're not as young as you used to be," she pointed out.

He grunted again.

Zenobia finished the leg and dropped the bone onto the table. "Let's sit and eat together, and perhaps plan a trip to Zingara."

"A trip with a hundred Black Dragons making sure every breath I take is a safe one."

She ignored his complaining. "But as you say, I smell of horses and sweat and the trail. So I'll bathe before we eat." She stood and walked toward the door leading into their bedroom and bathing quarters, undoing her clothing as she went, letting it fall to the floor. "Would you like to unsheathe your sword and come with me, my king?"

As Conan took three steps after his wife, someone knocked loudly at the door—two knocks, a pause, three more. It was the signal that his personal guard, Vaccharez, always used.

"What is it?" Conan shouted, frustrated. Zenobia finished stripping at the door into their chambers and smiled over her shoulder before closing the door behind her. "Damn it, what is it?"

"My lord, a visitor has arrived demanding to see you," Vaccharez said from beyond the door.

Conan sighed and went to the door, hauling it open. Vaccharez's eyes flicked past him toward the food-laden table, the fire, the scattered clothing.

"Apologies, my lord—"

"Vaccharez."

The big man relaxed with a sigh. He was a great warrior and bodyguard and had become a friend, but he was still uncomfortable with Conan's disregard of some of the trappings of royalty.

"Conan," he said. "I wouldn't have disturbed you if—"

"What visitor?"

"He won't tell us his name. He won't tell me anything."

"And so?"

"He says he must see you. He demands it." Vaccharez shifted

from foot to foot, uncomfortable but certain. Conan respected the man's judgment and knew that he had a talent to read a person as if their thoughts, desires, and schemes were laid out before him in a book.

"Demands?"

Vaccharez shrugged.

"Where is he?"

"In the treatment rooms."

"He's sick?"

"Sick. Injured. Mutilated. He says he's come all the way from Khoraja to see you, and you alone."

Conan's eyes went wide with surprise. Khoraja was almost a thousand miles away. Thoughts of his wife immersing herself in their giant scented bath played across his mind, but he was also a curious man and this was something far out of the ordinary. A mystery. He sensed change, something in the air. Maybe a problem not involving crop quotients and farm border disputes. Perhaps even adventure.

"I have examined him for any ill intent," Vaccharez said. "I know desperation when I see it, and this man is desperate. But there is something strange."

Conan raised an eyebrow.

"It seems he also has dispensation to call you Conan. Not King. Just Conan."

Vaccharez took them along a fast, quiet route to the treatment rooms, utilizing some of the palace's lesser-trodden corridors that wound around chambers and great halls, between solid, ancient walls, and beneath floors. Conan knew many of these byways, but as usual Vaccharez surprised him with some turns and diversions. It was simply so that they could move quickly and without being disturbed, but it felt like secrecy. Conan enjoyed that.

When they arrived at the treatment rooms, the two guards stood to attention, both slamming their short battle-spears on the ground in salute. Conan nodded and passed between them and through the door.

Vaccharez closed the door behind him after muttering to the guards, "No one to disturb the king."

The man was on a cot in the far corner of the first room. There were no other patients, but a leech attended him, a very old man whose name Conan could never recall even though he'd tended to several medical issues for him over the past few years. He was quiet and methodical, hardly speaking, moving silently, as if never wishing his patient to be aware of his presence. He was focused on his skill and talent, and the rest of the world was incidental. Conan respected that.

The man lying on the cot looked like he'd been through a dozen wars and barely emerged from the other side. His right hand was missing, the skin of his arm blazing red with infection all the way up to the shoulder. The red was darkening to a deep plum color here and there where infection had turned to rot. Conan was surprised his blood had not been poisoned and spread throughout his body. He was thin to the point of emaciation, skin stretched across his face and skull like a death mask on a corpse. Sunburn had blistered his exposed limbs, face, and neck, and where the leech had removed clothing to treat his wretched body, the skin was pale and slick like that of a subterranean slug. Several fragrant candles were lit around his cot, but the stink of corruption could not be disguised.

The leech bowed his head slightly at Conan but never paused in his task. His hands moved back and forth across the corpse-like man as he began to speak, administering healing balms, checking bones for breaks, assessing grazes and ruptures with expert fingertips. He had affixed several giant suckslugs on the man's arm to draw some of the rank blood, and they were swollen and pulsing black. "He's fallen into the sleep of the dead," the leech said. "He arrived on foot at the palace's main gate, and I cannot understand how he was still walking. The guards there said that upon uttering your name, he collapsed into darkness."

"Will he wake?"

The leech shrugged, still working. "Perhaps soon, perhaps never. I am doing my best to aid him. His flesh is shriveled and dried, and infection from his mutilated arm has begun to spread through his organs and bones. He's hot to the touch. I've given him some herbal decoctions of my own making to try and cool him, lest he melt his own brain, but they will take some time to work. I believe he was once a strong man, and that's why he still lives. But now he's exhausted, half-starved, dehydrated, and so weakened that—"

"Yet he came all this way to see me," Conan said.

"Not to see the king," the leech said. He leaned down and whispered into the stranger's ear, as if talking only to him. "To see Conan."

The man's eyelids flickered, eyeballs rolling behind them, then grew still.

"I am Conan," Conan said. "Speak, stranger."

The sick man's eyes flickered again, and then they cracked open. He stared at the ceiling, his mouth working, tongue swollen between tombstone teeth. The leech moistened the man's lips with a sponge, dribbled some water into his mouth, and held one hand against his forehead to settle him.

"There... there..." the leech said, and Conan was struck by the man's caring attitude for someone he had never known.

"Co... nan..." the man said, his croaking voice weak but clear. "I can't see you. Are you really here?"

"King Conan is here," Vaccharez said.

The man actually smiled, cracked lips leaking a pale, thin blood. "King. Oh, king. Of course you became king. Such greatness was always meant for you. That's what you said. That's how I found you."

"I don't know you," Conan said.

"Can I trouble you for… a drink and some food?" the man asked.

"I'll arrange for some soup and water, only water," the leech said.

The man shook his head. "I have not eaten in… days. Many days."

"Some soup," the leech insisted. "You're too weak for anything else."

"Ah, Conan," the man said, and an urgency seemed to bite at him. He lifted his remaining hand and reached, clasping at the air. Conan held out his own hand but the leech shook his head.

"I need to check him for illnesses," he said.

"I'm not ill," the man said. "I'm sick… with desperation." He turned and looked for Conan, wet eyes pale as they rolled in his skull. At last they focused on him, and something in Conan stirred—recognition, vague but there.

"A favor," the man said. "A favor for the friend you did not die with after all."

"Baht Tann," Conan said. The name tumbled from his mouth like a forgotten memory, excavated after so many years buried and almost lost. "Is this really you?"

Tann raised his hand again and this time Conan took it, much to Vaccharez's consternation.

"I know this man of old," Conan said. "He's safe." He wondered at that, how trust settled around him so quickly. Conan had known so much treachery in his life that trust and loyalty were more valuable to him than gold or gems.

"Really me," Baht Tann croaked. "And I have come to call in my favor."

"What happened to you?" Conan asked.

"Lean in, friend. My body and voice are weak, but my cause is strong. Lean in, and while your good leech fetches my water and soup, I will tell you my story."

As I fell, I knew that even if I survived I would not be able to take them on my own.

I haven't killed anyone in over thirty years. After Tangara—after you saved my life and we escaped that dread, cursed place where I believed all the gods had deigned that we would die—I went out into the world with only peace in my heart. I'd seen enough death, and dished enough of it myself. Given new life and a new chance thanks to you, Conan, I swore by Ishtar I'd make the most of it. Raiding, pillaging, and selling my sword would only bring new pain and fresh grief to others, and eventually to myself as well.

So I hit the river hard. It was lucky I'd kicked out from the cliff just as I fell. That dying bandit falling with me broke my fall into the water, my gem-knife still clasped in my severed hand stuck in his spilled guts. I almost died a dozen times more as the rough waters spilled me through rapids and over waterfalls, but four things kept me afloat, struggling, fighting for life.

The first is Grake, the bandits' leader, a brutish man who knows no pity and whom I see every time I close my eyes. Funny, at first I thought he was you, Conan, such is his size and strength and ferociousness. But he is a lesser man than both of us.

The other three reasons for me to live are called Larria, Davin, and Korum, my wife and our twin sons. No, no, I'm fine—these tears are good because they show I care. They show you that my family are all that matter to me. We've been prospecting for heartgems together for years, climbing cliffs and mountains and venturing into deep cave systems, searching for those elusive treasures. Once each season we travel to the meadow cities of Shem or the coastal towns of Argos to trade them with merchants from far away. It is a hard life, true, but it gives us freedom. As a large group, we've become self-sufficient and...

And now many of my friends are dead, put to the sword by Grake and his brutal men and women. Those who survived, including my wife and sons, will be slaving for them, sent back down those Khorajan cliffs, because we'd already found a dozen gems so there will be more. We were lucky enough to find a rich resource, and we'd already discussed staying in that remote place for the rest of the season and perhaps the one following.

For those slaves, there will be no safe climbing. No caution. Remember in Tangara, Conan, how little those Zamoran guards cared for us? I fear the same for my family and friends.

So as I struggled in that raging river, I decided I had to live. I knew that if I rushed back up to that escarpment and took on the bandits myself, I would die and achieve nothing. I'd been lucky once, airing the guts of that brute and using him to break my fall. I would not be so lucky a second time. And so I knew where I must travel to, and whom I had to seek out for help.

I eventually fought my way to the bank miles downstream, the great desert to one side of me, the plains of Shem to the other. I was exhausted, battered, and broken, but I knew I could not pause for a moment more. I made my plans. I didn't care about the great distance. Those many hundreds of miles I counted in how many moons it would be until I might be able to save my family. I lit a fire, sealed my wounds with flame, and screamed into the night as rage and hate filled me and determination fed me.

I set out in the darkness, a man who would not stop moving. And Death followed me, Conan. It danced in my wake and slurped up my tears and leaking blood with its forked tongue. It stalked me through Shem's northern mountain passes, peering from deep caves with blood-red eyes, growling, baring its glimmering teeth in godless moonlight. High in those passes, the snows came and Death chilled my muscles and bones, laughing when I attempted to light fires, creeping closer when I tried to catch a few moments' sleep. Down from the passes it drifted across the plains on the wings of stark-ravens. They circled me, harrying me as I ran. I grabbed one on the wing as it came for my eyes, throttled it, bit out its throat, and drank its blood. I tasted Death and swallowed it deep, screaming in defiance as it fed and sustained me rather than taking me down into dark oblivion.

Ten days after my fall, I found myself in a border skirmish in the mountains where Shem and Koth meet. For two days, Death was closer to me than ever before, ringing out in the sounds of clashing steel, blazing oils flooding through murder-ditches, the swooshing of bowmen filling the air with poison-tipped arrows. I crawled through a field of gluttonous reeds close to a raging river that were feeding on spilled blood, their leaves turned razor sharp as they hungrily sought more. My limbs were sliced, my face opened to the bone. I bled. I vomited at the stench of death, even while Death itself crawled and splashed after me, laughing, teasing, promising me my moment but never... quite... arriving.

Coated in the gore of countless dead, I finally descended into Koth and continued on my way. By day I rode on a horse I'd captured and tamed from those hundreds fleeing the field of battle. I called her Bolt, and she was a good horse. By night I was forced to give her rest, and I lay awake staring at the stars and willing them to give me speed and courage. I dreamed that Larria, Davin, and Korum were looking at those same stars and drawing their own courage.

I knew that they believed me to be dead. I hoped that grief

fed their determination to survive.

Bolt carried me far, until close to Ophir she was taken down by a river sprite. It rose from the marshes and came at us, and that was when I believed Death had chosen its moment to take me down. We fell, I struggled, Bolt died. The sprite must have been hungry for flesh rather than ready to tease and torture, because it burrowed into the horse while I swam and splashed and hauled my way through fields of mud planted with its previous dead. With each breath I thought it would come for me, but I survived.

My arm was infected. I could smell it and taste Death's laughter on my tongue, but I dared not stop to heal. I was given some herbal medicines by villagers in Ophir, curing balms that helped ease the pain and gave me the strength to continue.

You were on my mind, Conan. Always you. No one else would help me. No one else could. I knew that I was dying, but my strength never wavered. Death had stalked me all that way, from the base of those cliffs to where I was now, and eventually I made friends with it. I denied the fact of my own mortality. I would not allow Death to have its way, and as I crossed Aquilonia and came here to Tarantia, I became a ghost of the man I used to be.

And here I am now, that same ghost from the past. Come to call in that promise you made and the favor you owe me. Come to haunt you, perhaps. But here I am all the same. And now, my old friend, I submit myself to you as I never did to Death. With all my heart, and all my soul.

Even as Baht Tann had begun his story, Conan knew that he would go. A promise was a promise—even a promise given under such circumstances, forty years ago when neither of them had truly believed that they would survive. Perhaps such a vow carried even more weight.

Conan experienced a sudden vivid flashback to Bald Man and Beard debating his fate on that long-ago Zamoran battlefield. Lying there in the bloody mud, strength flagging and death approaching, he had dreamed of everything he might have done had he survived. In the four decades since that moment, he had lived all those dreams, and many more, yet still his hunger for adventure bit in hard.

"I will help you, of course," Conan said. He heard Vaccharez's gasp of surprise. "I will save your family and friends from this Grake and his bandits."

"Thank you," Tann said. "Thank…" He closed his eyes and the leech moved close and continued his ministrations.

There was no internal debate, no weighing of facts—he had made a promise, and Conan kept his promises. Yet he knew that everything would stand against what he had already committed to do—his throne, his position in Aquilonia, his advisors and councilors and subjects, and especially Zenobia and his son, Conn.

But his mind was made up. His broadsword was not an object of art to be kept hanging on a wall.

4

A King Alone

King Conan was not a man prone to examining himself in front of a mirror, but seeing how much Baht Tann had changed had shocked him into doing so.

His old friend was less than a ghost of whom he had once been. Conan had last known him as a warrior, hungry and weakened by captivity but still possessed of a fighter's mindset and body. They'd parted ways on the borders of Corinthia, and though Conan had thought of Tann a few times over the next few years, he had eventually faded away into the past along with many others. Now he had returned, a wretched shadow of his former self. By his own admission he was a changed man, traveling the land in search of precious and elusive heartgems. He had left violence behind.

Look where that led him, Conan thought.

In the decades since they had last seen each other, Conan had changed as well. Back then he'd still been a young man with a wandering heart and a soul ravenous for adventure, searching the world for purpose. He'd come to realize that he had already found that purpose by the time he and Tann crossed paths in that wagon on their way to the Tangaran salt mines, and after their escape he had ventured back and forth across the land and the seas surrounding it, from skin-clad barbarian to mail-clad mercenary, to thief stealing through shadowy streets and secret chambers beneath palaces and castles, to corsair sailing a dragon-prowed ship into battle and pillage. Chancer. Warrior. King.

"Soft king," Conan said. He prodded his flabby stomach, pressed his fingers against his chest, tapped his hip, and watched a ripple travel around his torso, trying to convince himself it was an imperfection in the mirror and not in him. He had never much been concerned about how he looked, but lately he'd noticed these changes. His muscles were still there, and he prided himself that he could probably take on and defeat any three warriors from the Black Dragons in combat—sometimes he even trained with them to reassure himself of this idea—but he was an older man now, and seeing the shocking change in Baht Tann brought the smaller, more subtle changes in his own body and heart into focus.

"You have a son," Zenobia said from the doorway.

Conan looked at her in the mirror. "He's strong. Conn will take my place when I'm away. Good practice."

"And a wife."

Conan grunted.

"And let's not forget a kingdom to rule."

He sighed. "I'll miss you both. But while Conn takes the throne, you'll be the real power. His advisor and guide."

"I just know what Councilor Ortan will think of that," Zenobia said, laughing.

"Ortan is older than the hills and twice as wrinkled," Conan said.

They both laughed, embraced, and took comfort.

"I do understand you feel you must go," she said. "I respect that. It's one of the many things I love about you. But make me happier and take an escort, at least. You'll be passing through Ophir and Koth, and neither place is a friend of Conan. And sometimes you do need help. Or have you forgotten how we met?"

"You saved me from twisted magic and a monster wizard's creations," Conan replied. "Neither figure here."

"You're so sure? You know that how?"

"One man alone will attract no attention."

"And when you get to Khoraja, and if Baht Tann's family are still alive, will you rescue them from a group of battle-hardened barbarians? Tann said there were twenty of them, maybe more."

"Yes."

Zenobia sighed and pushed away from him, gently but firmly. She looked him up and down. "You're already a man of too many scars."

"Scar tissue is hard."

"A promise, then. You make promises to your friends, and hold to them, it seems. Now make a promise to me."

Conan waited, silent.

"Promise me that you will return to us when this is done."

He thought about that, and about how she spoke those words with love. His answer came from the same place. Conan was an honest man, and he could not speak a lie, especially to the one he loved above all others.

"I promise that I will try."

Next morning, an hour before dawn, Conan kissed his wife and son farewell and went to check on Baht Tann one last time. The wounded and sick man was still in the same cot in the treatment rooms, and the leech continued to tend to him, seemingly untiring and unwavering in his commitment to this stranger he did not know. Conan mused that he could do with more people like the leech in his council.

He asked how Tann was faring.

"He may live, but he'll more likely die, my lord," the leech said, keeping his voice low so that Tann could not hear. "I've never seen such strength and determination. He should have been dead a dozen times already, from blood loss, infection, a corruption of his humors. There are bites all across his body, and I believe two of them were from lion spiders. A drop of toxin from one of those should kill a man twice his size. He's suffered his way through so much to come here, my lord." The leech looked Conan up and down and the ghost of a smile touched his lips.

"Clothes do not make a king," Conan said.

"Oh, I know that, my lord. It's heart and soul, and you have plenty of both."

"I'll speak with him before I leave. Is he awake?"

"If he isn't, nudge him from sleep. It's time I bathed and turned him again. For now, I'll leave you with your old friend, my lord. He is a man who is lucky to count you as friend."

"You're a good man," Conan said.

The leech bowed his head and walked away, and Conan sat on the edge of Baht Tann's cot.

He might have been asleep. His eyes were half closed, and his breath rasped, fast and light. His body beneath the light blanket was never still, twitching in discomfort and pain, or perhaps at memories that haunted his days and nights.

"Baht," Conan said, and at the sound of his voice Tann's breathing paused and he opened his eyes.

"You look like a nomad," Tann said. His laugh was a stony croak.

"Always have been," Conan said. "I'm leaving now."

"It's been so many days," Tann said, and he started to shiver again, his clawed hand reaching out for Conan. "I should have stayed, gone back, tried to fight them, and—"

"And died. You're not that man anymore."

"But you are, Conan?"

Conan grabbed his hand and held it, but not hard. He feared that his old friend's bones would crumble beneath his grip. He said no more, but he put his hand to Tann's forehead and nodded.

Then he stood to leave, feeling Tann's gaze on his back as he walked from the treatment room. He picked up the things he'd left by the door—his traveling pack, his broadsword safe within its sheath, and the knife given to him by Zelata—and without a backward glance he left his comfortable, cosseted present and went to discover his destiny.

There were several ways into Old Tarantia and thence to the royal palace itself. The ancient, wide suspension bridge that led to the rest of the great city was always bustling with travelers and traders, eager to sell their wares and take advantage of the safety that came from being so close to the palace. The Old Tarantian docks were similarly busy, and there were always queues of boats waiting to be registered and checked before being allowed to moor and disgorge their passengers and cargo. Elsewhere, several long footbridges crossed from the plains to the north and east of Old Tarantia, used by travelers from beyond the city itself. All of these routes were guarded by the Black Dragons, highly trained warriors committed to protecting the throne and whoever sat upon it.

Disguised though he was, Conan could not risk using any of these routes to leave the city. He wore the clothes of a traveler—scruffy boots, worn trousers, a tattered leather singlet, and a robe that was more holes than material. On his back he carried his traveling pack, one that he'd hardly used in decades but had kept lovingly oiled and stored for such an occasion as this. Sheathed across his back was his broadsword, its handle wrapped in old oilcloth so that the finely carved ivory was hidden from casual view, and he wore the knife on his belt. Both weapons were within easy reach. Yet despite these precautions of disguise and readiness, he knew that if he tried to cross the suspension bridge, buy passage on a boat, or seek egress over one of the smaller footbridges, he would be recognized. He could not disguise his bulk, nor his piercing blue eyes.

But he knew other ways out of the city.

Down through the depths of the palace, where it was rooted in the rock of the world, he became a man of stealth, slipping into shadows when he heard people approaching, crouching in doorways to let Black Dragons pass by on their way to and from their quarters. He skirted around busy kitchens, scooping up some fruit and dried meats from a trolley left unattended and dropping them into his pockets for later.

Deeper still, he forced open barred doors that had been locked for years, lighting a torch and brandishing it to see away troubled shadows that would haunt this place forever. These were the palace's deep dungeons, mostly unused now but in the past home to dreadful tortures and agonizing deaths. He could sense ghosts down here, and the dagger grew warm at his hip. Shapes skittered into the shadows to avoid the flickering light cast by the flame, and he saw the glint of eyes watching him from side corridors and high in the cavernous ceilings. Sometimes the eyes were in pairs, red-tinged and angry at this intrusion. Sometimes there were a dozen of them set close together, pulsing in slow, lazy blinks.

He kept moving, one hand on the knife handle, because the fact that he was king did not matter in these forgotten, haunted depths. He passed several gated dungeons and did not glance through the bars. Whatever depravities these wraiths had been subjected to were their own, and he gave them the privacy to suffer in peace.

As he wound his way through the deep roots of the palace and moved out beneath Old Tarantia itself, he started wading through water that grew deeper, then deeper still, and he knew that he was beneath the river at last. Ancient hands had built these tunnels and catacombs, and more recently the royals preceding him had used them for their own nefarious and brutal ends. Conan's closing-up of these spaces had been a statement, but he was a man always ready for change. If they ever required opening again, their dark depths made ready to receive prisoners and enemies, he would be the first at the gates.

Now, this was his secret way out of the city. The frisson of danger that accompanied every step set his senses alight and his soul soaring. There were no guards down here to see that he was safe from aggressors or potential assassins, no Black Dragons clearing the way for him—not even his friend Vaccharez, who had committed life and soul to Conan's safety.

Being so alone felt good.

As he passed beneath the Khorotas River, the waters flooding the tunnel grew deeper and colder. He felt slick shapes darting past his legs and feet, and he waved the light around him to keep whatever they might be at bay. Fish, probably. Only fish.

At last, he reached the end of the tunnel network and a set of stone stairs spiraled up toward the surface. He counted the steps as he climbed, and just before reaching two hundred he arrived at a wide landing area. Breathing hard, he wiped sweat from his eyes, moving the torch around and locating the old oaken door that would open onto the outside world once again.

He only hoped he'd come the right way. He had passed a dozen junctions, staircases leading up and down, and he knew that there were even deeper routes that ran further, and to more mysterious places. But where he was now was in a system of natural caves, not tunnels dug and built by ancient races. Far more ancient than even the oldest worked stone of Tarantia, they were a place and law unto themselves, and there was no saying what might live in them.

Starting to crave daylight, Conan heaved at the rusted bolts on the oak door. They were stuck fast, rotted in place, so he drew his broadsword and pried at them, working the heavy tip beneath their metal plates and gouging the wood around them until they popped free. He slid the sword through the circular metal handle and it turned, creaking and complaining, until the door popped open with an angry puff of dust.

He passed through, closed the door behind him, and found himself surrounded by great mountains of grain, thousands of bags of it piled high all around. This, then, was one of the many dockside warehouses along the riverbank across from Old Tarantia, a few hundred steps from the great bridge. He sighed with relief. It seemed that he had navigated the right way.

He was away from Old Tarantia and the palace and all the people who knew him. Now he had to work his way through the great city of Tarantia itself, and not be recognized by all those who knew of him.

He made his way through the warehouse, and as he approached the wide doors the fresh light of the morning sun drew him onward, and the bustle of the streets outside gave him cheer. Shaking off the shadows of the underworld, Conan pulled his cape's hood over his head and set out into the throng.

He enjoyed the experience of witnessing the city as a lone traveler once again, instead of as king. Usually, if he passed this way he

was surrounded by a retinue of guards and attendants, and their movement left a wake, his presence having an effect on everyone and everything around him. Now he saw the city in its normal state—raucous, loud, bustling, the wide streets thronging with its denizens. Traders sold fruit and vegetables, crafts and tools, waving them above their heads and trying to lure people in to part with their hard-earned luna. Some sang songs, others were funny, all offered a better deal than others further along the street. Buyers wended their way around these sellers, sometimes engaging but more often using their own judgment as to whether something was worth buying or not.

The scents of street food made Conan's stomach rumble—spices and herbs coating a variety of meats and cooking in hot fat, marinated vegetables roasting over open fires, exotic fruits sliced and laid out on slate platters, adding their own sweetness to the air. Music drifted in from where taverns spilled into the streets, and the hoppy hint of ale made his mouth water. His presence here did not cause waves and he left no wake in his path, although some did glance at him and step aside. A stranger the size of Conan, in clothing so obviously worn and tattered by a long time spent on the trail and bearing a broadsword on his back, caused more than a few people to move out of his way.

Beyond the streets, the tall buildings and spires at the city's center caught the bright sunlight, exaggerating their blue and gold colors and shimmering rainbows high above the city. Conan glanced back only once, and saw the mighty palace on the hills of Old Tarantia looming high over the rest of the city. He had never been lured there by the palace's riches, but he always felt a sense of awe when he viewed the conglomeration of tall, grand buildings from outside. So much effort, so much heart had gone into its construction. So much pain, too—the lives of so many slaves. He grunted and turned away, knowing he might never set eyes on the place again.

He kept his gaze down most of the time, trying not to appear too threatening. He smiled when someone caught his eye, bought some spiced flatbreads from a trader and bantered with her, and then found himself leaving the bustling center of the city and heading toward the outer suburbs. There were fewer people here, and he sped up. He was a man on a mission.

Khoraja was a long way to travel on his own, over nine hundred miles, and Baht Tann's memories of his own traumatic and extraordinary journey were hazy and clouded by grief and pain. He must have been traveling for thirty or forty days at least, and Conan's journey might be of a similar length. His friend's wife and sons might be dead by the time he reached them, if they hadn't already been murdered, died from maltreatment, or been sold into slavery.

Yet he had to try, and he would do his best to cross that distance as quickly as possible. He was more than aware of the dangers he would face, despite the fact that he'd been king for a long time, protected by the Black Dragons, fed and watered by a huge staff of servants, and with a soft bed to sleep in each night.

Damn, he'd lived a soft life for too long! Conan tried to be as honest with himself as he was with his friends and loved ones, and he knew that all of this was not only about fulfilling the promise he had made to Baht Tann. This was also about him.

At the city's eastern edge, he purchased a horse from a farmer who bought from tired travelers and sold to those venturing once more away from the city. The one he wanted was a strong, fine stallion, but Conan was already trying to cover his tracks. He pretended that he could not afford that animal, and when the dealer refused to haggle, he chose instead a steed that looked almost as old and soft as him.

"Her name is Ella," the horse dealer said.

"Ella." She neighed and turned her ass to him as if to say, *Who are you to use my name?* Conan said, "I like her already."

As the sun reached its highest point, he rode the moody mare away from the city and out toward the eastern plains that led eventually to Ophir, hoping to make twenty miles before sunset. He sensed how strong Ella was, despite her mulish countenance, and it took only an hour for her to fall into a decent pace. He did not push her too hard, but neither was he soft with her. It seemed that she respected that.

Conan and Ella, man and horse, left Tarantia behind them, and hours later the setting sun cast their shadows down the long road ahead.

Conan ate in the saddle. He folded the dried meat he'd taken from the palace kitchens into the flatbreads he'd bought in the marketplace. Consuming that simple meal out in the open air of the countryside made him feel good. Ella snorted when she smelled the food, but he kept her moving. She'd have her feed when the time came.

As the sun dipped below the horizon behind them and shadows rose from the ground, he chose a place to camp close to an outcropping of rocks. He tied the horse's reins loosely to a tree, giving her plenty of room to move around, and while she grazed on rich grasses he walked the area, making sure they were alone and that there were no snakes or more deadly creatures hidden in the nooks and crevasses of the rocks. He found a small stream on the rocky mound's far side and refilled his water bladder, sniffing first to check that the water was not tainted.

As he drank, he saw three shooting stars streaking overhead from west to east, disappearing below the distant horizon. Perhaps the gods were watching him, or maybe observing eyes belonging to more eldritch entities. Conan wished he could defy their silent scrutiny and ride with the stars, but he concentrated only on what he could control. And right now he was hungry again and growing cold.

It had been a long time since he'd had to hunt for his own food. While Ella continued to graze close to where he'd left his traveling pack—though he retained his broadsword on his back—he crept around the rocks and started looking for signs of game. There was a scattering of deer scat, but it was old and crumbling between his fingers. He found several pigeon nests high up on the sloping rock face, but they contained only scattered feathers and the dried remnants of broken eggs—some other predator had been here before him. Close to the stream, he felt the ground change texture beneath his feet, and when he knelt and ran his open hands through the grass, he felt rabbit droppings. They smelled fresh.

He built a snare, using a thin willow sapling close to the stream and a leather cord from his belt pack. It flipped from his hands twice while he was tying it down, lashing across his face and raising welts, but Conan was patient and persistent, letting his forgetful hands catch up with memories of trapping food in the wild a thousand times during long-ago travels.

Eventually the snare was set, and he went back to where Ella now stood dozing. He smoothed her coat where he'd removed his saddle, and she whinnied softly at his touch. He felt that they were already becoming friends.

Conan had missed working with horses. Those at the palace were always trained and broken in by his stable servants, the animals made into willing servants themselves, but Conan always preferred a ride that was its own beast. A horse should always go the way it wished to go. His gift as a rider was to make it believe it wanted to go in the direction he desired.

Keeping one ear open for the snare around by the stream, he went about building a fire. He was pleased to find that this still came naturally, though it took a dozen strokes from the flint to cast enough sparks into the dried kindling he carried in a pouch in his pack. Soon, though, he had smoke and a flame, and he gathered some fuel from the gaps beneath looming rocks, using his broadsword to sweep it out in case snakes or spiders lurked there. He found enough dried wood to last the night and set it down a few feet from the fire.

He sat sipping from his water bladder and stared across the flames into the deepening darkness. He let his mind go free, and like a well-treated steed it moved the way he wished. Still awake, Conan allowed himself to dream of past times when he had traveled alone in other lands for different reasons, until the sharp whip of the snare stirred him to alertness once more.

He dashed around the rocks and saw the small shape struggling in the leather cord's noose. With a muttered thanks to the land, he broke the rabbit's neck and untied the snare, pocketing the cord.

Skinning and gutting the beast took moments, his hands moving as if they had their own memory that had not softened and grown lazy. If he thought about what he was doing, his hands would stray, his mind interrupting and telling him that he'd had his food caught, prepared, and cooked for him for too long. But Conan's muscle memory was all of the wild, and he reveled in the feel of blood on his hands and the smell of honestly caught game spitted and cooking over a fire he had made.

With grease on his chin and a full stomach, he glanced around the fire. Ella stood motionless, snorting and farting softly in her sleep. The remains of the rabbit still hung over the fire, dripping melted fat that spat into clear blue flames before smoking away to nothing. Beyond the flickering light, a deeper darkness pulsed and ebbed with shadows. And something more.

Conan stood and disappeared into the dark, there one moment, gone the next. He moved so quietly and smoothly that

Ella did not stir, and neither did the fading fire's flames. He was a wraith.

A few heartbeats later, he was around the other side of the pile of rocks, consumed by shadows but using his other senses to find his way. He could hear leather stretching, carelessly held weapons scraping stone, soft breathing. He could smell the sweat of unwashed bodies and a warm garlic taint on the air from whatever meal they'd last eaten. And then he saw the partial silhouettes of his stalkers cast by the campfire beyond.

He must have turned a stone with his foot or perhaps trodden on a stick, because they stood and spun around in shock at Conan's sudden appearance.

He swung the broadsword from above his right shoulder, intending to take their heads. His heartbeat was barely raised, his breathing steady, and he was focused on his attack. No one creeping around and spying on him at night could have good intent.

Steel clanged and sparked as a sword was raised in defense, parrying his powerful blow. He was surprised at their speed, and he looked to one side, knowing that in the dark he should rely more on peripheral vision. He pulled the sword down toward the ground, hoping to slice through their wrists, but then someone called out.

"My lord!" The man who had deflected his blow lowered his sword and bowed his head toward him. "It's Vaccharez and two Black Dragons. Have mercy! We're here to ensure your safety."

Conan tensed, holding his sword raised once more, calculating the angle and speed of the blow he'd need to kill them. The other two silhouettes also bowed in supplication, and he wondered if this was some ploy. Though he recognized the voice, he knew that there were glamors that could fool his hearing. And Vaccharez would never defy his orders and sneak out after him.

He swung, and his broadsword hummed through the air in anticipation of blood. The shapes parted and rolled and he missed them all, turning slightly as the heavy sword's momentum almost caught him off balance.

Rusty and tired! he thought, berating himself. Fight like Conan, not like a street urchin.

He crouched, sword held before him to defend against the counterattack that must surely come, when one of the other figures spoke.

"My lord, it's Elize!" the woman said. "I trained with you two moons ago on the archery range. And Vaccharez speaks the truth."

Conan paused, doubt worming in. He remained alert, tensed and ready for battle. "Who won?" he demanded.

There was only a slight pause. "Er... I did, my lord."

Conan lowered his blade and stood upright, but still kept it ready to swing up in defense. Vaccharez was his bodyguard and friend, and the Black Dragons were sworn to protect the crown and whatever king happened to bear it, but he knew better than to trust mere appearances.

Then the truth settled around him and he smiled in the dark.

"Councilor Ortan sent you," he said, although he knew that was a lie. Whether or not they now revealed the truth would decide their fate.

"No, my lord," Vaccharez said, and he chuckled. "Your wife, Queen Zenobia, instructed us to follow you and keep you safe."

Conan laughed aloud. "I am safe!" There was no reply. Vaccharez and the others would have known that Zenobia's order to them went against their king's wishes. "There's some rabbit left," he said with a sigh. "Eat before you return to Tarantia."

"Thank you, my lord," Elize said, standing and sheathing her sword. The other two did the same. "But we will not be returning—"

"This is Quille," Vaccharez said, interrupting Elize and touching the other Dragon's shoulder. "She's one of the finest fighters we have with a shortsword."

"Quille, you allow your weapons to touch stone," Conan said. "Elize, your leather belt is not tight enough. And Vaccharez, you smell of garlic."

Cowed, the three warriors followed Conan back to his fire. Ella stirred only slightly, offering a disinterested glare before lowering her head again. Conan sat across the fire from the warriors, and they each pulled off a few fingers of flesh from the cooked rabbit.

That is how three soldiers of the Black Dragons ate a meal with their king and Conan spent his first night in many years alone beneath the stars, not alone at all.

5

A Tale of Grake

With Conan before him, Grake's greatest day has arrived.
He is caked in warm, sticky, congealing blood. Shattered bone shards speckle his left forearm, and a splash of brains has sealed his right eye shut. However much he wipes it, he cannot clear his vision. The brains belong to someone else. He wonders whether it is friend or foe, but Grake does not care. In truth, there is no friend or foe anymore. There is only Grake and everyone else, and everyone else is about to see just how great he is.

Around him are three dozen corpses, freshly opened and leaking goodness and life into the ground. Most were killed by him in a fighting frenzy, his energy and rage aggravated and enhanced by the quesh he took just before the fight. He keeps worrying that he will run out of the Khitain drug one of these days, but the pouch that was given to him by the age-grizzled, three-armed wizard in the darkness of an ancient keep exactly two hundred and twenty-two miles east of the Vilayet Sea has never emptied. The wizard told him it was the leathered scrotum of a demon and the quesh was its unholy seed renewing, renewing, renewing, day after day. Each time he wets his fingers and dips them inside, they find quesh and his muscles are fed, his soul set aflame.

I will be the greatest warrior this land has ever known, Grake thinks, a familiar desire that has been as powerful as the quesh at drawing him onward through life since he was very, very young. It is a desire that became a quest, and then an obsession. Now, he is ready to feed the obsession and mount that pedestal at last.

There are a hundred witnesses left over from the recent battle. Most of those on either side are wounded and bloodied, but the skirmish has now ended. The real fight is about to begin.

Conan shrugs his shoulders and cricks his neck, and his muscles pulse and writhe like independent living things. Blood makes a tapestry of his body. The art is brutal and beautiful. He stares at Grake with utter confidence, because Conan has just killed fifteen warriors who all went for him at once. Heads rolled, guts spilled, screams rose, limbs fell, and now Conan stands amid the wreckage of flesh and bone.

Invincible, Grake thinks. I am invincible.

He takes another pinch of quesh from the pouch around his neck and sniffs it. Stars explode in his head. His limbs become mountain ranges, their muscled terrain displaying the geography of the future.

His future. Because he will be king of this land and all others, ruling from atop a throne of fallen warriors, with Conan's cleaved and boiled skull serving as his crown.

Conan comes at him and Grake steps to one side, kicking out with one foot and sending the great warrior sprawling in gore. Conan cries out and rolls, lashing out with his broadsword. Grake smashes it to one side, striking so hard that the steel shatters into a thousand shards that catch the blazing sunlight as they arc through the air.

"Grake!" those watching cry, starting to chant his name even before he's struck the final blow.

Conan begs for mercy. He fouls himself. He is a fallen man of scars, and when Grake slices off his head he will take possession of every myth and legend that Conan has given rise to over his long lifetime.

I am the greatest warrior this land has ever known, Grake thinks, and he does not hesitate. His sword jars his arms as it slices through Conan's thick neck.

"Grake!" the watchers cry again. "Grake!"

He picks up Conan's head by the long black hair and holds it up for the crowd to see, one foot on the dead man's broad chest. He looks into Conan's piercing blue eyes as they grow pale and the life fades from them, and he hopes that in those last moments all Conan sees and knows is the man who has bested him in battle and who will be known as greater than Conan ever was.

"Grake!" they chant, "Grake! Gr—"

Grake woke and sat up, drawing his knife and grabbing the man's throat.

"—ake! It's me, Korn!"

Grake froze as his reality gathered around him again. Then he gave the warrior's throat a final, harsh squeeze before letting him go.

"You woke me from a fine dream of the future," Grake said. "It had better be for a good reason."

Korn staggered back a couple of steps, coughing and spluttering, as Grake stood in his small tent and pulled on his clothes. He opened the entrance flap and pinned it wide. It was dawn, the sun already blazing across the desert far to the east, watery images dancing across the distant horizon. It was also hot, and Grake was sweating. He looked down at his feet as he slipped them into his boots, imagining Conan's decapitated corpse beneath them. Not yet, he told himself. Not yet, but soon.

"One of… the slaves is… refusing to work."

"Huh. Then you'll have killed them already, of course."

"Well…"

Grake finished dressing, tightening the leather cords on his loose robe. He shrugged his big shoulders, flexed his muscles, ran fingers through his long hair to rid it of knots and insects from his brief sleep. He had been up in the night with Sornia, riding and sweating and keeping the slaves awake with their noisy congress. The second part of the night had brought familiar recent dreams of besting Conan in battle. It had been a good night of rutting and resting, and he cursed that he had been woken to Korn's indecision and weakness.

"Well what?" Grake snapped.

"Well, the slave is the tall streak of piss from Corinthia. He's the strongest of them, like a damned spider on the cliffs, and he's already found two heartgems."

"Then he's earned his time with us," Grake said, looking outside again.

The slave Korn was talking about was seated close to the edge of the cliff, legs crossed, arms resting on his knees. He was bleeding from the battering he'd already received, but when one of Grake's people hauled him upright and let go, his legs folded and he sat back down. The other slaves were huddled in a small pack behind the fence enclosing their compound, men, women, and children watching the display of defiance.

They saw Grake and all looked down at their feet. They knew better than to catch his eye, especially when things weren't going to plan on top of that Khorajan cliff.

Grake ducked back into the tent and started strapping on his sword. Korn nursed his bruised neck. Grake smiled at him, but there was no humor in it and no apology. Korn watched, eyes wide, as Grake took a pinch of quesh from his pouch and sniffed it high into his nose.

It's rot-root from the deep mines of Stygia, he'd heard the warriors in his band of cutthroats and barbarians whispering.

No, it's crab spice from the pirates beyond the Western Sea, others would say.

It's dark magic, Sornia would say, loud enough for Grake to hear. And you'd do best to respect it, and Grake.

He sniffed again, then placed his hands on Korn's shoulders. He was a good man, a warrior who'd raided and pillaged with Grake for almost three years down through Zamora and Koth. But his strength stopped with his muscles and his will to fight. None of it leaked into his brains. He had violent wisdom but no finesse when it came to dealing with anyone he wasn't out to kill.

"Korn," Grake said. "Korn, Korn. He might be a spider on the cliffs, but he's a thorn in our side above them. We need supplicant slaves to gather the heartgems for us, and his seed of defiance, once bloomed, will lead to less work, more revolt among the others, and worst of all, hope. They can't have hope because it gives them a vision of freedom on their horizons. With no vision of hope, they will always work harder seeking it. So this will be a lesson to them, and one to you as well. Learn from it. And trust me, once this is done, they will all work harder."

Grake turned and burst from the tent, and he heard Korn following behind him. The others from his group—hulking warriors, tattooed barbarians, brutal cutthroats one and all—were standing around their clifftop encampment, eyes on him. Sornia stood behind the tall man who had woken that morning and decided that refusing to work was the way to go. She was short and lithe, head shaved on one side, long hair on the other tied in a snaking plait weaved with razor-knives, tattoos across her throat and shoulder displaying battles she had fought. On her right arm were curved red tattoos for each foe she had bettered and killed. There was little room for more.

Grake smiled at her, then looked at the slaves and picked out Baht Tann's wife and two sons. They were good workers, though the boys had taken a few days to get used to being lowered down the cliffs to search for heartgems. The mother had told him that only adults worked that way, and he'd almost killed her there and then. Instead, he'd made it clear that a slave who did not work was of no use to him.

She'd been quick enough to tie her brats onto the end of a rope after that.

"Korn tells me that you have decided not to work today!" Grake said as he marched across to the kneeling man.

"I'll work if you give us more food and water," the man said. "If we're stronger, we'll work better. If we work better, you get more heartgems."

"Well, now, that almost sounds like you're bargaining with me," Grake said, smiling down at the man sitting cross-legged before him.

"It's a bargain if you choose to treat it that way, but—"

Grake moved like the wind, like lightning, like the pulse of the world was beating in his veins. He groaned in sensual delight as he plucked his sword from the scabbard on his back and swung it in a beautiful arc, drawing art on the air and singing songs with his limbs. The blade parted the man's head clean down the middle, both halves of his waggling tongue flapping in the wind as he failed to finish what he had started saying, and then it continued down, splitting his jaw and neck and spine and coming to rest jammed in his pelvis.

One more sniff of quesh and I'd have cleaved him all the way through, Grake thought. But perhaps this was better. It was more grotesque.

Someone screamed. Someone else shouted, telling the children to look down at the ground. Even Sornia took a step back, away from the ruined man and closer to the cliff edge.

Grake planted one foot on the dead man's groin and pushed, tugging his sword free as he did so. "I grant you permission to not work today," he said as the parted man's guts and organs spilled across the ground. A scorpion skittered across the spreading pool of blood and into the steaming wet chest cavity.

Grake leaned down and wiped his sword on the man's trousers. *Schwick, schwick!* and it was mostly clean again. But he felt its hunger for more blood, so he kept it in his hand.

"Does anyone else not wish to work today?" he asked. No one answered, so he walked toward the slave compound, resting his sword on the rough bamboo-and-wire fence that kept them contained. They stank. He didn't mind. It was the smell of work, the stench of profit. "Anyone?"

Silence.

Grake threaded the sword through the fence and pressed it beneath the chin of Baht Tann's wife. He had not learned her name. It didn't matter to him. A twist of his wrist and her head was raised. She stared at him, expressionless.

"He'd better return soon," he whispered. "I'm waiting to see him, and the man he brings."

"You're out of your mind," the woman said, and both of her children glanced up at her with wide eyes. They knew Grake and what he could do. They had all just borne witness, after all.

"I've too much to do, too much to become, to be out of my mind," he said.

The woman glared at him, and he saw that look in her eye that she'd retained since the first day he and his group had arrived and Baht Tann had gone over the cliff. It was a look that said, You will lose. You will die.

But what she did not know—what not even any of his

warriors knew—was that Grake would not be alone when Conan arrived. Oh, he would wield the sword, he would split the skin and slice the flesh and crush the bones of the greatest warrior the land had ever known, for sure. But though Grake was a man of ambition, drive, and almost supernatural strength thanks to the Khitain drug that never ran empty in his pouch, he was no fool.

Help was coming.

Grake killed his first person when he was nine years old. It was his father, a brutal old man who constantly beat Grake and blamed his son for his own failings. So Grake knifed him three times in the gut, knowing that dipping the blade in dog feces beforehand would ensure the old bastard died a slow, horrible death due to infection.

Three years later, Grake climbed the mountains into Khitai with a band of marauders, attacking villages, butchering anyone too weak to be sold into slavery. They took their victims back over the mountains to the shores of the Vilayet Sea, selling them to slave traders who would sail them across to Turan. It took Grake a year and the murder of four members of his group before he became leader.

When he was sixteen, the small band of hardened marauders was ambushed and slaughtered by strange simian beasts from the eastern extremes of Khitai. Grake was the only survivor, and he fled into a complex network of caves to escape the attackers' wrath. He learned that they were spirit-sinks, creatures in whom the wraiths of those many people Grake and his group had murdered gathered and exploded into acts of vengeance that would have been sung in songs for generations to come, were anyone left alive to compose the words.

In the darkness beneath the huge mountain ranges between Hyrkania and Khitai, Grake found deeper truths. He practiced and advanced his art of war, defending himself against blind cave dwellers, unknown creatures of the dank darkness, and others who had made those monstrous caverns their home. He also encountered wandering lost wraiths, but he was not afraid. Fear gave them power, and instead in his arrogance he found himself holding power over them.

He spent a long, lonely year beneath those mountains, exploring six hundred miles of caverns, tunnels, crevasses, and long-forgotten ruins that told of a deeper history than he could ever comprehend.

In one of those caves, occupying a half-fallen structure that might have last seen the sun a hundred thousand years ago, he found a wizened three-armed blind man. They became friends. And it was this old wizard who gave him that stiff leathery pouch that was a source of his quesh.

Emboldened by the drug that gave him great strength and an unnaturally long life, Grake went up into the world once more. He was stronger than he had ever been, filled with a thirst for blood and vengeance, and craving notice. He did not wish to continue life as a forgotten cave dweller. He had no desire to spend his time in the shadows of the past, hiding from the present and afraid of the future.

Grake sought to be known by one and all as the greatest warrior the land had ever known.

He raided and fought his way around the coastal regions of the Vilayet Sea. He crossed paths with like-minded bandits and joined forces, and they hewed and hacked their way through any who stood before them. They stole and lost great riches. They gained reputations and saw them fading away once more, and so Grake went on his own once again, learning more and more about his art of war and destruction by seeking those stronger and more powerful than him, and killing them.

He picked up many wounds that should have ended the story of Grake. The quesh kept him living, moving, fighting, and killing, and pursuing his ambitions across the deserts, plains, and steppes, until finally he found himself on the eastern borders of Stygia. His injuries healed into scars that told his story in knotted words of hardened flesh and distorted skin.

In Stygia, he met a woman named Mylera. They became lovers for a while, and in her Grake met his match. She approached sex with the same insatiable hunger that she displayed for every moment in life that took her closer to the future she sought— screaming, biting, scratching, and hauling herself through every instant toward her ultimate aim.

She sought the death of King Conan of Aquilonia, the Cimmerian barbarian who had murdered a king for his crown. She raged about Conan as she rode Grake into sweating, exhausted submission, and her fury was so deep that sometimes he saw fire in her eyes, flames deep in her soul that writhed and danced in the shape of the man she wished to kill.

Grake expressed his doubt about Mylera's ability to kill such a great warrior, and if it weren't for the quesh that he sniffed and snorted, her passionate admonishments might have been the end of her.

And she screamed secrets into his ears as they united in furious congress.

Mylera's father had been a knight in Conan's army. He had died protecting Conan during a skirmish between an Aquilonian force and pirates raiding the Zingaran coast, stepping in between the king and a monstrous sea creature enslaved and used by the pirates. Conan had not honored his death. He did not even know his name.

I am remaking myself, she told Grake. I have destroyed who I was, and I am reforming myself into a human demon of grief and rage that will take her vengeance to King Conan, when the time is right.

Sometimes she disappeared for days, and when she returned to him she was stinking of dark magic.

Grake knew. He had inhaled those scents himself, deep down beneath the mountains bordering Hyrkania and Vilayet. But Mylera started to scare him, and though that was something he would only ever admit to himself, it was enough to make him move on. He had never been a man beholden to one place or one person.

So he left Stygia and reached the coast, raiding, killing, stealing, pirating, remaking himself in his own personal way. Mylera's hatred for Conan had instilled something in Grake's heart which nestled there, a seed of something waiting to bloom.

To become the greatest warrior in the land, he had to kill the land's greatest warrior.

And so Grake had carried the seed of that idea for years— One day I will kill King Conan. A patient man, he waited until the time was right and the opportunity might present itself.

Now, on that clifftop in Khoraja, he was anticipating Conan's arrival and what it would bring.

Ten days after Baht Tann floated away down the river, he had sent a message hawk toward Stygia. He had no way of knowing if it would reach its destination and deliver its message into the right hands, but something told him it would. Grake had waited a long time for fate to coalesce around him, and with every shred of his existence he felt that happening now.

The hawk would find his old lover Mylera. His message would be read. Mylera would come and help him destroy Conan.

And then he would destroy her, and bathe in the glory of his conquest.

6

His Face Tells Stories

Three days later, Conan reached the Tybor River, which marked the border between Aquilonia and Ophir. His mount, Ella, was becoming stronger and more agile with every mile they covered, and though she was still cranky, Conan believed that they were developing a good relationship. He knew that he was heavy for her old back, but she was stronger than she looked. He treated her well. She did as he instructed with rein or knee. Still, he remained careful not to stand too close behind her when they stopped for the night. He respected her grumpiness.

Behind him rode Vaccharez and his two companions, Elize and Quille. Conan's insistence that they turn around and return to Tarantia had caused some friction between them. He could see how awkward they found disobeying a direct order from their king, but he also knew the strength of an instruction from Zenobia. They were conflicted, and in the end so was he.

Vaccharez was an old friend, and Conan also found himself liking Elize and Quille. They carried a quiet strength and great skills. Knights of the Black Dragons spent their whole lives training for their task, and he knew that were he to require any help out in the wilds, these three people were the best to bring it.

It had taken a brief internal battle while sat around the campfire that first night for him to settle the issue. On the one hand, his commitment to Baht Tann was feeding Conan's desire to venture back out into the world again, not as a king but as a wanderer. He wanted to set his wild side free once more, unconstrained by duty or age and unhindered by the expectations of those who knew who and what he was. On the other hand, he knew for sure that his mission would be filled with peril, even before he reached its culmination. The fact that Zenobia had chosen and tasked these three with ensuring his safety had not made him as angry as it should, because it showed her love and concern for him, but also her respect for his dignity. She knew what type of journey he wanted this to be. If she had cared only for his safety, she would have sent an army.

So Conan had agreed to let them come with him. He'd been ready to silence them if they spoke too much, and berate them if they attempted to assert any type of control over his movements or decisions, but Vaccharez led them well. For the past three days they had ridden along behind him mostly silent, and it was only when they camped for the few darkest hours of night that the three soldiers had allowed themselves to loosen a little, though they remained on their guard. They chatted among themselves, and Conan sat silently and listened.

In truth, he was quite enjoying their company. Though he had rediscovered his trapping and survival skills, he had yet to face down a dangerous foe. With their journey about to take them into Ophir, and thence across Koth, that would almost certainly change. He could have taken down the three Black Dragons easily enough that night at the campfire, but they had been following their king, and their conditioning had not allowed them even to begin defending themselves against him.

Though he hated the feeling, he remained a little uncertain how well he might fare against true aggressors.

Standing on the bank of the Tybor River, Conan stared across the flowing waters toward the opposite shore. Around them were the dilapidated remains of old fortifications, built after Ophir had sided with Koth against Aquilonia. That was many years ago now, and the enmity had lessened with negotiations and new trade and security alliances, but these scars of conflict still marked the land. There were old timber watchtowers, fallen and rotting into the ground. To their right and further downstream, Conan could just make out the stumpy remains of an ancient stone bridge that had been destroyed by Aquilonian forces to protect against another invasion. It had never been rebuilt, and it stood as another fallen memorial to that great war.

A war that Conan and his allies had eventually won.

"Do you recognize me?" he asked, turning to the three soldiers.

"Of course, my lord," Quille said. "You're our king!" Elize nodded. Vaccharez only smiled, because he already knew what he meant.

Conan grunted. "Huh. Then I'd better disguise myself better. In Ophir, my face tells stories."

"Neither of you have been to Ophir," Vaccharez said to his two companions. "There's peace between our lands now, but there are still many who remember war. Those mental scars run deeper than physical wounds."

Conan brought a long, thin scarf from his travel pack slung on Ella's saddle. He flicked it out, holding it up as the breeze fluttered it open, then wrapped it around his head.

Vaccharez continued, "If King Conan is recognized once we cross into Ophir, it's a gamble as to whether he'd be welcomed or…"

"Or not," Conan said. He tucked the scarf's loose end into itself and looked at Elize.

"A stranger!" she gasped. "But where is the king?"

Quille's eyes went wide at her jocularity, but Conan smiled.

"Your king is in Tarantia," he said. "From now on, I am your traveling companion, equal to you in all measure."

"Of course, my lord," Quille said.

Conan raised an eyebrow.

"It might take... some time to get used to it, my... Conan." Quille looked away.

"Get used to it by the time we reach this river's opposite shore," Conan said, and he nudged Ella down the bank toward the flowing water. She whinnied and turned her head, looking up at him with one eye as if to say, You expect me to walk across that? He kneed her again and clicked his tongue, and she took a few hesitant steps down and into the water.

The river was wide but not deep, and soon they were across and into Ophir.

"The fastest route toward our destination will involve crossing the meadowlands, where we'll find many towns and fortresses," Vaccharez said. "The safer way will be to switch south a little. The land there is more sparsely populated and—"

"The fastest way it is," Conan said. "Baht Tann's family have already been slaves for too long." He started riding and the others followed. Elize came and rode by his side as if he were a normal companion, and he was pleased at her company. She and the others had come after him already dressed casually rather than in their Black Dragon uniforms, and they all blended into the landscape as normal travelers. Armed, yes, but that was more common than not.

Ophir troubled him, with its history of antagonism toward Aquilonia. Though half his age, Vaccharez was correct in his assessment of current relations. Yet that did not mean that King

Conan traveling with a sparse guard would not prove a tempting target for Ophirean vagabonds or old knights still harboring scars and resentments from that long-ago war.

What really worried him was Korshemish in Koth, and the dread Scarlet Citadel, twisted into nefarious use by the long-dead wizard Tsotha-lanti. Darkness bled from his memories and filled his thoughts when he recalled his time in that place, trapped in his cell in those unlit, dark-magic-tainted basements. He had killed down there and almost been killed, but Conan had long believed that he'd brought something out of those dread dungeons with him. It nestled in his mind, a corrupt seed of sick thought and deed, and it took only a fleeting memory or an unhindered dream to disturb that seed and set those terrible memories free to haunt him once more. His inner strength meant that he could push back and keep the darkness at bay.

He said nothing of this to Elize and the others. The time would come for that when they crossed into Koth in another few days.

They moved away from the river and into the afternoon, and now that Ella was riding stronger, Conan set them at a jog. It was still many hundreds of miles to Khoraja and whatever he might find there, so the faster they ate up the ground beneath them, the better. The landscape was relatively easy going, consisting mainly of open meadows, rolling hills, and farmland. They followed established routes, which were faster, and away from the river they started to encounter other travelers. Conan kept quiet, sitting astride Ella with his head bowed and the scarf low over his eyes. Elize threw enthusiastic greetings, while Vaccharez and Quille hung back together, keeping watch on their surroundings. Most people they met were farmers or locals, some armed but of no real threat.

However much Conan and the others tried to appear benevolent, their swords were obvious. Vaccharez also carried a heavy crossbow and Quille wore a bow and arrow-quiver. Some people returned Elize's greeting with barely a nod before hurrying on their way.

That first night in Ophir they camped near a small lake, in the shadow of a huge fallen tree that was home to a few skittish lizards and a mournful owl. Vaccharez and Quille fished for dinner, and when they returned Elize had started a small fire. Its flames reflected in the tree creatures' eyes where they hid in crevasses in the trunk and watched these unwelcome visitors.

Conan chose to sit back and observe them set camp and cook, not because he was king but because he was unsettled. For the past hour he'd smelled something strange. Maybe it was some unusual crop that the Ophireans had started growing, or the scent of spring pollen coming from huge trees that huddled around the shores of the lake, tall with purple leaves, that he hadn't seen before. Wherever the curious scent came from, it had him on edge. So he kept watch.

Conan always trusted his hunches.

Vaccharez picked up on his caution, and as the fish cooked he sat down close to him.

"Something wrong?" he whispered.

"A feeling."

They sat quietly for a while. Watching, listening.

"It seems peaceful," he said.

Conan grunted.

The shadows closed in around them as the sun set far across the landscape, splashing the way they'd come with glorious color. He looked to the horses, his Ella and the three younger, fitter steeds that the Black Dragons rode. They stood motionless with their heads down, not grazing—listening. They should have been hungry.

The fire spat as fat dripped on it. Quille said something. Elize laughed.

Conan inhaled long and deep. The smell was stronger and closer than ever, and he knew that the trouble he'd sensed coming was now with them.

"Prepare!" he said quietly, reaching for the sword by his side.

"For what?" Quille asked.

A high ululating war cry broke the peace.

"How did you know?" a shocked Elize asked as she snatched up her own sword.

"I smelled them," Conan said, stamping out the fire. "And now they're here."

As Conan and the others moved away from the fading flames so as not to provide a target silhouette, more war cries sounded around them as their attackers streaked in from the shadows. Conan counted eight or ten before he leaped forward and swung his sword, feeling the satisfying wet crunch as it shattered a ribcage. He went with the momentum, slicing the sword out of his victim and closing his eyes to prevent the spraying blood from blinding him.

The attackers were a mix of sizes and races, and Conan guessed they were chancers, a gang of bandits attacking travelers to steal from them without knowing who it was they were fighting.

He ducked a mace swing and jabbed with his sword, gutting the assailant. Glancing around, he saw Elize fending off two foes, fighting them both with grace and easy, flowing movements. She caught one across the throat, rolled, buried her sword in the other's abdomen. Vaccharez and Quille were back against the fallen tree, tackling three bandits who confronted them with long pikes. As ever in combat, he strived to know how his comrades were faring, but his main fight was always for himself.

Conan marched into the path of several more attackers, taking the fight forward rather than waiting to defend. He swung his sword two-handed, parried and ducked, and his muscles felt warm and strong, as if their memories of old conflicts had flowed to the fore. He downed one warrior with a strike to her shoulder, and as she fell his sword jammed in her clavicle. He stepped with it and sensed the heat of a body coming at him from the right. He ducked, felt the swish of a blade passing a hand's breadth above his head, then snatched up with his other hand and clasped the attacker's arm. As he stepped on the dying attacker beneath him and hauled his broadsword from her shoulder with a crunch of bone, he twisted the arm grasped in his other hand and heard it crunch from its shoulder socket. The attacker cried out and Conan butted him hard in the face, then slammed his sword up through his jaw and out through the top of his head.

Someone cried out, and it was a voice he knew.

Vaccharez was pinned to the fallen tree by a pike through his chest, and several more shapes were crouched atop the trunk.

"Crossbows!" Conan shouted. He ducked and rolled and felt a bolt kiss across his upper right arm.

Quille clambered up onto the tree and hacked down two of the crossbow wielders, and Conan drew a breath to warn her about more on the other side.

Too late. Quille tumbled from the tree with three bolts in her right side. She fell heavily, reached for her fallen sword, and then two figures fell on her, hacking with knives, reveling in their murder and uttering that strange high cry once more. The sound was frenzied and ebullient, filled with the joy of the fight and a hunger for blood. These are more than just bandits, Conan thought.

"Bastards!" Elize shouted as she cut them down, dispatching both with a forehand and backhand sweep of her blade.

A horse neighed in alarm, and Conan turned in time to see two of the Black Dragons' steeds peppered with more crossbow bolts. Ella looked up at him as if to ask permission, then she turned and started cantering away.

You go, Conan thought. *Be safe.* He fought on, hacking this way and that, always moving so as not to provide a target for the crossbows. He grabbed one skinny marauder and crushed his throat and larynx, driving his fingers in deeper and cracking his neck. He held the corpse tight against his body as he ran at the fallen tree. He heard and felt bolts hitting the shield of flesh and bone, then he grunted and heaved the body hard, sweeping his sword across the top of the tree. Flesh ripped and bone splintered, and two shapes cried out, fell, and struck the ground on the other side.

"Conan!" Elize shouted. He ducked and spun, just in time to avoid a battle-ax swung by a huge, hairy man. The attacker growled and swung again, from high up this time, and Conan held up his sword flat in both hands. The ax struck the blade and sparks flew, illuminating the madman's face. His eyes were hollow black pits.

Wolfspar root, Conan decided. *Maybe that was the smell that had unsettled him and warned him of the approaching danger.* These were berserkers on a mission, drugged up on dried wolfspar, focused and fearless.

He kicked at the man's shins, then heaved up with both hands, driving the ax handle into his nose. The man grunted and stumbled back, colliding with Vaccharez's corpse, still pinned against the tree. Conan swung his blade and the man's head tumbled into the dying fire, his beard sparking and spitting flames.

Conan looked around their chaotic camp, scattered with the dead and dying. Elize was down, lying on her back with two cutthroats darting at her and away again, uttering that mad cry and probing with pikes that she parried with her sword. He saw the glimmer of bloody open flesh across her legs and knew that she did not have long. If she could no longer stand, it was only a matter of time until—

Someone leaped at him from atop the fallen tree and he cursed his clumsiness. He punched back with his free hand and felt the cool sting of a blade opening the flesh of his forearm. He pivoted on one foot and swept the sword behind him, but the shape was on him then, kicking and headbutting and stabbing in a mindless frenzy, eyes wide and black in the reflected light from the embers.

Conan bit his attacker's face, clenching his jaw tight and shaking, and he felt sharp impacts across his hip.

Fool! he thought. Clumsy, rusty fool!

He slammed forward into the tree, then pressed his attacker against it and pushed sideways, scraping skin and flesh against the cruel bark. The man did not even cry out, continuing his mad attack until Conan managed to bring his sword around and slide it through his side, severing his spine.

He stood back and the man slumped lifeless to the ground.

His world seemed to tilt. He blinked blood from his eyes, unsure whose it was, and turned in time to see Elize pierced and pinned to the ground. She cried out, and her two attackers seemed to be the only ones left standing.

Conan roared, and they both looked his way.

With her dying breath, Elize let out a loud cry and thrust her sword up into the gut of one of her murderers. Blood leaked and sprayed and combined as they died, huddled together on the ground.

Conan's vision blurred, the ground tipped beneath him, and the final surviving attacker came at him. Conan ran forward and stumbled, using his momentum to take the woman down and crush her into the bloody mud, and he butted her three times in the face until bone cracked, then three times more until his face was wet and warm.

Breathing hard, Conan tried to find his balance, but all he found was darkness.

I'm riding Ella. She's injured, but she has me laid across the saddle and she's carrying me somewhere safe. How did I get into the saddle? The others are dead. I'm in so much pain. There's human flesh stuck between my teeth. Strength bleeds from me.

Conan struggled to open his eyes, and their lids parted with a bloody wet pop.

Something was still moving beneath him, but he no longer thought it was his steed Ella. This was something else.

I will not die like this.

He braced his hands and pushed himself upright, and he was looking down at the mortally injured woman beneath him. Her face was deformed, bones crunched and splintered. In the moonlight, he could see that her eyes were flooded black, either by the blood of internal wounds or the wolfspar root he could smell on her short, panicked breaths.

As he looked down, her one good eye rolled in its socket and fixed on him, and her right arm rose weakly from the ground, knife still clasped in her hand.

Conan lifted his left hand and fell again, weakness crumpling him onto the dying bandit. The knife pricked at his side twice, three times, and he roared in fury, gathered every shred of strength he could muster, and pushed himself up onto his hands and knees. He grabbed the woman's arm and slammed it to the ground. The knife bounced away and her arm broke, but she barely uttered a sound.

"Who sent you?" Conan demanded, blood dribbling from his mouth. He tried to assess his wounds, but everything hurt. Instead, he focused on this last living enemy, because he needed information from her before she died.

This had not been a random attack. The way she focused her one good eye on him, like a python readying to strike a long-intended victim, told him that.

"King... Conan..." she said, and she spat a phlegmy laugh.

He grabbed her bloody face and squeezed. "Who sent you? Tell me and I'll give you a fast warrior's death."

The woman coughed blood. Her eye rolled. She stank of wolfspar. It dulled pain and aggravated fury, but there was no more fight in this dying killer.

"King Conan... kill him and earn... more riches than... imagine."

"Kill me for who?"

The woman frowned, as if that memory would not come. Then she died.

Conan rolled onto his back and groaned as his wounds started to announce themselves properly. Despite the pain, he knew that his priority was to get away from here. Lying wounded among so much death would attract more trouble, if not from wandering scavengers who would steal from the dead, then from wolves, bears, or other creatures of the night that might have heard the fight or smelled the carrion. He was not sure he could defend himself currently against man or beast.

And what of my quest? he thought.

One thing at a time. First, he had to survive.

He spied his sword close by and grabbed the handle. It felt good in his fist, like the touch of an old friend, and as he dragged it to him its tip made a *shhhhh* sound across the blood-soaked ground. He was still cautious and alert in case there were any enemies still alive hiding in the shadows, watching, waiting for their moment to finish him. He didn't know how long he'd been unconscious but thought it hadn't been long, just a few moments, because little around the camp had changed. Scattered embers still glowed from the fire he'd stomped on, smoke curling lazily into the still night. The bodies of friend and foe remained motionless, and there were no animal scavengers yet at work on the opened flesh, spilled organs, and bloodied soil—the surest tell that it had not been long.

He examined his body for any wounds that might prove fatal. His senses were still blurry and uncertain, and when he felt across his stomach and hips he realized why—he was soaked with blood. He was shocked by how much, and he hoped that much of it was not his own. Then he found the gaping wounds in his right side.

By Crom, I'll not die this night! he swore. But he wasn't certain. Not at all.

Hugging his right arm tight against his wounds to try and stanch the flow of blood, he pressed the sword into the ground with his left hand and pushed, shoving himself up onto his knees. The pain was exquisite but he held in his groans, more conscious by the moment of the dangers that lurked in the darkness.

Someone had hired these killers and promised them good pay for his head. With the work not yet done, he had to assume that he was still the target of an unknown foe.

He took a moment on his knees, then stood, tugging his sword free and holding it ready. The scarf he'd worn to disguise himself hung loose across his shoulders and he shoved it out of the way. But he kept it on, because once he believed himself safe it would be useful to try and bind his wounds.

So would everything he had brought in his travel pack, but the pack was gone from its spot by the campfire. He didn't have time to search for it.

He stood motionless for a moment and surveyed the carnage. Close to Elize's corpse, he found her own pack, and he shrugged it onto his left shoulder. He also collected Quille's water pouch. He considered bringing the crossbow that remained propped against the tree close to where Vaccharez had been sitting, but it was a limited weapon, and once he was out of bolts it would be useless. He would rely on his broadsword and the shorter blade that remained sheathed on his belt. He glanced at Vaccharez to make sure his friend was dead, feeling a pang of sadness but quickly dismissing it. Grief could not aid him.

Black Dragons taken down by common bandits! he thought, and he was not sure where his anger was directed. But though common, these bandits had been driven by something more—a promise of riches, and the power and fearlessness imbued by wolfspar.

Leaving the camp and heading north around the lake, Conan found his companions' three horses butchered in the long grass. With them was Quille's bow but no arrows, so he left that as well.

A little further on he discovered Ella. She was lying on her side, breathing slowly and softly, her exhalations shimmering the grass around her head. Several crossbow bolts protruded from her neck, buried almost all the way in. The attackers had shot her at close range. She struggled at Conan's approach, then stilled when she saw it was him. He stroked her head. Then he drew his knife and slit her throat, because there was no saving her and he didn't want the scavengers that must surely arrive soon to eat her alive.

Conan sat on his dead horse's flank for a while, securing the scarf tightly around his muscled waist and binding his wounds. It hurt, but he knew he had to lessen his blood loss. He felt dizzy, nauseous. The wounds were deep, and infection was likely. He was alone in Ophir, and though his mission still preyed on his mind, survival was his main concern. For that, he had to find help.

Injured and bleeding, Conan walked through the night, afraid that if he stopped to rest he might fall asleep, and thence into death.

The Last Song

As dawn cast its color across the eastern skies, Conan hid himself in the marshes spread across the wide plain at the foot of a low range of hills. He had smelled the tang of marshland from miles away and steered himself there, partly for the cover the dense reeds and difficult terrain might afford him and partly for the natural balms he sought. He found a small rise on which to pause and take a drink from poor Quille's water pouch, and in Elize's pack he found some dried pig skin to chew on. It tasted sour and old, but he needed the nutrients.

Sat among the reeds, he took some long, deep breaths to settle himself. He guessed he'd traveled eight miles through the night's witching hours, always on guard, always listening and sniffing for any signs of pursuit. If any of the sellswords hired to take his head had survived, he did not believe they were following him. And if there were carnivorous creatures who had picked up his scent leading from the scene of slaughter, they were leaving him alone for now. He figured that there was more than enough fresh meat scattered by that lake and fallen tree to satiate their ravenous hunger.

Passing into the marshes, he had walked through the water to hide his scent trail, careful to make sure it did not reach the wounds in his stomach and side. He was already hot and shivering and worried about infection, fearing that parasites would make their homes in his open flesh.

While stopping a while to eat and drink, he remembered the woman Olivia, whose father, the king of Ophir, had sold her to a Shemite chief because she'd refused his arranged marriage. He had killed that chief for his own revenge in another marshland far away and long ago, and by doing so he had set Olivia free. Conan frowned, because he could not remember what had become of the woman. Time misted memories. It was strange how being away from Aquilonia on his own brought so many of those old memories up out of the darkness.

Once the food and water had quelled his dizziness, he took off his leather singlet and unwound the tightly tied scarf from around his injured torso. There were several ugly stab and slash wounds across his right hip and higher up on his stomach, and removing the temporary dressing caused some of them to start bleeding again—but that was what he wanted. There were two shallower cuts that had scabbed over, and he picked at the scabs, wincing as the dried blood peeled away and fresh blood flowed. He worked the flesh around the wounds with his fingers, encouraging the bleeding in the hope that it would clean out any infections, though he knew it was a vain hope. Some of the wounds were deep—in one, he thought he could see the paleness of a rib—and any infection would have already burrowed its way deep into his body.

Still bleeding, Conan used his knife to dig around at the base of some of the reeds. The wet soil there was a rich reddish-brown, reflecting hues of daybreak. He rolled a palmful of soil into a ball and placed it in his mouth, chewing until it was a thick pulp. It was gritty and stringy, containing many fine roots from the reeds that his teeth shredded down. Once chewed, he spat the mess into his palm and pressed it into his wounds. He hissed in pain but pushed it in as far as it would go, digging and chewing more, repeating the process several times until the worst of his injuries were packed with mud. That would help to ease the bleeding and clean some of the raw flesh, at least.

Next, he needed medicine.

He had to walk for another hour in the brightening day before he saw the low-growing spright tree in the distance, on a rise of land above the marshes. Once he'd reached it, he was thirsty again and feeling nauseous. He could no longer ignore the fever that was growing behind his eyes, drawing sweat from him and setting his limbs shivering. Though it was yet early in the year, he hoped that the spright tree's fruit would be enough to fight off the growing infection.

He spent the morning climbing the tree and picking its scant fruit from the higher branches. He cursed his injuries, his weight, and his bulk as the branches bent and moved beneath his weight, but he succeeded in gathering enough of the tiny berries to make a decent broth.

There was not much dry kindling with which to start a fire, so he ripped the end of the bloodied scarf and cut off some threads, laying them in the sun to dry for a while. The fire sparked first time, and soon he was using Elize's metal drinking mug to boil the water and berries together. After letting it cool, he sipped the sour decoction, drinking it all down.

He had once fought six rabid otter-people in the Border Kingdom of Cimmeria, his sword dashing from their wiry fur, their teeth clacking in deformed mouths. Their spiked claws were dripping with venom, and he had beaten them through brute strength. Back then he had been a far younger man, stronger and, more importantly, less mindful of the dangers he charged into headlong. He'd killed one otter-man with a lucky strike through the eye, then used the corpse to batter the others to death. Only when the fight was over had Conan found his wounds. Wandering delirious across those wild frontier lands, he'd chanced upon a family working a marshland and making a living catching freshwater eels and selling them at market. He'd woken to find the family—mother, father, and three young children—staring down at him and chewing, and for a nightmarish moment he'd believed he was being eaten alive.

Many years later, in the coastal regions of Kush, he had been wounded while fighting a rival crew of pirates and he'd wandered inland in delirium. An old woman had found him and forced him to drink a foul brew, waving aside his complaints and telling him he would die if he did not. With no reason to trust her, still Conan drank, and a day later his delirium lifted and he headed back to the coast. His crew and ship were long gone, but Conan was not a man of regret or stillness and he headed away into other adventures.

He was pleased that after all this time he remembered how to prepare and use reed-root soil to pack wounds and see away dangerous infections, and how to brew the fruit of a spright tree into a medicine that would calm fevers and level the mind. He had not considered either of the skills in all the years he had been King Conan, but they came back to him now. Words from his past whispered such knowledge, and he recognized his own voice.

But despite his ability to harvest from the land to treat his wounds, he understood that his injuries were severe and that they would have already killed a lesser man. He needed fresher and stronger medicines, the means to stitch together and dress his wounds properly, and a horse to continue his mission—because Conan had never for a moment doubted that he must go on. Perhaps the Black Dragons coming after him had been a mistake after all and he would proceed better on his own.

If I'd been on my own during that attack, I would be dead, he thought. Yet if he'd been traveling on his own, perhaps he would have camped in a different place, taken a different route. Maybe he would have been more alert to dangers, and sensing that strange odor of wolfspar root on the air he might have paid more attention to the danger it represented.

Either way, he would continue on his way and rescue Baht Tann's family if they were not already dead, fled, or sold into slavery elsewhere in the land. Today he was in agony, but Conan was no stranger to pain. He was a man of scars, and he knew that come the next full moon he would not even remember the pain from these wounds.

If he found proper medicine. If he treated his cuts and gouges correctly.

So he went looking.

Conan walked from the marshes into dusk, and that evening he trapped a rabbit and ate it raw, lest the smell of cooking brought trouble once more.

At a breath past midnight, he heard a song.

> *With a poison heart and a soul to match,*
> *Xelta rode out of the gloom,*
> *But farm and mine-folk of Reaper's Catch,*
> *Sent him packing to his doom.*

Conan ducked down by the side of the rough trail he'd been following since just after sunset. He'd had to slip from the track and hide several times when he saw people approaching, but the route was not well used, though it wound up into the low hills where the land was now more often farmed than left wild, where heavy-horned cattle that bore various brandings seemed to roam free. He knew that soon he would come to areas of greater populousness, and that was what he wanted. A lone farmhouse, a traveling group, even a small village—any one of them he could raid for the medicine and horse he required. He would ask first, but if they said no he would bring out his sword.

Now, perhaps he had found what he was looking for.

But Xelta's doom was not assured;
Death only made him madder.
When he returned to Reaper's Catch,
He did so meaner and badder.

Conan frowned. Was he hearing things? If so, his imagination was creating a song that was hardly worthy of airing.

A couple of voices sounded in the distance, quieter than the singer and the plucked string instrument that had accompanied him. At first Conan thought they were arguing, but then he heard laughter, high and hearty.

"Well, you do better!" a voice shouted back. "Pompous cock."

Conan settled himself more comfortably within the cover of a bank of shrubs. The voices and music were coming from further along the road, and if he squinted and looked to the side he could see the glow of a campfire flickering in the night and reflected from distant trees. Whoever these people were, they did not seem concerned at hiding themselves. Conan knew as well as the next man that not every road, path, and land was filled with danger and death. It just seemed that peril and violence always seemed to find him.

It made what he had to do next that much easier.

He swallowed more of the sprightberry mix he'd put into Quille's water pouch, swilling it around his mouth and drawing energy from the decoction. He wished he'd searched the bodies of the cutthroats for some wolfspar root, but he cast that thought aside. It might have given him strength and rage, as it had done for them, but wolfspar was notorious for driving its user mad.

Conan needed no drug to fight. Wounded though he was, the thought of his quest gave him power. That, and his promise to Zenobia that he would do his best to return home.

The song continued, in a woman's voice this time and unaccompanied by instruments.

Xelta, demon of dark and fire,
Sought to build his blood-red throne.
He craved the heft of forces higher,
And sat on a seat of...

The song trailed off.

"Bone?" a man said. "You were going to say a seat of bone? And you laugh at my rhymes!"

More banter reached Conan, and he readied himself. He made sure that his singlet was tied tightly around the wounds in his stomach and side, and took in a dozen deep breaths to fire himself up. He could not appear weak, and he definitely could not let them see that he was injured. He held his sword in one hand and knife in the other. He did not wish for a fight, but he was more than ready for one.

His barbarian days of raiding and pillaging returned to him, and as he rushed through darkness toward the camp, he knew that he would present an intimidating visage when he burst upon them.

He approached through a copse. A horse neighed. A voice rose in surprise. As Conan strode into the light of their fire, he said, "I need your food, water, all of your luna, and a horse."

With a glance, he took in the camp and those in it. There was a covered wagon pulled by two huge horses, unshackled now and grazing contentedly nearby. A one-legged woman clothed in bright colors sat on the wagon's seat, lounging on cushions and smoking a big clay pipe. Five others stood or sat around the nearby campfire that had been built within a circle of large stones, all of them appearing relaxed and unprepared for any threats. One was a short but strong man, a Bossonian with a heavily scarred face, and in his arms he held a long, thin stringed instrument. A stocky woman tending the fire might have been a Pict, with her dark skin and heavily muscled limbs, though her clothing was much finer than most Pictish barbarians he had come across. Close beside her, laying a gutted pheasant on hot rocks beside the fire, was a pale man with brown hair and Stygian-style tattoos across his face and neck. A woman wearing a strange mask made of animal skin, her arms covered in raised swirls, sat back against one of the wagon's wheels, and Conan knew a pirate when he saw one. In shadows to the left of the camp was another man, tall with short hair and strong arms, and about him Conan could make out no details.

The covered wagon might hide more threats, perhaps with bows or crossbows. Conan had checked the shadows surrounding the camp upon his approach, but that didn't mean there weren't others from this group out there somewhere, hiding in the dark for a shit or sex, and the sudden change in the atmosphere of the camp—the silenced instrument, the cessation of banter, the tension zinging the air—would alert them to danger.

That was why he had to act quickly.

He strode toward the fire, keeping all six travelers in his line of sight. He'd spied some blades here, a sword there, and two spears were affixed to either side of the wagon's steering seat, ready for the person driving the wagon to pluck them up at any time. But his plan was to not give them time to fight.

The Pict woman reached for a burning brand from the fire. The man in the shadows came forward and a sword whispered as he drew it from its scabbard.

Conan stood before the fire and pointed his sword at the woman, his knife at the man, and shook his head.

"One chance. Then I kill you all."

The one-legged woman sitting on the wagon laughed. The tattooed man cooking the pheasant smiled.

Conan felt the held breath. The camp was frozen, all six of them looking at him, the large fire lighting the scene and casting dancing shadows across their faces. Even the two horses had stopped grazing and were watching to see what might happen. Whatever came next, he would ignore his wounds, deny his weakness, and channel his strength and fury through his bones and muscles and into his blades.

The Bossonian first, then the two by the fire. He tensed and coiled his muscles, ready to leap through the flames.

Something struck his head. He blinked, momentarily dazed, and the man in the shadows crouched and flung something else. This time Conan was ready and he crouched too, twisting his body aside. Then he jumped over and through the campfire, ready to fight.

The Pict woman and tattooed man were no longer there. Conan ducked and went into a controlled roll, feeling his stomach wounds stretch and protest as he came up on one knee, swinging his sword at a shape that dashed at him from the left.

Steel sang as swords clashed, then Conan kicked out at a shape and felt his foot connect. There was a grunt and the figure fell, gasping for breath.

As Conan went to stand, a foot struck him between the shoulder blades and shoved. Conan was heavy, immovable, solid, and he slashed backward with his knife, stabbing down at his attacker's leg. The blade met nothing. He went to stand and dizziness struck him, and he roared as he pushed himself to his feet, sending his broadsword singing at the air, eager to taste blood. It struck another sword and was deflected, and Conan heaved it back, striking someone with the flat of the blade.

A voice shouted to his left and he turned that way, swaying on his feet. He felt no pain, but his body betrayed him. The world tilted and he staggered to the right, spinning as he went to pretend he had intended the movement. He could show no weakness.

Someone tripped him with a heavy wooden club to the shin, and he tumbled forward, landing on his elbows with both blades still raised and ready.

The same wooden club smacked across the back of his neck and he saw stars. Flames. The flow of blood in a vision, and it was his own. Not yet, but soon. His senses swam. He stood and roared and swirled and cut down two of his attackers in a frenzy, blood spraying the air and sizzling on the fire, rent flesh slapping on the ground, and then he realized he had imagined the move. He was face-down in the dirt.

Someone stomped on his hand so that he could not lift his sword. He heaved, lifting their foot a little, then the foot's owner applied all their weight and crushed his hand to the ground.

He felt the cool kiss of steel pressed to the back of his neck—a pike, its point ready to break his spine.

Conan tried to rise, to fight, to defy the damage his body had sustained and the wretched weakness that damage had seeded in him. He managed only to turn his head, and saw the one-legged woman coming quickly toward him from the wagon, a heavy stick beneath each arm acting as legs, pipe clasped tight between her teeth.

"Yer most dead," the old woman said from the corner of her mouth. "Only proper to help ya on yer way."

"Jemi, you don't mean that," a man said, and Conan recognized the Stygian lilt to his voice.

Jemi laughed. "'Course I don't. Only he don't afford us no niceness, do he?"

Someone else gasped. "I knew it. I knew it!" It was the Bossonian, now kneeling and pressing his face to the dirt a few feet from where Conan lay trapped on the ground.

"Knew what, Fennick?" Jemi asked.

"My dearest friends of the Last Song," Fennick said, staring into Conan's face with wide eyes. "We find ourselves in the presence of a king."

At that moment, Conan expected to die. He vowed to writhe and rage and fight, but...

...but the fight was gone from him. His blood burned in his veins like poison. His muscles barely worked. His senses faded in and out, giving his own strange singsong interpretation of what the travelers he had chosen to raid said and did. He waited forever for the ax strike that would sever his head, or the sword to plunge into his back between his mighty shoulder blades to cut his spine in two. Neither came.

Instead, they cared for him.

He was confused, perhaps delirious. Maybe the gentle roll onto his side was to better access his man-parts to slice them off and cook them over the fire in plain sight. Perhaps the coolness across his mouth and lips was venom rather than water, something to keep him awake and aware while they hacked off bits of him to feed to creatures of the night.

But no, he was on his side so that when he vomited it did not clog and clot his throat and fill his lungs. The coolness across his lips really was water, and he drank it down. And when he felt the clumsy dressings removed from his wounds and looked down, he saw the Pict barbarian woman holding cold fire in her hands, muttering unintelligible shamanistic conjurings and laying the blue flames across his wounds. They burned for a heartbeat, and then numbness took away the pain as the cold flame nestled in the slices and holes slashed and hacked into his flesh.

"You're... helping me," he said, and the Pict woman glanced at him with a strange smile.

"Don't expect a Pict to act such, eh?"

"He doesn't know you, Kaz," the tattooed Stygian said. "He doesn't believe we don't want him dead."

Conan said nothing.

"Gratitude is the usual response," the Stygian said, crouching beside Kaz where she administered the strange cool fire she continued to conjure.

"My thanks," Conan said. He was still suspicious, still uneasy, but his wounds and weakened body gave him no choice but to submit to their ministrations.

"Right, and well," Jemi said as she came into view behind Kaz and the tattooed man. "Ya only had to ask."

"Who are you?" Conan asked.

Last Song, he thought he heard her say, but maybe she was inviting one or other of them to start singing again.

The fire cooled and calmed, they gave him more water, and his body conspired to overrule his cautious mind, sending Conan into a peaceful sleep.

8

A Tale of Mylera

The hawk rose high above the majestic cliffs where Khoraja met the great deserts that led, eventually, to Kuthchemes and the borderlands of Turan. It barely flapped its wings, drifting high on thermals created by warm air from the desert washing against the cliff face and rising like a great, invisible wave. It circled as it climbed, instinct turning its eyes down to the ground far below for any potential prey. When it saw scampering, fleeting things with its incredible eyesight, its brain told it to fold its wings and dive, membranes saving its eyes from damage, wings tucked tight against its body, claws held out before it to deal the killing blow. But a stronger urge kept it aloft, some vague instruction, an order trained into it by human hands and minds.

When it was high enough to feel a coolness settle around its feathers, it flew south and west. It moved quickly, riding the airstreams that carried clouds and dreams way above the land. Sometimes it flapped its wings and moved faster. Other times it drifted, looking down occasionally at the leather pouch on its left leg. Whenever it looked there, its mind shivered and tweaked its path a little to the left or right, following an urge as strong as any instinct to migrate, hunt, or procreate.

On the third day, the hawk felt hungry so it circled down toward the winding silver ribbon of water far below. It followed the river's course for a while, passing rapids and waterfalls, until it reached a wider, calmer flow. There it spotted a shadow beneath the water and plunged down. The fish it caught was small and feisty, and the hawk ate it on the wing.

As it climbed up and away from the River Styx, three spark kites closed in and attacked. The hawk had unintentionally drifted into their patch, and with young fledglings in their nests on one of the hundreds of small islands in the Styx, the female kites were vicious in their defense. Though the hawk was three times their size, it did not have their maneuverability, and it was a little heavy from its recent meal. As it tore one kite apart with its talons and beak, the others drifted in and ripped out the back of its neck.

They glided away as the hawk fell. One of them circled back and watched, ensuring that the threat was truly dead. The hawk splashed into the river and floated away downstream.

Its huge wings spread across the river's surface, the bird's body bounced between rocks and over small waterfalls for seventeen miles before a mudcroc ripped it apart with one deadly bite. It swallowed most of the carrion whole, but the hawk's left leg and one wing escaped its maw and floated on.

The wing got stuck between two rocks at the head of a set of rapids, until one day, when the river levels lowered at the end of that long, hot summer, a young boy traveling with his family group found it. He plucked three feathers from it and made quills. With these three quills, he wrote a history of his father, and his father before him, and they were tales that became legends. As the boy grew into a man, he sometimes wondered if the spirit of that fallen bird had informed those tales.

The hawk's leg floated on through the rapids and downriver, and days later it was swallowed by a salmon. It stuck in the fish's throat and choked it to death, and the salmon was snapped out of the water as an easy meal by a giant red bear. The bear gulped down the fish without chewing, and two days later it was killed by a priestess of Set named Belindra Zarn. She took the bear apart and spent three days and nights harvesting its blood and organs, bones and skin, restocking her denuded cellar and planning to use its parts to continue her dark-magic pursuits.

Seven days later, one of her students returned from a thirty-day fast on the Stygian steppes, her mind clear, her blood fresh, her intention never as focused. This student's name was Mylera. Zarn refused to let her sleep, rest, or eat, and instead said that that day they would form a mind spell. She sent Mylera to her cellars to bring up some ground red-bear liver, a mudcroc scale, and a handful of dried testicles harvested from an ancient Keshani battlefield many centuries ago.

In that cellar, something drew Mylera's eye to a shriveled hawk's leg hanging from a wooden beam. Its skin looked misshapen and deformed, and when she moved closer she saw that it wore a tight leather sheath. Inside the sheath was a fold of paper. On that paper, a message to her.

Many message are sent by dove or hawk, wolf or snake, scorpion or spider. Most never find their home, and these stories rot with their bearer or continue to wander the land, looking for an ending. Some that do reach their destination mean little and have no import.

Some—a few—wend and weave to their intended targets by luck or happenstance. These are the messages that change worlds.

Mylera knew that she could not run. If she did, Zarn could reach out across vast distances and punish her. It was what that dark priestess of Set did, and what Mylera had been learning from her for these past few years. Prior to that, she had worked in a brothel in Khemi, drawing on twisted, perverted desires to bend men and women to her will. Before that, she was at a healing place in Sukhemet, treating victims of disease and scourge while absorbing their trauma and examining their minds. Their pain gave her power. Their weakness allowed her to root through their distracted thoughts, using skills she was still learning to winnow down to find their deep truths.

Besides, she had no wish to flee and abandon Zarn, because she owed her thanks. When Mylera had arrived in Belindra Zarn's circle of influence over five years ago, her fledgling talents had been chaotic, unfocused, and dangerous because they were so untempered. She could touch minds but not steer them, read thoughts but not instruct, live other lives but not impress her will upon them.

Seeing and feeling is not knowing, Zarn had told her that first day, when the offspring of a traveling group hung butchered over a fire, their skull pans sliced open and emptied, brains boiling together in a pot of mystic fluids whose source she would come to learn over time. Knowing, truly understanding, is seeing what they see and controlling it, feeling what they feel and changing it. Reaching out to read is not enough. I will teach you to reach out and steer.

"You know this Grake?" Zarn asked when Mylera revealed the hawk's message to her.

"I remember him vaguely from years ago," Mylera said. "I rode him for a night. A strong man, ripe with ambition, but boring and unimaginative."

"In bed or in life?" Zarn asked with a wry smile.

"Both."

"And now he's sending you a message that makes you want to leave before your training is complete."

Mylera looked down at her feet. Zarn was a mentor and teacher, but she was also a bad woman. Mylera remained afraid of her.

"I tease," Zarn said. "No learning is ever complete. Even I still seek truths that elude me."

"You?" Mylera asked, shocked.

"Yes, even this old witch of Set. Magic demands focus from beginning to end, and my mind sometimes…" She waved one hand at the air, a gesture that left a hint of a shadow behind. "Wanders."

"I'll come back," Mylera said.

"Maybe. Maybe not. That's not for you to say or me to see. But your desire to go would corrupt your learning. You've come far, though you have plenty still to learn, and a little knowledge is dangerous. So if you decide to leave, I'll send you away with my blessing. But you have to tell me why."

Mylera's eyes went wide. Had she really never relayed her story to Belindra Zarn? The tale she must have told Grake and others like him over the years? It seemed strange, but it also made some twisted sense. Zarn was someone who could give her something of true value, and Mylera had never wanted to appear fractured, damaged, or ready to break apart. She was a woman building herself afresh, and she had feared that revealing past traumas to her greatest teacher might interrupt that process.

"Of course," Mylera said. They sat on carved wooden chairs outside Zarn's woodland cabin, the firepit between them. Many a skull had been opened and boiled over that fire, and now it was Mylera emptying her darkest histories, and willingly. "The note Grake sent tells me that King Conan of Aquilonia is making his way to the sheer cliffs of Khoraja to fulfill a vow. Many years ago, my father was a knight who fought in Conan's armies against pirates raiding along the coast of Zingara. Conan led his army as a favor to Aquilonia's neighbor. These pirates were from out of the far west, further than our horizons stretch, and they brought new, terrifying magics with them. Yet powerful though the pirates and their ships were, they were nothing compared to the creatures they conjured up out of the deep. I wasn't there, of course, but my father's knight friends told me about it, when they brought me news of his death."

Mylera paused and went quiet, because it had been some time since she had shared this story, and never in this much detail. Usually she spat it out in the throes of lust or in the dark corners of dingy taverns. Now, Belindra Zarn was sucking it up like a thirsty horse taking water from a stream.

"Great, wet monsters," Mylera said. "A travesty to nature and all the things of the world. Difficult to behold, because human eyes cannot understand their nature. They bore countless tentacles with barbed suckers, ravenous beaks, and eyes that had seen far more and further away than anyone on that battlefield."

"Creatures from beyond," Zarn whispered, leaning forward in her chair, her eyes going wide. They looked elsewhere, beyond the haunted forests. "I've heard of them, and how their magic dances between the stars."

Mylera continued. "Terrifying though they were, certain though the pirates were of their success, Conan and his army stood fast and attacked. My father was the bravest of them all. He stepped in front of a monster bearing down on King Conan and fought it, giving his life for his king. And Conan..."

Mylera almost growled. This part was what fed every beat of her heart and chilled her soul, and made her who she was becoming—a broken woman, slowly being made whole again in a visage of pure vengeance.

"Conan did not care," she said. "He didn't honor my father's death. Didn't even know his name."

But Zarn was no longer listening. She stood and dashed inside, and when Mylera followed she found her teacher running her hands across the faded spines of ancients texts gathering dust in the far corner of her cabin, muttering to herself, searching for something beyond Mylera's ken.

"A magic from the stars," Zarn said between excited breaths.

"I seek Conan's heart in my clenched fist," Mylera said. "I see his head on a spike in my dreams, a spike made from my father's sacrifice."

"Yes, yes, go with my blessing," Zarn said. She paused in her search, distracted, staring at Mylera like a wise woman staring at a child. Then she went to another corner of the chaotic room and rooted around in a wooden chest, bringing out a leathery bag that Mylera had never seen before. It bore tattoos. She dug around in the bag, pulled something out, and offered it to her student.

"Here," Zarn said, holding out a small glass vial, its contents a pale green.

"Is that… creore?"

"You see?" Zarn said with a smile. "You're already wiser than you think. But I'm not offering you anything good, Mylera. You should know that."

Mylera knew what she was being offered. Creore was a deadly magical potion. It was perhaps the rarest fluid in all of the known world, containing juice from the liver of an albino bat that lived a mile belowground in the south of Stygia, blood from the absorbed twin in a blind boy's brain, and semen drawn from a bear-man in the deepest jungles of Zembabwei.

"There are three drops in here, three chances to help you perform the magic you've spent your years learning from me. You're far from ready, and without this you'll fail without a doubt, but use these three drops wisely, and only if you have to. The first will scorch you with an agony you've never even imagined.

The second will cripple you. The third will likely kill you."

I don't care about pain or disablement or death, Mylera thought. All I want is revenge. But Zarn knew that already, so all Mylera said as she took the precious vial was, "Thank you."

Zarn had already turned again to her library, moving back and forth, back and forth, until her finger alighted on a spine. She paused, gasped, and pulled the book down, blowing dust from its spine. "Zingara, you say?"

"Zingara." It was the last word Mylera spoke in her dark teacher's presence.

Before the moon set that night, she was already on the trail, heading northeast toward Khoraja. And while she went, creore vial safe on a cord around her neck, she planned to put everything she had learned to the test.

At midnight on that first night, impatient, Mylera prepared to cast her first spell.

With Conan away from the safety of Aquilonia, perhaps he was more vulnerable, and with three drops of precious creore in her possession she was convinced that she now had the talents, skills, and means to exercise the dark arts she had been learning for just such an occasion. It would be the first such spell she had ever cast without Belindra Zarn holding her hand, and her very first use of the precious creore.

She had come across a lone man traveling a well-trodden path between local villages. Luring him into the fields with a whispered suggestion of sexual wonders at the back of his mind, she slit his throat, then didn't even wait for him to bleed out before hacking off his head. A little while later, his head was spitted above her campfire, the top of his skull sliced off so that his exposed brains slowly boiled.

Mixed with his brains was one single drop of creore.

The arcane invocations were those she had learned from Zarn, but they were spoken in Mylera's Aquilonian accent that she still bore after all these years. As the brains bubbled and merged with the special potion, Mylera breathed in the steam and sent her thoughts and desires adrift.

The skin of the world wrinkled and became fragile, riven with cracks and fissures. It flexed and wavered. Reality was uncertain and vague—she knew that—but now she could sense and feel that as well, with every cell of her body and spark of her soul. She saw the world as it really was, a palatable dream of reality overlaying the awful, unbearable truth of time, distance, and deep cold eternity. She smelled the burned-flesh scent that haunted the emptiness between stars. She heard the low, almost gentle background *hushhhhhh* of that strange place, like a distant wind or an indrawn breath taking eons. And she tasted the never-ending putrescence of time beyond understanding that her general vision of reality usually tried to smother so that she could exist without going mad.

It's awful it's horrible it's wonderful, she thought, and as she breathed in further lungfuls of steam, smoke, and creore from the boiling brainpan of the dead man, she felt distance and time mix and merge.

Mylera knew that now she could begin to travel.

She thought of Conan. Zarn had taught her this skill—how to urge her mind and thoughts to travel across distances and find the subjects of her desires or hatreds. She had not seen him for many years, but his image in her mind was rich and fresh because she dreamed of him most nights. Huge, tall, heavily muscled, with long black hair cut straight across his forehead and smoldering blue eyes, he was a man primed for movement. In her imagination, he stared past her at something she could not see, and there was a deep intelligence to his gaze.

Beneath the veil of reality, the world that existed was sparse and featureless, inhabited with her own thoughts and aspects of herself. She drifted across vast open plains of nothingness in the blink of an eye, weaving around and over mountain ranges, skimming across the still, stagnant waters of motionless rivers and inland seas. There was no distance here, but there was direction.

Toward him.

She drifted, keeping that image of Conan rich and sharp in her mind, and soon—she could not judge time, so it might have been moments or eons that she searched for him—she closed on the subject of her hate sitting by a cold blue fire in the vast wilderness.

Mylera was cautious not to get too close—not because she feared him, though she did, but because she did not want to alert him to her intentions.

His mind was strong. She was inexperienced—not weak, but traveling like this felt like riding a horse for the first time—so she skimmed past Conan and found others nearby, three hidden figures who also had strong minds and a focus on the traveling man.

Not them, she thought. I could try but they are strong, I fear I would fail, and then my advantage would be at an end.

So she pulled back and drifted further beneath the skin of the world, until she found a group of mindless fools, brutal men and women with weak minds that she knew she could infiltrate and steer. She wiped these people's selfish, shallow intentions and planted her own, reinforcing them with a promise.

King Conan travels east. Kill him and earn more riches than you can imagine.

This was her skill. This was the spell she had been working on and building for years. She felt their minds change and reform around her demands, just as the reality of the world shimmered and flexed as she traveled behind and beneath. But she was tired now, and her senses were becoming hazy. Somewhere deep down and far back, she felt pain building, like a storm in the distance waiting to sweep across her.

Mylera pulled back, sweeping across desolate emptiness toward her body, her mind on a rope that now reeled in. As she went, the emptiness and darkness grew even more intense, and horror squeezed her mind.

I am seen, she thought, and she was vaguely aware of her stomach clenching as she vomited across her campfire. She felt staggering, huge intelligences observing her with indifferent minds, and she thought, This is what dwells in the true reality beneath the world we believe in.

Her mind almost left her then. Madness stalked her, fed by the sheer unknowable size and depth of the presence she sensed around her, its age and coolness. If Mylera had dwelled a moment longer, insanity would have scrambled her brains, but she hauled herself back in and—

—collapsed close to the fire, vomiting again and again until her stomach knotted and she retched only air. Her muscles cramped and contorted her body into a twisted thing, reflecting her damaged mind.

She had never felt such agony. She cried out, kicked and writhed, and one of her thrashing feet knocked a stone from around the fire and sent it crashing into the spit she'd fixed above the flames. The severed head tipped and rolled, spilling boiled brains into the flames, where they spat and burned—and perhaps that saved her.

The spell fell away, her awareness became all her own, and her brief but terrible peek beneath the veil of the world melted away into dreams.

Does Belindra Zarn feel this? she wondered. Is she so tortured each time she makes a spell? Or is she right and I'm not yet ready?

She remembered the words of her mistress, a true sorceress of Set: The first will scorch you with an agony you've never even imagined. The second will cripple you. The third will likely kill you.

Mylera had been scorched, but she did not care. She wanted Conan dead, and perhaps she had already planted the seed of demise with her first true spell. Perhaps she was stronger than Zarn believed, because soon the pain faded to a background ache. She eventually fell into a troubled sleep, and the bubbling brains boiled away, leaving a luminous green trace around the inside of the broken skull.

While she slept, Mylera cried out in childlike glee when she dreamed of Conan gutted and defiled beside a Kothian trail.

Awake, cooking a captured serpent over her newly stoked fire, the dead man's charcoal-blackened skull staring at her through crumbled sockets, Mylera was filled with crippling self-doubt. It had haunted her ever since she'd made the decision to flee Aquilonia, and it was worse now. She had been too quick to cast the spell. She should have waited until she was sure.

I will never kill Conan.

It was a phrase that appeared as if from nowhere, torturing her as much as the idea of her father's brave, horrific death.

I will never kill Conan.

It cast shadows over everything she did and all that she achieved, the dark arts she learned, the plans she set, the determination with which she approached every single solitary task and undertaking that would take her ever closer to avenging her father's useless sacrifice for a man who didn't care about him and had never known or honored his name.

I will never kill Conan.

The dark spell she had cast yesterday, the minds she had touched, would likely not work. Though she had attempted to seed her desire in a dozen corrupted minds, it was her first true spell, and she had also felt the weakness of those minds. Whatever Conan was, he was far from weak.

But she had to try. And she would gather her strength and try again, and again, even while she traveled across Shem toward Khoraja, where Grake—a man she hardly remembered—waited for her. If she killed Conan before reaching Grake, all the better. If not, perhaps together they would—

She froze with a chunk of smoking serpent halfway to her mouth. Eyes wide, mouth slack, she remembered a man she had met in one of the Shemite meadow cities on her long journey to Stygia many years ago. This one she had not shared her desires with, because he had scared her more than any man she had ever met. His eyes had been dark, black, almost impenetrable, like spyholes into the endless cosmos that she had felt a whisper of the previous night. His bald head was tattooed with spiderworks of words in a language she did not know, and he'd told her this was his story as yet unfinished. She had seen those words changing as he and she spoke over the space of an evening in a lakeside tavern, tucked away at the back to avoid upsetting other patrons. Just another stranger on her long road from Aquilonia to Stygia, but he had stuck in her mind. Not because of his ever-changing and unfinished story, which she had not been able to translate, but because of who he had said he was.

A student of chaos, like her. An adventurer in the arts of darkness, like her. His name was Krow Danaz, and he had once been a young pupil of the evil Kothian wizard Tsotha-lanti, a great man whose had found death at the hands of Conan.

Krow Danaz also wants Conan dead, Mylera thought, and the cooking serpent hissed and spat as if in agreement. *Conan is strong, but vengeance is stronger. Maybe three of us together* can succeed in destroying him at last—me, a stupid warrior named Grake, and the dark magician Krow Danaz.

Perhaps she could send mind bats to find him. Unlike last night's questing spell, it was a much simpler glamor that could be used to touch the memories of someone she had already met, and thus relay a message. Each contact between souls left a trace, the remnant of a line that connected soul to soul, past to present.

Together we'll be a triptych of death for King Conan of Aquilonia—the Cimmerian, the barbarian, the pirate and sellsword.

"Conan the dead," she said, and laughed into the fire.

9

A New Song to Sing

A song called Conan up out of a haunted sleep. He was eager to open his eyes and escape his dreams of fleeting demons and friends lost to blood and steel. Reality was usually more welcoming.

But he kept his eyes closed for a while longer, listening to the mournful song. It told the tale of a mythical warrior from Vanaheim who had tamed a winged beast and used it to attack his enemies from above. Conan knew the tale. He'd learned it as a child, when he was already scarred from battle and had notched a dozen kills on his sword's pommel. He listened to these traveling musicians recounting the story in their own way, and there was something about their voices and the way the music ebbed and flowed that calmed him. They sounded strong, confident, unafraid of the pre-dawn darkness that even now was being painted with the day's early light far away across the eastern horizon. They had confronted him, a danger from the shadows, and instead of killing him when his wretched injuries and weakness pulled him down to the ground, they had tended him.

They know me, he thought. The Bossonian had recognized him as King Conan. Yet still they left him covered in furs as they went about cooking breakfast over their fire and singing their songs.

This song ended with that ancient warrior flying his mount too close to the sun and being blinded by the glare, and every enemy he had made over his decades of raiding and pillaging returned to stab and prick at him, ducking his blind sword-swings, until he was a man of open wounds. Then they threw him into a fire ants' nest and let the land's smallest creatures burrow into his opened skin and flesh and sting him to death.

The old woman, Jemi, sang this last part. Though it was a brutal death, her lulling voice made it sound like peace.

Conan opened his eyes. They were camped in the same place as the previous night when he had come intending to raid them, and their camp was not broken down. The two big horses were still grazing away from the wagon, the roaring fire had been fed, and he could see five of the six travelers he'd seen before. The Pictish woman, Kaz, was somewhere out of sight.

"I know you're awake," she said from behind him.

Conan didn't answer. Without moving his head, he looked around for his sword, his pack, his knife. He could see none of them. He was naked beneath the furs covering him, and the injuries in his stomach and side throbbed. They had been treated and dressed, and he remembered that cold blue fire flowing on and around the Pictish woman's hands as she'd laid them on his wounds.

"You're lucky you're not dead. Most of the cuts were deep but treatable. One knife stab chipped your hip bone. One sword slash opened you to the gut. I had to stuff it back in. Half a finger's width more and your gut would have been cut and you'd have poisoned your blood with your own shit."

Conan sensed each wound as she described them, felt the

ache in his hip from the fractured bone, the gnawing pain in his stomach from his abused intestines.

"Your witch's fire calmed the wounds," he said. He expected her to spit and rage at being called a witch. Most Pictish shamans attributed their skills to the ancient gods, not to knowledge of the mud and flesh, fire and water of the land.

"Halazar's balm," she said, as if it needed no explanation.

"You're named Kaz."

"And you are King Conan of Aquilonia."

"You're mistaken. I'm just a traveling—"

"I couldn't give two shits between king and peasant. It's not me who recognizes you."

"The Bossonian," Conan said, remembering the man leaning down and staring into his face as he lay bleeding into the ground.

"Fennick," Kaz said, her voice softening. "He was born on the Thunder River. He used to be an archer, and he served you in your campaign against Nemedia. He carries scars from that war, and if you're nice to him he'll tell you the story of each one."

Conan sighed. It was pointless trying to deny his identity. Kaz the Pict seemed unconcerned at having a king lying at her mercy. Indeed, no one in the camp seemed particularly perturbed at having been confronted by royalty. Their song had ended, and Fennick was standing close to the fire while the woman with the animal-skin mask stirred something in a large metal pot suspended over the flames. Fennick kept glancing at him, but Conan saw only curiosity in his expression, not deference.

Conan went to push himself up into a sitting position. He heard shuffling movement and Kaz appeared before him, reaching out and pressing down on his shoulder to dissuade him from moving. He glared at her. She shrugged, stepped back, and watched as he sat up. He groaned, steadied himself with both hands on the ground. The world swayed and turned, then leveled again.

The others around the campfire saw his movement and glanced his way. Kaz signaled to them with one hand—a very small, gentle gesture. They continued cooking, feeding the fire, and Fennick strummed his stringed instrument again, picking out a calming tune that settled all across the camp.

"Two shits between king and peasant, but you're happy to treat a Cimmerian for his wounds?"

Kaz shrugged. "Ancient grudges don't concern me."

"Maybe they concern me."

She studied him for a while, as if truly seeing him. Then she half-smiled. "Weak and feeble though you seem, I know your reputation, King Conan. Our song for you would be a long one, filled with tales of barbarism and heroism most wouldn't believe belonged to the same man. I could have killed you a dozen times through the night, but you could have killed me a dozen times more. I think this Pict and this Cimmerian are beyond old grudges, don't you?"

Conan chuckled. At her mention of a song for him, another question came to mind. "Jemi called you and your friends the Last Song?"

"We travel, write music and words, perform it for ourselves and others. Our songs are about famous or infamous dead people. Or, like that piece you just heard, 'The Sun Behind his Eyes,' mythical figures from legend. Our purpose is to bring music to the world."

Conan raised an eyebrow.

"I know, I don't talk like a Pict," she said. "I've traveled."

"I believe you all have," Conan said. He looked at the others again and saw the truth in what he'd suspected from the first moment he stumbled and fell by their fire. "You're all warriors."

"Not anymore," she replied, voice low and soft. "We've left a life of violence behind."

"Why?"

"We all have our reasons. The others' stories are not for me to tell."

"Then sing me yours."

Kaz smiled. She sat close to Conan and leaned in, nodding down at his stomach. He sat back a little and allowed her to lift away the furs where they'd gathered at his waist. She examined his wounds, leaning left and right so that the firelight lit them. Dawn was blooming in the east, adding its illumination.

She sat back, sighed, and swayed a little to the music, eyes half closed, strong arms resting on her crossed knees.

"So?" Conan said.

"We sing only songs of the dead," she said. "My song's not yet written. But I'll tell you my story, if you're truly interested."

"I'm interested in anyone who helps me," Conan said. It was strange, being spoken to as an equal by someone he didn't know—a road rat with no home, and a Pict at that—but he found that he liked it. He liked her. So often back in Aquilonia people bowed to him, revered him, and he'd never really been comfortable with that. It was why he sometimes donned his old singlet and furs and a fully masked helmet and spent time wandering around the markets of Tarantia, staring up at its silvery spires with wonder instead of boredom. It was why he loved training with the Black Dragons, telling them to fight him as an enemy, not their king. He thought of Elize and how she had beaten him at archery, and felt sad. The loss of his friend and bodyguard Vaccharez made him sadder, even though in the end the man had failed in his primary task.

"Very well. Here's my story, and one day this will be part of my song. I was born into one of the outland tribes in the Pictish wilderness. My father was a warrior, my mother came from lands far across the western seas. He brought me up; I never knew her. In my youth I joined a band of raiders working the Black River, charging protection to those using the waterway for trade and travel, and sometimes picking off a boat or two if times were lean. I became adept at camouflage, an excellent swimmer. At fifteen I was attacked by river snakes and I almost died fighting them off. Got bitten nine times, slit the bites, and sucked out the poison myself. At seventeen a mudcroc took me down into its nest, and I was under water for so long fighting it and trying to escape that my people thought I was a ghost when I finally surfaced. When I was twenty, we boarded and took a sloop from far to the north. We killed everyone on board, but the last man waved his hand and all of my raiding party but me fell dead on the deck, blood and brains boiling from their popped eyes. He walked around and kicked and pushed them all into the water. I couldn't move. I was transfixed, and remained transfixed by him for the next seven years. He taught me his shamanistic ways, his dark magic. He said I was marked by snake and lizard, and he saw their stain in my eyes. He expected nothing in return. Nothing but my soul."

Kaz looked at her hands resting on her knees, as if remembering all the things they had done. The blood that stained them. The deeds that haunted their bones.

"After seven years he tried to call in that debt, but my soul was my own. And by then, I'd found music. It set me free, fed my soul and made it whole, precious. Purged the hate and need for war that had been festering there. I fled, as far and fast as I could, and a year later I found Jemi and the Last Song. Fate brought me here. Music has more power than sword or ax."

Conan grunted. It was quite a tale. "My wounds would disagree," he said.

Kaz smiled sadly. "I don't expect you to understand."

"What does that mean?"

She looked him up and down, and once again he was struck by how these people treated a king. Keep a hold of yourself, Conan, he thought. Don't stand too proud or too high, for you are always just a man.

"Look at you," she said. "You're a man made of scars."

"I see more than a few on your arms and face, Pict river raider."

"Mine remain a warning to me," she said. "I sense that yours are worn with pride." She stood up and walked to the fire, and Conan heard her and the others chatting. They looked at him as they talked. He felt no threat coming from them.

The Last Song, he thought, and it was a strange idea, that a group of former warriors, sellswords, and barbarians might find peace in such music. But he supposed the telling of history had a power all its own.

Conan went to stand, groaned as his wounds stabbed and weakened him, and ended up crouched over, supporting himself on his hands and knees.

Jemi stood and came over to him, moving smoothly on her wooden crutches. The stump of her left leg—gone above the knee—was festooned with colored bindings, and the rest of her clothes were no less exotic. "Kaz says ya lost a lot of blood."

"I have plenty."

"Ya wanna lose more? Get up, start prancing around, yer likely to."

"I have things to do."

"King things?" Jemi asked. "That why ya been all cut up and sliced open?"

"My business."

"Ah, right. Well, sorry, yer majesty." Jemi chuckled, and Conan felt a prickle of indignation. He bit it down.

"I have to go," he said, and he moved again to stand.

The world turned again, and then he was on his face once more, Kaz crouched by his side with a water canteen. "Did I…?"

"Passed out again," she said. "Only for a few moments, but long enough for Tathar to eat your porridge. We'll make you some more. But if you head off on your own, you'll end up falling into a river or passing out and letting the local wildlife have their pickings from you."

Conan sighed and drank down some more water, then Kaz took the canteen away.

"Why are you doing this?" he asked. He looked past Kaz and saw that the others were standing around now, closer to him than the fire. Jemi smiling on her crutches. Fennick watching him wide-eyed, still nursing the stringed instrument but only holding it now, not playing it. It sat on his shoulder like a replacement bow. Conan thought it looked good on the Bossonian archer.

Behind him was a man he assumed to be Tathar, the Stygian tattoos across his face harsh in the growing dawn light. His expression was unreadable—typical for a Stygian. Conan had never met one he could trust, and he didn't think that was about to change.

Then there was the pirate with animal skins still obscuring her face, and beside her the tall man he yet knew nothing about. What marked him beyond average was the terrible slew of scars now visible across his face, and the necklace of withered ears that seemed out of place for a peace-loving musician.

Peace-loving maybe, but they all have stories of blood and war, Conan thought. And that was when an idea started to bloom. Tired, queasy, and weak, still his mind was working on the reason he'd come here and the distances he'd yet to travel.

Maybe his place could be with the Last Song. He had to nurse that idea and let it find its own weight, because he was not the one in control right now. That was Jemi. It was in her attitude, and the way the others seemed to gather around her in a semicircle and defer to her.

Strange. Conan suspected that she was the only one among them who had never taken another person's life.

He had pressing matters in the east, with a band of slavers

and cutthroats holding his old friend's family hostage. His injuries pinned him where he was, and caution—a sense he rarely acknowledged but which had kept him alive all these decades—pricked at his impatience and calmed it. He remembered the words spoken by that last living attacker he had taken down after his Black Dragon traveling companions were butchered.

King Conan… kill him and earn… more riches than… imagine.

Someone knew that Conan was on the road, and they had already tried to kill him. What better place for a warrior king to hide than with a traveling musical troupe?

They remained in that camp for another full day, and Conan became more and more twitchy, expecting another attack at any moment. He had not told Jemi and the others many details about his mission, though he knew that they were curious. All he'd said was that he was not on official royal business. He'd told them that he'd encountered a group of road bandits, and that he'd been taken down with a lucky strike from a dirty sword.

Maybe I was a fool to think I could do this alone. If Zenobia hadn't sent Vaccharez and the others to keep an eye on him, he might well be dead.

Someone out there wanted that. If he started thinking about who across the known world might wish him harm, the names would be many, the list long. There was no use in trying to figure out whom it might be. But he couldn't help thinking it was linked to Baht Tann and his kidnapped family. No one else knew he had left Aquilonia on this long journey.

"Not Baht Tann," he muttered to himself as he lay healing by the Last Song's campfire. "He wouldn't have betrayed me." Many so-called friends had turned on him in the past, and there were graves both marked and unmarked in a dozen countries paying testament to those betrayals, but he believed everything Tann had told him. That matter of shared food and water, that small promise cast in blood, meant the world to them both.

Not Baht Tann, then. But who?

Someone was spreading the word about his having left the palace and his throne, however temporarily. He would have to be on his guard.

Being with the Last Song gave him time to rest, at least. They might have turned their backs on a life of violence, but that didn't mean their skills did not remain. If a threat manifested, he was sure the Last Song would know. They played their music and sang their songs, but they possessed a comforting alertness, a graceful confidence in their surroundings. Tathar the Stygian often strolled the fringes of their camp, looking outward. The quiet man, Gannar—an Aesir sellsword, so Conan had discovered—placed telltales further from the camp that would make a loud noise should someone attempt to close in unobserved. And the mask-faced pirate, whom Conan had discovered was named Allymaro, disappeared for hours at a time. Jemi said she was their hunter, and she always returned with game for their fire, though Conan suspected she hunted more than game; they might have given up their years of blood for new years of song, but she always took her shortsword with her.

The Last Song ensured their camp was secure and under no threat. In that security, Conan allowed himself to rest, just a little. And as he rested, that idea of how he might enlist the Last Song on his journey finally took root and bloomed.

"Jemi," Conan said. "I have a proposition for you all."

"Huh." Jemi jumped in surprise. She'd thought Conan was

dozing, but he was actually watching her where she sat a few feet from him. She was whittling a stick of elder, patiently carving it into a thin, long flute. He'd seen her doing this over the course of the day, and between working on it she tucked it into a notch on one of her crutches. She'd probably carved those herself, too, Conan mused. Jemi seemed the sort of person who was very self-sufficient.

She hadn't yet offered her own story, and Conan had not asked. He realized that the people of the Last Song placed high value in histories. That was what had given him this idea.

"It's some give and some take," Conan said.

"We're not looking after ya for take," she said.

"I understand. But I'm asking more of you."

"Huh." She looked at Conan, then down at the flute she was working on. She placed it to her lips. The notes she blew were out of tune and painful, but it got everyone's attention. Jemi waved them over, and as they came from across the camp she held up her flute and examined it. "Got to tune ya better," she muttered.

The Last Song gathered around Jemi and Conan. Jemi and Kaz sat, Fennick crouched down, Allymaro and Tathar stood. Gannar held back, running his fingers back and forth along the necklace of dried, shriveled ears around his neck. Conan meant to ask him about those, if and when they ever had time alone.

"Our guest has a proposition for us," Jemi said.

All eyes on him, Conan sat up against the tree where they'd made his bed. He grimaced as he did so but did not let out a groan.

"You all know who I am," he said. "I'm older than all of you. You know me as King Conan, but before that I've been much more." He looked at each of them in turn as he spoke. "Barbarian. Sellsword. Pirate. Thief. Some think they know my story, and parts of it are told far and wide across these lands, but only I know it all. Even my wife has been told only the... less distasteful parts."

"I've heard whispers," Allymaro said. Her voice was a growl from behind the animal-skin mask. Conan wondered what the mask covered and how damaged she might be. If what he was about to suggest was accepted, perhaps he would find out.

"I'm journeying east, to fulfill a promise to a friend," he said. "The road is dangerous, its end more so. I'd like you to come with me."

"We've all put down our swords and axes," Tathar said. "We're musicians and storytellers now, not fighters and killers." He spoke with passion, even anger, and as Conan wondered at his story, he realized that most of these people were still a mystery to him. He suspected that their tales were long, dark, and deep.

The others muttered agreement and nodded at Tathar's words, presenting a united front. Conan was impressed by them, but curious as well. He'd met old warriors seeking the path of peace before, but he'd never quite been able to understand that philosophy. He wondered if an ember of bloody desire burned in their hearts as it had always blazed in his own.

"I respect that," Conan said. "That's why I'm asking you to come with me as the Last Song, not as warriors."

Jemi raised one eyebrow. The others shuffled a little. None of them spoke.

"I've been attacked once. Might be again. Traveling with you will be the perfect cover." And no warrior forgets the feel of steel in their hand or a bowstring on their fingers.

"Ahhhh," Jemi said. "And in return, we get your stories."

Conan nodded.

"I know one story well, King Conan, because I fought with your forces against Nemedia," Fennick said.

"But to know so much more will make it our greatest song," Kaz said.

"When I'm dead," Conan said.

"Of course," she said, and offered her half-smile.

"Which won't be for some time."

"Like you said, Conan, you're much older than most of us."

Ally laughed out loud. Jemi chuckled. Even Tathar smiled.

"We're a democracy," Jemi said.

"I understand," Conan said. "But I'm leaving tomorrow, with or without you all. Either way, you have my gratitude."

The Last Song headed back across camp to gather around their wagon and confer. Fennick was the last to go, the Bossonian archer smiling back over his shoulder at Conan. "Quite a song," he said. "Quite a song."

10

Not My Face

The Last Song had been on their way to the coastal ports of Argos to entertain sailors and gather stories and legends for new compositions. They were nomads by nature, following no real route and setting their compass through passing comments and the direction of the winds. Choosing to change their plans and accompany Conan eastward was not a difficult decision for any of them, but neither was it a firm commitment. Jemi told him that they would travel across the border regions into Koth, and from there they would decide how much further they would go.

Conan was grateful. He knew that when he was healed and well and able to travel under his own steam once again, new decisions would be made. Though he carried myths and tales around him like a cloud of ghostly revenants, he was still but one man. The Last Song told the stories of eons.

Thus he found himself in the back of the Last Song's wagon as they made their way across the marshy, dangerous border regions where eastern Ophir kissed northern Koth. At his request they had skirted far around Korshemish, and Jemi had seen something in his eyes when he asked that. But though Conan had promised them tales of his past, he was not yet ready to tell them about the Scarlet Citadel, and the dreadful things he had encountered in those hellish basements. Perhaps soon. Maybe if he grew to really trust them.

They kept the wagon's canvas cover folded down so that he could see their way and watch the skies passing by. Jemi sat on the wagon's seat and steered the two steeds with a gentle hand while Kaz sat beside her, nodding gently as the soporific movements lulled her in and out of sleep. More than once, Jemi reached over and grasped the Pict woman's jacket to prevent her from tumbling to the ground.

The others walked, chatting or at peace in silence.

Conan felt no such peace. He was frustrated at the speed they were making, angry at his body for not healing faster, and concerned at the possibility of further attacks, and the Last Song's casual bearing did nothing to lessen his fears. Even with Allymaro sitting in the wagon with him, he could not relax.

Alongside Conan in the wagon bed was everything owned by the traveling musical troupe. There were instruments of all shapes, sizes, and kinds made from wood and wound gut, bone and ivory, and intricately worked metals; six different traveling packs of different sizes and designs, probably one for each of them containing personal items and clothing; the battered metal pot they used to cook meals over open fires; a large water vat that swished half full; sundry packs of dried fruit and sachets of herbs and spices, some of which he recognized, many he did not; rolled sleeping mats and a pile of animals pelts; and weapons. He saw swords and axes, a heavy mace, and several bows and arrow quivers. There were also the two pikes on either side of the wagon's front seat. His traveling companions might have moved on from their violent pasts, but they also understood that many of the folk they encountered on the trail would still tread that blood-red road.

"Crossing inta Koth," Jemi said without turning around.

"No border guards?" Conan asked.

"Huh. No border. We know the quieter routes, the secret passes. These marshes're remote an' dangerous, an' most travelers stay away."

"Why?"

"The banshees, mainly."

Conan asked no more. He'd heard tales of the Penperlleni banshees but had never heard or seen them for himself, and he had no real desire for that to change. But he recognized what Jemi and the others were doing for him, keeping him secret and safe.

"So maybe now's the time to work on your disguise," Allymaro said, and she pulled a leather bag into her lap. She untied the string and opened it out, and inside were three masks similar to the one she wore. They were finely made, with intricate stitching and delicate cuts, but something about them made Conan shiver. Similar but unique, they each carried the character of the animal their skins had been taken from, treated, dried, stretched, and scraped before being worked into a mask.

"Did you make these yourself, Allymaro?'

"People call me Ally. And yes. I have more, if you'd like to see."

"I'm... not sure they are for me."

"Afraid to hide your true self?" Ally asked.

Conan looked away, out of the wagon and across the increasingly marshy terrain, where a low mist now blanketed the ground, breaking around copses and small hillocks. They followed a raised trail that rose up and down, sometimes the wheels splashing through water or thick mud, other times crunching on dried and compressed stone.

"Apologies," she said. "Your business is not mine."

"I'm well used to disguises," Conan said. "But I sense these masks are more."

Ally stared at him from behind her own mask, green eyes never wavering. As if they were eating him in, savoring him to see if he could be trusted. At last she brought up both hands behind her head and unfastened her mask. She held it to her face for a moment more, unfastened, as if deciding whether to reveal her own true self.

Conan stared at her.

Ally took off her mask.

He did not look away, though he wanted to. He kept his composure and refused to offend her by closing his eyes.

Allymaro's face was a mask of horror. Her skin was ridged and scarred, bloated and cast hard. Her piercing green eyes existed in shriveled pits. Her nose was missing, leaving a grotesque hole that dripped and dribbled. Her lips were darkened purple and split in many places. Half of her hair was missing, and her scalp was zigzagged with dark lines where blood had leaked and dried.

"I was born on the Baracha Isles," she said. "I've seen in your gaze that you recognize what I once was."

"A pirate," Conan said. "I was one also, and they called me Amra the Lion. But I wasn't like you."

"No, not like me. I was born a pirate, brought up on the seas, lulled to sleep by the ocean's violent waves. My mother wore me in a sling while she stormed boats and raided coastal towns along the Zingaran coast. By the time I could walk and talk, I had seen things no child should see. I grew into the life, and when I was nineteen I was drafted on to a new boat by a new captain. We went further afield, attacking the Pictish coast and taking prisoners to sell as slaves in Stygia. But there was something inside me that didn't belong—empathy. Even kindness. Emotions that made being a pirate painful.

"One day when I was almost thirty, I jumped ship in Khemi. I'd almost made it out of the city when I was caught by slave traders and hauled back to my crew."

Conan grimaced, and looked away from her at last. He knew the oath of the pirate. "Usually they kill deserters," he said.

"My captain was particularly brutal. He wore shrunken baby heads on a belt around his fat waist, the offspring of women he'd sold into slavery. In a cruel world, that man was pure evil. He waited until we were back out to sea before issuing my punishment. They strapped me to the foremast and sent divers down onto the coastal reefs around Argos. There they harvested a certain type of fish called the redtail. You've heard of them?"

Conan shook his head.

"Then you're lucky. They're parasitic, attaching to their victims with suckers along their stomach and abdomen. He stuck seven redtails to my face and left them to die in the sun whilst stuck to my skin. Dying, they sucked my blood. Once dead, they quickly expanded in the heat while rot took hold. One by one they exploded, and their toxic and acidic guts and innards melted my face. He left me up there for three days."

"But you escaped," Conan said.

"No. Not really."

He frowned but asked no more. She was looking down at her hand holding her mask, the one thing that hid her horrific truth from the world.

"A Zingaran naval sloop engaged us a few weeks later and our ship was holed. In the confusion, I cornered the captain in the hold and bit out his throat. Then I fled."

"So you did escape."

"No one escapes a crew such as mine, Conan. They came after me—the survivors, at least. For three years I hid, ran, hid again, moving across Zingara, Aquilonia, Nemedia. They gave chase, because honor drove them, and their blind loyalty to their bastard captain whose flesh I still had between my teeth. I killed seven of them, two in one night. And still I run."

"But you're with the Last Song now."

"And I have been for nine years. Disguised, peaceful, lamenting my losses. Sometimes we perform the song I wrote about my captain, but only when we're alone."

"You think the survivors still pursue you?"

Ally shrugged, then slipped her mask back on. "I wear different masks because I have to believe so, yes. I've renounced my former life, but if any of them ever find me, I'll take their heads and spit down their throats."

Conan watched as she fixed and adjusted her mask.

"So, let's think about your disguise, former pirate Conan. You won't take a mask, but there are other things I can do for you, if you'll let me?"

Conan held out his hands, palms up, inviting her to try.

Ally came closer and looked at Conan from different angles. She reached out and almost touched his face, running her hands over the contours of his head while not quite touching him. She was close, and he glanced at her piercing green eyes behind her mask. What horrors she had endured. What depredations. She had hinted that she still possessed the heart of a warrior, if the need arose, but it was her peace and empathy that defined her now. She reminded him of Zenobia, and as she moved around him and started working with his hair, he realized that no woman had been this close to him—this intimate and personal—for years other than his wife.

He breathed in deeply and drew in Ally's scent, and it was redolent of the sea. He stared ahead, through the wagon's open flap while she tried to make him look like someone else.

She wound his long black hair into a tail, separating it into three strands that she wove around each other until it hung heavy and thick from the back of his head. It felt strange, but he liked it. It pulled at his forehead and temples, smoothing his scarred and aged skin.

Ally sat back and reached into her bag. Conan thought she was going to try to fit him with one of her masks once again, but instead she pulled out a thin silver headband. She polished it with her jacket sleeve, then reached out and placed it around Conan's head.

"It will draw the eye," she said. "Anything to distract."

"Where's Conan!?" Jemi asked, looking over her shoulder, and she laughed out loud.

Kaz startled awake beside her and turned around, and when she saw Conan she gave him the ghost of a smile. Then she stretched her arms, and as her mouth yawned wide a terrible high scream erupted all around them. Kaz and Jemi pressed their hands to their ears, and Ally grimaced and hunched her head into her shoulders.

The Penperlleni banshees. The sounds were high and piercing, more than mere screams. They were inside Conan's head as well, scraping at the inside of his skull with sharp-nailed fingers.

The wagon rocked as Fennick jumped onto its side and Gannar held onto the back. Conan thought they were reaching for weapons, but he should have known better. Ally was ready, and she handed each of them an instrument from the rack on one side of the wagon. Fennick took the long stringed instrument he'd been playing the night before, and Gannar grabbed a thick, hollow tube of bamboo, with a mouthpiece at one end and various holes and hollows along its length.

Jemi started shouting and Kaz joined in, and Conan realized that they were singing. Ally joined them, accompanied by Tathar's deep voice from beside the wagon, and Fennick and Gannar quickly started playing their instruments. The strings twanged and rang, the bamboo instrument boomed and chimed, and though there was very little finesse to their playing and singing, Conan felt the discomfort in his mind easing.

"The horses!" he shouted. "What about the horses?" But if anyone heard him they did not answer. He half-rose from the wagon floor and saw that the horses were already wearing blinkers over their eyes and mufflers over their ears. Jemi had come this way knowing what they might encounter, and she'd been prepared.

Conan reached for his sword, lying on the board by his feet, but Ally fell on it, hand splayed and fingers holding the blade down. She was still shouting her song, and she waited for Conan to look at her before raising her eyebrows and shaking her head.

Conan was not used to shunning his sword while confronting a threat.

He looked around them. The old trail they followed wound across the top of some higher ground, while the lower areas of this border marshland shimmered with water, swathes of tall reeds, and other plants that favored wet ground. At the scream of the banshees, a thousand birds had taken flight all around them, speckling the skies and fleeing in all directions to escape the dreadful sound. Conan wished he could do the same.

Ally nudged him, still singing loudly. Fennick's fingers plucked heavy notes from his strings, and Gannar's cheeks billowed and grew rosy red as he blew into the length of bamboo, his fingers dancing across the holes as he brought forth a tune. Conan realized that there was no real pattern here, no one tune they were playing or song they were singing, and when Ally nudged him again he joined in.

Conan had never claimed to have a singing voice, and he proved that now, but as soon as he started shouting a bawdy old campfire song from his early years in Cimmeria, the screeches of the Penperlleni banshees receded a little in his mind. He sang the same verse over and over because they were the only words he knew. His wounds throbbed with the effort, and he knelt on the wagon's bed and looked around for approaching danger.

He'd heard about the banshees from a knight in the Black Dragons. They wore a person down with their cries, drawing energy, dulling senses, numbing their victims until they were almost powerless.

Then they would strike.

The Penperlleni banshees were blood drinkers, vampires whose bite often followed their dreadful shrill screams. Once blood was drained, they preserved the flesh of their victims in dirty marsh water, letting it rot before they sucked it from the bones.

Conan shouted and shouted, the rest of the Last Song sang and played, and then he saw the first of the banshees.

It drifted into view across the marsh, moving through the low-lying mists and leaving hardly any wake. It seemed to disappear as soon as he saw it. Its voice was close, slicing the air with screams. Another appeared, then another, and this time he saw them clearly. They were floating things with no discernible limbs, skull-like heads swathed in long gray hair, torsos clothed in loose ragged cloaks, and they floated above the brackish waters and through the yellow mists like ghosts.

Jemi took a breath and gently flicked at the horses with her whip. They needed no encouragement to move faster. Perhaps the two strong steeds had caught sight of the banshees through the sides of their masks, heard them even though their ears were muffled, because they started trotting along the trail. The wagon bounced and jolted, its contents falling from racks and clattering to the floor.

Conan eyed his sword but left it where it was. He could grab it up in an instant if the banshees came closer, though he wasn't sure how effective tempered steel might be against them. He wasn't even sure how real, how corporeal they were.

Conan and the Last Song sang and played, the horses trotted, the wagon jarred and bounced, and a while later Jemi brought them to a halt atop a high hillock at the edge of the marsh. In the valley beyond they saw grassy plains, heavily wooded areas, and here and there the more regular patterns of farmed land.

Breathing hard, their songs ceased at last. Gannar leaned against the wagon, breathless from blowing the bamboo. Fennick kept his instrument at the ready, like a warrior holding his favorite weapon.

"I feel like I've heard the worst song ever," Kaz said.

"I think that was me," Conan said, and they all laughed. "So they're definitely behind us now?"

"They don't leave the marshes," Jemi said. "But we should, an' quickly. Let's not take a chance." She looked back at Conan from where she sat on the wagon's steering seat. "Ally should finish yer disguise. We're in Koth now, and we'll be headin' inta farmland soon enough, before that gives way to the Kothian Desert. We'll meet people. They'll wanna know who we are. And the last person you c'n be is King Conan."

11

A Tale of Krow Danaz

"Another rock," Krow Danaz said. "Another. And then another." A weak cry came from the man who had attempted to steal from him. He was on the floor, his arms and legs splayed and tied to iron rings cast into the flagstones. Elsewhere in this dungeon of torture were meat hooks suspended from the ceiling, a pit filled with acid, a closed and locked cubby where Danaz kept a dozen jars of poisonous insects and toxic minerals, a covered hole in the floor where old victims were even now rotting down into slick soup, and a rack upon which he had once watched a traitorous slave slowly pulled to pieces over the space of three long, wonderful days.

But for this thief, Krow Danaz had ordered a crushing.

"And another! Now!"

Two slaves hurried back and forth between the pile of small, square rocks and the heavy wooden platform that had been laid across the victim's stomach, groin, and legs. They placed the rocks and the man beneath cried out again, an agonized exhalation that held very little breath.

"Betray me and die," Danaz said. "Steal from me and die. Try to escape me and die. Do as you're told and…?"

"And we relish your mercy," the two slaves said, voices low and matched. They knew what to say. They always did.

"Mercy for me," the man groaned. "Mercy for Kaneg, I beg—"

"You have no name," Danaz said. "You lost that when I brought you here. Using your name on me now, trying to inspire a mercy you don't deserve, you know what that brings you?"

Poor Kaneg shook his head.

"Another rock."

One of the slaves picked up a rock and handed it to the other, who placed it on the stack on the wooden board.

Something cracked—a bone, though Danaz did not know which one. Maybe his hip joint. The man cried out, high and brief. Danaz smiled. He was excited by the pain he witnessed, thrilled by the power he wielded. It was fuel for life.

"More rocks, and don't stop," Danaz ordered.

More rocks, and more, and there were more cracks and cries. Skin burst, fractured bone protruded, blood flowed, and the man was barely conscious now. Danaz thought about pausing and letting him linger, but he had work to do. Experiments to attend to. Dark magic to create. There would be more tortures to watch and enjoy. Among his slaves, it was easy for him to find reason for punishment.

The rocks piled high on the wooden board, and eventually it sank down with a great *crunch!* and crushed the man to death. His breath went with a final weak croak, and rats scampered in from the shadows to lap at his blood and chew at his open flesh.

"Bring me his liver before the vermin get at it," he said. "I'm peckish. I'll have it fried with some onions." He watched as the slaves went at the body with knives, slicing open the shattered torso and extracting the precious organ. Danaz's mouth was watering.

"Now back to my laboratories," he said. The two slaves came to him, turned him around in his wheeled chair, and pushed him from the torture dungeon. From behind he heard the sounds of chewing and crunching as things larger than rats came up out of the depths to feed on the carrion. He also heard the fast, frightened breathing of his slaves.

Fear kept them subdued. For Danaz, fear was the greatest weapon.

The castle of Kerrodan Xen was in ruins a thousand years before Krow Danaz took up residence in its extensive basements. Nestled in the border regions between Shem and Koth, its purposes were long lost to the mists of time, its name known only through whispered myths and stories carried down through the ages, most of them red-tinged with blood and pain. As centuries passed, its name changed from lips to ears, its stories growing and mutating. Such is the effect of deep time and brief lives.

The remnants of the castle's upper battlements consisted of a few walls swallowed in undergrowth and ivy, with a forest of trees growing among the fallen stone piles. In a few places walls still stood abutting each other, but most of the structure was tumbled away to war, cataclysm, or misfortune. Like all things living or inanimate, time had had its way with Kerrodan Xen.

Toward the end of the extensive travels that marked his later life, Krow Danaz did not pause at the castle because of what it showed aboveground but for what was below. Beneath the ruins was a vast labyrinth of dungeons, basements, and natural caves, many of them lined with the remains of countless dead. Femurs formed curved ceilings, ribs decorated walls, and he walked on the hollow-eyed faces of upturned skulls. In the corners of some of these deep rooms he found the tunnels that led to caverns, and thence deeper still, deeper than he had ever dared go. He was already sickening by then, the wasting disease that ravaged his body working its evils on his bones and muscles, and those first few days belowground almost became his last. He'd gone way down, and when his torches burned out and he lost the advantage of sight, the darkness closed around him like a solid weight.

Something found him and bore him back up to the light.

Danaz still did not know who or what had saved him. He remembered its smell, like that of an old, damp dog. He recalled how it felt beneath his fingers as it carried him—dry scales and moist joints between its muscled limbs. In his darkest dreams he heard its voice as it sang to him in an unknown language, its tone deep and sinister, its intentions mysterious. That thing brought him up and saved him, and when it turned and retreated back to the depths whence it came he suffered an unbearable sense of loss.

Yet he dared not descend to search for it, because he suspected—no, he knew—that it had saved him from even worse horrors that existed down there. He'd heard them, soft rumbles as primeval things turned over miles beneath the surface of the land. He'd felt the soft warm drafts of their irregular breaths passing through the basements and carrying a dank promise of madness and death, a promise that had existed before this modern time had ever come into being. Perhaps they had gone down when times changed and humankind came to the land. Maybe they had always existed in the dark.

He heard and felt them still.

So Krow Danaz stayed in the basements of Kerrodan Xen, and over time he came to realize that this was the place he had been searching for ever since his master and teacher Tsotha-lanti had been murdered by the new Aquilonian king Conan many years ago. In those years following, he had wandered across Koth and Shem and south to Stygia, but he had never found anyone or anything that made him want to put down roots. His master's death had set him adrift, in body and soul. Even when the foul sickness settled over him, he continued moving, wanderlust showing him much of the land and yet nothing that impressed him.

Until, that was, he made Kerrodan Xen his home. There he continued the experiments that he'd begun many years ago under Tsotha-lanti's guidance, and the more he learned and studied and encased himself in those dark arts, the greater he felt at home. At last, he had found somewhere he belonged. At last, he had discovered true purpose in his shriveling, fading life.

In his accelerating journey toward death, his aim was immortality. Necromancy became his focus. Sometimes he slaughtered one of his slaves and resurrected him or her, studying the effects of life-from-death. He refined his spells, and at all times the memory of his master was with him, whispering in his ear, praising good choices, admonishing him when an experiment went wrong. He was perfecting his dark arts so that when he died, he might rise again, immortal, endless. A god.

Tsotha-lanti would have been proud. And if his master had not been killed before his time, Krow Danaz's skills would have been much more refined. He had acted as father as well as master, and for that Danaz had always considered how pleasant it would be to find vengeance against Conan, the warrior who had taken his master's head.

Yet as time drew onward and Danaz found himself diseased and weakening, revenge became a vague thought. It did not drive him, was not his obsession, and as the years passed in those basements and catacombs beneath Kerrodan Xen, it faded into something of a dream.

Until the coming of the mind bats.

Krow Danaz was in one of the larger basement chambers, where he had established his main laboratory for practicing and refining the arcane art of resurrection.

The glorious image of the crushed slave fresh in his mind, he settled his wheeled chair beside the stone slab where another slave lay. She had once been a fine specimen, a strong farmer from Argos who had come to him along with a haul of captives from his favored Shemite slave traders. She had learned like the rest of them that her name and identity meant nothing here, and the diminishing potion he gave her—a special creation of Danaz's, designed to subdue and subjugate by melting the personality portions of the mind—wiped much of her past. She became one of several prime slaves, attending to his personal needs such as washing, dressing, eating, and the occasional sexual perversions that took his fancy, but lately he had perceived the spark of something he did not like in her eyes. Just now and then, when she thought he was looking the other way, he caught some sad recollection of her past in her distant gaze.

Sometimes the diminishing potion failed over time, and slaves who regained memories of who they once were could become problematic, even dangerous. But Danaz never wasted a good slave.

Lying on the slab, frozen by a stab of purple lotus juice, the woman's eyes were wide and defiant as mechanical pumps sucked her lifeblood from arteries in her arms and legs. The warm fluid spurted through tubes and filled glass beakers placed on tables to either side, each beaker gently warmed, the blood drawn back and forth between containers via a series of pumps and smaller plastic tubes. Danaz observed her body's reactions as the blood left her—first a shiver, then a violent clenching and unclenching of muscles still untouched by the purple lotus. Then she uttered a terrible, rattling breath and her lifeless body relaxed on the slab.

"Good," Danaz said. "Good! And now keep the blood warm and flowing, keep it alive, and soon her eyes will be open and burst afire once more." He wheeled himself away from the dead slave and approached a large table covered with papers and books filled with his own writings, along with dusty tomes he'd collected over the years of his travels. One large volume lay open at the table's edge, and it was here that he made his observations, drew diagrams, and composed his incantations of resurrection.

As he flipped through the pages to search for the correct incantation for this situation, his mind was assaulted. He cried out, head thrown back, and his wheeled chair drifted away from the table. He clawed at his temples, trying to press fingers inside his skull to scratch away the horrible invasive sensation. Two slaves emerged from the shadowy recesses at the room's corners, wan empty eyes wide, and closed in. Danaz lashed out at them.

"Do not touch me!"

He felt his mind being opened and examined. Mind bats! He knew of the art but had never been interested in it himself. The dead were his domain, whereas mind bats were intended to infect the minds of those still alive.

"Damn you," he said through clenched teeth. Someone was targeting him! Someone knew of him, sending their thoughts his way, and there was no way of telling how malevolent these thoughts might be.

Danaz grabbed the wheels of his chair and heaved, turning himself slowly. If only he were still strong! His thin arms strained as he pushed himself toward the door, intending to head deeper into the basements, where perhaps—

In the blink of an eye, Krow Danaz was somewhere else.

The tavern was busy, bustling with drinkers laughing and singing around the large circular bar, others sitting at tables gambling with cards or other games, and a trio in one corner playing bone flutes. A few people danced in front of the band, hypnotic movements in time with the lulling music. Away from the bar in the tavern's shadowy recesses, people huddled and made nefarious deals, planned dark deeds, or rutted on wooden benches or tabletops.

Krow Danaz was in a far corner, sitting at a table with several empty tankards before him. A woman sat opposite, and he remembered her. He had been here before, years ago, and now he was here again. He looked down at himself—withered, ill, dressed in dirty rags, but not in his wheeled chair.

"You sent mind bats for me," he said, and he tried to lunge at the woman. He did not move; his body did not obey.

"I mean no harm," the woman said, smiling. "Yes, the mind bats are mine. They've brought us back to this place, where we met many years ago and talked the evening away. You frightened me then. Those…" She pointed to his bald skull and the dark tattooed words that decorated it, phrases that would change over time given his mood or disposition. "And they frighten me still. But there is something I have to tell you. An opportunity I must impart. I think you'll like it."

"Mylera," Danaz said. He remembered her. It was strange because they'd merely passed a brief evening together, drinking and talking, and he hadn't thought of her since. He had been much younger then and more innocent, healthier in flesh and mind. An ex-pupil of Tsotha, true, but not yet driven away from the world by the dark arts he practiced. But her name was fresh in his mind, as if they had just met and introduced themselves.

He reached for a tankard, but his hands did not move. Clever. The mind bats were giving him a memory to live in, but he was not really there.

"I seem to be your unwilling listener," he said. "But be quick. I'm busy. A dead woman is awaiting my ministrations."

He saw something pass across Mylera's eyes, a shadow of fear. It set his soul aflame.

"Conan," she said.

"Ah, yes. That's right. You hate him. You want him dead."

"You do too?" she said, eyes wide.

Krow Danaz shrugged. "You, me, and half the world, I'd suggest. But I've not wasted my life craving his demise. His time will come, while mine…" He trailed off. There was no need to tell this strange woman of his experiments, his writings, his journey toward immortality.

Mine will never come.

She waited for him to finish what he was going to say. After a moment of silence, she continued.

"I'm going to kill him. I know where he is, where he'll be, and someone else I know is scheming his murder. I believe the three of us together can succeed."

His interest piqued, Danaz imagined waving a finger as if to gesture, Go on, tell me more, yet still he did not move.

"He's heading for Khoraja, on a mission to rescue the family of a friend from slavers and bandits. The other one I know is called Grake, and he holds this family prisoner. They're bait. We are the executioners."

Laughter, music, and the sound of clinking glasses filled the background to this memory-scene, but really it was just him and Mylera, the woman from long ago. He was no longer furious at her intrusion—angry, yes, but also intrigued.

"You've learned a lot since we met," he said.

"Mind bats are the least of it." She was evidently still

unsettled by him, and he liked that. He thought of the resurrection spell he was about to cast, and the words marked across his skull squirmed and shifted to spell something new. Mylera's eyes widened a little and she looked away.

"Khoraja," he said.

"The cliffs overlooking the great desert," she said. "There we can meet and you can avenge your dead master, whose head Conan took."

"And you can avenge… your father. I remember now."

Mylera nodded.

"A triptych of terror to finally kill Conan," Danaz said, and he remembered his master, Tsotha-lanti, those deepest black eyes, the total control he exuded over the powers he carried. His head, parted from his shoulders by a sweep of Conan's sword and carried aloft by an unnatural eagle, never to be seen again.

Mylera had lit a fire in his belly that he had believed long dimmed.

"I have not seen the sunlight in years," he said.

Mylera stood across the table from him, and he felt a strange tickling inside his skull as the mind bats began to fade. First the tavern around them dissipated into a white mist, all sound and vision fading to nothing, then the table between them disappeared, leaving only him seated and Mylera standing before him.

"Unless you're a vampire, the sun won't hurt you," she said. "I'm making for the Khorajan cliff escarpments. I hope to see you there."

Without waiting for his answer, she was gone.

Krow Danaz gasped as he opened his eyes onto a familiar cold subterranean room, barely lit by torches whose flames flickered from endless drafts.

Mylera, you witch, he thought, but he was impressed. When they'd met, she had been but a woman, now she was something of a sorceress—one who had come to him for help. Danaz was a crippled man in a wheeled chair who had shut himself away from the outside world in order to pursue his dark ambitions... but he also had an ego. He liked the fact that she had remembered him.

He liked even more the opportunity she had extended to him. If it was real, perhaps he might finally avenge his long-dead master and wipe Conan from the face of this world. That would be another step toward ending his own wretched existence and becoming something more, something far greater than he had ever been. Greater even that Tsotha-lanti.

"But first, one more trip into the sun."

He called it Spidderel. It was a creature he had created in one of the huge birthing vats he'd started experimenting with soon after he arrived at Kerrodan Xen. Back then, he had been interested in transmogrification—merging species, expanding size, aggravating certain tendencies—and the vats held a special growth fluid he had developed from a luminous compound discovered deep in one of the caverns beneath the castle. Several monstrous beings had been the result, all but one of which he had destroyed when his interests had wandered away from such things.

Spidderel, he kept. It was more intelligent than the others, and more importantly its psychic link to him was far stronger. Some of the other beasts had threatened to drift beyond his control, and he'd never liked the fact that they had their own brutal, primeval drives that held more power and allure than his own desires. Spidderel was different.

He called it up now, breathing in magical fumes from

sixteen human-fat candles lit with flames from unnatural fires. He wasn't sure how deep it had gone—since moving on from these experiments and destroying the other creations, he'd given Spidderel freedom to go its own way, down into the labyrinth of tunnels and caves deep beneath the castle—but it didn't take him long to make contact. He sensed it waking from a deep hibernation and rising, scampering, dragging itself up out of the endless shadows to do his bidding. And his first bidding was to end his current time at Kerrodan Xen.

He could not leave this place in the hands of untrustworthy custodians.

Screams echoed through the underground as Spidderel slaughtered and ate the slaves. Some hid, others ran, some even tried to fight back, but Spidderel tore them all apart. Danaz saw nothing with his own eyes, but he viewed through Spidderel's strange vision as it bit and slashed, crushed and imbibed all those who remained in the ruined castle's underworld.

Then it came to find him, and he was ready.

"My, you've grown so big!" Danaz said as the ten-limbed monstrosity hauled itself through narrow hallways and crouched in the wide archway to his chambers. It was spattered with blood, globs of human flesh hanging from stiff spines up and down its legs. Its great armored body was scarred from encounters with unknown foes of the deep, and Danaz wondered what trials and adventures it had been through over the several years since he had granted its freedom. But he would not pry; he would let that be Spidderel's story.

"It's time for us to leave this place, for a while," he said. "Time for us to feel the sun on our skins. For you, for the first time! And perhaps at the end of our journey, I may see an old foe's head spiked on one of those great, beautiful limbs of yours."

Spidderel hissed and clicked and skittered through the archway, lowering itself down so that Danaz could pull himself out of the wheeled chair and up onto its back. Such a ride. Such a steed.

The world was not ready for this.

Much as the idea of a touch of sunlight had been growing more attractive since Mylera's visit with her mind bats, Danaz knew that to begin with they would have to travel by night.

12

A Second Chance

Mylera met a small family of travelers as she crossed into Shem. She welcomed their invitation to take food with them. She told them that she was adept at foraging, and after the meal she and the father went searching for mushrooms and root veg to refill their supplies. He knelt to harvest a spread of honey mushrooms, and she slit his throat. While he clawed across the mossy ground after her, she returned to their camp and killed the mother and two children.

Thus, on day three of her travels, Mylera had a strong horse, a travel pack of clothes and equipment for the wild, and a full belly. She rode hard, heading northeast across Shem toward Khoraja.

Yet all the while, a thought was nagging at her. She was bothered by the sense that Conan was still alive. *I'd feel differently if he were dead*, she thought. *I'd know it. I'd feel free.*

And if he does still live, I need to be the one to kill him.

Conan had haunted her dreams the previous night. She saw him arrogant and aloof from his people as King of Aquilonia, watching as her father sacrificed himself for him, laughing as the monster from deep beneath the waves took him apart with its tentacled limbs and pecked out his heart.

Then she imagined Conan pierced by Grake's sword, shivering as steel parted his ribs and ruptured his organs. Grake laughed and blooded himself across the face and chest. He was the land's greatest warrior now.

A blink between dreams, and then Conan was writhing beneath twisted magic as the tattooed Krow Danaz hung suspended in the air above him, standing on limbs of lightning and boiling Conan from the inside out with a dark spell.

Whatever she dreamed, Conan was dead. But...

...but I need to be the one to kill him.

That night, eating remnants of the food stolen from the murdered family, warming herself with furs their children had used while sleeping beneath the stars, Mylera sat by her campfire and rolled the small vial that she kept on a chain around her neck between her fingers. It now contained only two drops of creore.

The first will scorch you with an agony you've never even imagined. The second will cripple you. The third will likely kill you.

Belindra Zarn's words came back to her again and again, the warning stark. Indeed, the first time she'd used creore it had hurt, a blazing agony that had caused vomiting and paroxysms through her body, but two days later she'd felt fine. The pain had been fierce, but she had recovered with no permanent reminder of her experience.

Apart from being seen, being noticed, beneath the veil of reality.

She shook her head and threw another log onto the fire. Sparks erupted and faded again. She could not dwell on that shattering, indifferent gaze she had felt upon her. Whatever it had been, she would gladly risk it again and pay whatever price was necessary to see Conan dead.

"I'm stronger than you think, Zarn," she said, and the campfire danced as if in excitement at her words. She believed that Krow Danaz would come, that Grake was waiting for them and for Conan on those Khoraja clifftops. "They want to witness the light fade from Conan's eye, for their own reasons. I just want him dead, close by or at a distance. Dead."

It was that more than anything that made her decide to perform another spell. Stronger this time, more targeted toward Conan, whether he was traveling alone or perhaps with those three others she had seen and sensed following him.

This time, she would ensure that it worked.

She slept for a few hours, and then before dawn announced itself to the east she was riding again. As the sun peered above distant hills, she saw a town in the distance, temple spires poking at the sky as if to impale the light. She found a well-traveled road and headed toward the settlement.

For what she wanted to do later that day, she was going to need a head.

13

A Song Too Soon

After a day riding in the wagon and a night sleeping close by, Conan said that it was time for him to walk.

"Your wounds need rest," Ally said.

"I know about wounds," Conan said. "I've had plenty. I'll walk."

"But your gut was poking out of a hole in your stomach. We had to stuff it back in."

Conan looked around at the others breaking camp. While they'd all taken turns on guard duty—Conan insisted on being included, though Kaz had sat up with him—they'd also slept deeply. Jemi said it was because of the banshee songs they'd had to endure for so long the previous day. Those unearthly wails had wormed into their subconscious, and deep sleep was a reaction from their bodies and minds to expunge them.

"If it pops out again, I'll be sure to ask you for help," Conan said.

"Fool." Ally turned to walk away, then spun back to face him again. Conan had experienced just a few moments of disgruntlement at their treatment of him, but he'd quickly shoved that aside; the false trappings of civilization had rarely sat well with him, and he'd always believed that the higher up the pyramid of civility someone claimed to sit, the more dishonorable and corrupt they were likely to be. Being an equal to these songwriters, wanderers, and former warriors made him feel more at ease than he had in some time, even knowing there was someone or someones out there conspiring to kill him.

After all, that was the story of his life.

Ally prodded him in the chest. "Kaz and I, and all of us, have worked hard to fix you." She held out her hand, palm up, turning it this way and that as if holding a cool blue fire. "Kaz doesn't use her talent very often. Just for special cases. It reminds her too much of her troubled past before the Last Song. It hurts her. You're wounded, we're helping you, so if you're so stubborn that—"

"It's not stubbornness," Conan said. "I need to move, I need to heal, and by Crom I'll walk if I want to." He kept his voice low and even, but the others around the camp stopped what they were doing and watched the exchange. Jemi was climbing up onto the wagon's seat, and she laughed. Fennick heaved their rolled sleeping mats and cooking pot into the wagon's rear with ease. Gannar watched motionless from within a copse, the shadows hiding his expression.

"I thought Aquilonia's god was Mithra," Ally said.

"If I need one, Crom is mine."

Conan realized that Ally was right, they were helping him, and right then he didn't want to do or say anything to risk that changing. But there were only a few days' travel until they reached Khoraja, and he had to be the best he could be when that moment came. Sitting motionless in the back of the Last Song's wagon was not an effective way to ensure that.

"I've been injured many times," he said.

"We saw your scars, and heard the tales you were telling us at the campfire last night."

"I know my body and how to heal. I must move."

Ally sighed, nodded, and turned away.

They moved out and Conan started walking ahead of the wagon and its two reliable horses. They were trusty steeds, big hill horses from the Nemedian uplands, brown and white in color and with heavy hair around their lower legs, tails, and manes. He'd worked with such creatures before and knew that, though not fast, they were extremely strong and persistent. Jemi told him that they'd used these two for three years and they did not tire.

That needs to be me, Conan thought, and years ago it would have been. He had gone against Ally's advice to walk, and she was right about his being stubborn. He must not appear to tire now. He was grateful for the Last Song's help, and he was becoming fond of them and their mission, if not their strange outlook. They carried enough weapons in their wagon to raid a small town, and the more he got to know them, the more he realized that they were all experienced fighters, warriors, and barbarians in their own right. They could take what they wanted. Instead, they traded and sang for it, as they were doing with Conan—as recompense for helping and protecting him, he was slowly giving them the material to write his own song.

Many people had composed poems and songs about Conan. He'd heard them in Aquilonia, smiling indulgently while he sat on his throne and listened to another wretched minstrel giving his, her, or their version of his life or a portion of it. They all got the details wrong, too focused on his crown to dig deeper into the truth. They saw him in different ways, none of them clear and incisive. Sometimes it amused him, but mostly it just bored him.

He was still confused by the Last Song and their ways. Why

sing songs about taking on demons or enemies or beasts of the shadowy world when you could go out there and fight them in real life? Yet he perceived a solidity to their existence. Firstly in their intentions, because they were true to their cause and mission. Their songs were rich and beautifully imagined for the most part, deep and soulful recollections of the lives and deaths of those about whom they sang and played. Yet he also sensed the hardness beneath their peaceful exterior. They played and sang and laughed, but if the occasion called for it, they could also bite.

While Conan walked ahead of the horses, twenty steps in front of him Tathar led the way. The tattooed Stygian was quiet and solemn, and Conan wondered at his story. He was no fan of Stygians as a rule, and had killed more than a few in his time, yet Tathar seemed different. There were dark places in Stygia, and dark people, but Tathar seemed like someone who had come through into the light on the other side.

As Conan sped up toward him, a song started from behind. Fennick played his instrument, which he called a fitar, strumming softly across the strings as it rested on his shoulder. Beside him, Gannar was doing the singing this time, the Aesir's northern accent gruff and clipped.

> *Into the castle cast in red, so they led him bound,*
> *Covered in blood and filled with dread.*
> *Conan, king and warrior past, opened his eyes and found,*
> *Things down there that would see him dead.*
> *Scales and venom, fur and claw,*
> *Darkness clothed his world,*
> *And he was meant for torture...*

Fennick continued strumming while Gannar frowned and looked to the sky.

And he was meant for torture...

"I'm not dead yet," Conan said back over his shoulder.

"Just composing," Gannar muttered, not even looking at Conan. He stared at the sky as if the words and verses that eluded him might be read in the clouds.

"Not. Dead. Yet." Conan turned and marched on until he was walking beside Tathar. He heard a few chuckles behind him and bit back a smile. Looking sidelong at Tathar, he saw a similar expression on the Stygian's face.

This was as close as they had been. With a glance, Conan assessed the tall man's facial art, colorful tattoos that spread across his cheeks and down both sides of his neck, disappearing into his jacket collar and promising much more beneath. They seemed chaotic, random images of creatures, sigils, and unknown words from a language Conan did not recognize. In his time as king, he'd learned to read a few Stygian words, but he could translate nothing here.

When Tathar glanced sideways and saw Conan watching him, the smile slipped from his lips. He presented a blank canvas.

"They'll still sing," Tathar said, his voice heavily accented with a broad Stygian drawl.

"I don't want to hear my own musical eulogy."

"They're not singing to anyone but themselves. It's how the Last Song works. We have to write somehow. Fennick is playing, Gannar composing, the others will be creating silently. A good song builds over time, like a good story. You are still creating your story, Conan. Over time."

"You don't usually say much. That was a lot."

Tathar shrugged.

They walked in silence for a while, the air between them heavy. It was Tathar who broke it. "You don't like Stygians."

"I've met few that gave me cause."

"That's fair. I understand. I don't like kings."

They walked. The wagon's wheels crunched along the gravelly trail behind them, the horse's hooves clopping, the Last Song walking and talking and sometimes singing random phrases to a strum from Fennick's fitar.

The north Kothian landscape at the foot of its border mountain ranges consisted of wide-open arable lands, and Conan kept a wary eye on their surroundings. His senses of the wild were coming alive again after so long being cosseted in Tarantia's royal palace and its modern streets. A bird took flight to their left and he looked to see if something had startled it aloft. A creature scampered across the trail ahead of them, a long low shape that he could not identify, yet he perceived no threat from it nor could he tell from where it had run. He sniffed the air for evidence of distant campfires or the scent of travelers closer by and glanced into cool shadows beneath the occasional copse or larger woodland.

"Jemi is the only one among us who does not come from violence and blood, you know," Tathar said.

Conan said nothing. He had already realized that for himself.

"When I met her, I thought she was weak," Tathar continued. "She said things that sang true with me, and some of the others were already with her then. I stayed, but I thought it was me driving things, making my own choices. In truth it was Jemi, always her, right from the moment we met. I've come to realize she's the strongest of us all."

"She hasn't told me her story," Conan said.

"She might. She might not. It's hers to tell, and hers alone. Do you want mine?"

Conan glanced at Tathar and offered a small nod. It was good to know who he was allied with, and it would pass the time.

"I was a knight defender of Stygia," Tathar said. "I served Set first, the sorcerer-king of Stygia second, like all good soldiers.

From a young age I trained, and I made my way up through the ranks to become a unit commander. I had two hundred soldiers under my command, eighty cavalry and one hundred and twenty foot troops, each of them a skilled warrior in their own right. We fought in many campaigns, large and small, in our fierce protection of Stygian lands and people. My own unit was stationed near the coast, close to the border with Kush, and we were involved with several border skirmishes with that nation. We were more prepared, more professional, and better trained, and we always prevailed. Apart from my last combat.

"They came out of the sea. Six of them, great beasts beyond my powers of description, all of them drawn by an immortal witch who had long harbored desires over Stygian land. I can't recall her name. I think the trauma of that day wiped that from my mind, but I still see her when I blink, when I rest, when I try to sleep. She was tall and heavily built, her long hair knotted and thick like seaweed, and her skin was covered with hard shells, like barnacles across the bottom of a boat. Her eyes were black and wet, her arms and legs covered with spiked suckers. And the things she brought with her…

"They were like nothing I have ever seen, and nothing I ever imagined before that day even in my deepest, darkest nightmares. The size of the largest horse, they had multiple tentacles with suckers and spikes, horns and eyes. There were eyes all over them, Conan. They looked like the witch's eyes, obsidian black and filled with a depth I cannot comprehend. They crawled out of the sea and followed their mistress, and at first I thought they were acting like obedient dogs. Then I realized that it was they who held the strings and she was the puppet. The dark void I saw in that witch's eyes was terror. Those things were in charge.

"We attacked, and when arrows hit the monsters the shafts simply sank into their bodies and disappeared with no effect. Their tentacles unwound and whipped and thrashed out, curling around my foot soldiers and bearing them aloft and ripping them apart. They pierced my knights' horses and expanded, tearing them inside out. Heads rolled and splashed into the sea, bobbing until common sea creatures took them down. That rocky beach was painted red, and I hear it remained that color ever after. Nothing seemed to hurt those strange beasts as they slid and rolled and squirmed up the stony shore, wiping out most of my unit in the space of a few breaths.

"Then I had an idea and I turned our attack onto that sorceress. They protected her with all they had, and I lost twenty knights in the blink of an eye. But as they died, so they covered my own attack, and I cleaved her from head to stomach with one sweep of my sword. As she fell, so they screamed.

"I've never heard a sound like that, and I still hear it when I sleep. I still see them in my dreams, even though they crawled back into the sea and the waters closed over them, and moments later the only evidence that they had ever been there was the bloody remains of my unit spread across that damned beach. The witch was gone to a black puddle, smoking and stinking as it cracked and melted beach pebbles, then burrowed deeper, draining down out of sight and memory, but maybe not out of life. That place was forever damned.

"Somehow, I was the only warrior left alive. The monsters had gone, but I carry the memory of their disgusting intelligence with me. Because they saw me, Conan. They…"

Tathar trailed off, and Conan stared ahead as they walked to give him privacy for tears.

"I have seen something like them," Conan said. "A crew of pirates brought such things ashore in an attack along the coast of Zingara many years ago. I led my army from Aquilonia and we drove them back into the depths, at great cost."

"You've seen them also?" Tathar sounded young and vulnerable, unguarded in his questioning. Perhaps it was shock, or maybe even relief that Conan did not think him mad. "Then they must haunt you as they do me."

"I'm haunted by many sights, Tathar, and countless ghosts. I keep them in the past, where they belong."

"Then you're lucky. These are wards to hide me from such evil forces." Tathar gestured at his tattooed face, where symbols and words and images made a map of his horrible memories. "A fool's ploy, I realize now, but back then, in those mad years after that battle, I was willing to try anything. Because I will meet those things again—I know it for sure, and I'm as certain of that when I'm awake as when I see them in my dreams. They marked me. She saw me, their puppet sorceress, and then they saw me as I cut her in two and drove them back into the depths. And they marked me. They'll be the cause of my death, and I feel that drawing closer with every breath I take. Meeting Jemi and the others gave me a distraction—music is my only comfort—yet between songs I still feel their horrible, unknowable eyes upon me. My life since that moment has been an indrawn breath, and I'll scream when they come." He fell silent, his story told, and Conan did not offend him with some casual platitude.

They continued walking together, leading the Last Song into the east.

Around midday, they approached a small town. It had several buildings at its center, tall white walls and round glass windows shimmering in the sunlight, and a boundary wall pocked in several places, with wide-open gates. The roads leading to these gates were busy with traders. People on foot, on horseback, and in wagons transported goods toward the town, where they would be traded or sold in the central marketplace.

Jemi called a halt and parked the Last Song's wagon by the

side of the road, shaded by a copse. Conan noticed that she was careful not to look as though she was hiding from view while still finding shadows where she could sit away from the sunlight and prying eyes.

He was glad that they'd stopped. His stomach wound ached, spasms of pain singing up and down the nerves on his right side. While he was too proud to suggest a rest—especially after Ally had berated him for walking instead of riding in their wagon—he uttered a soft groan as he sat on a fallen tree beneath the lush green canopy.

Empty bags over their shoulders, Jemi and Gannar headed into the town to stock up on supplies. Conan was impressed with Jemi's strength and how she did not let her missing leg define how she lived her life. It would have been easy for her to rest her crutches and send someone else. As it was, the tall, yellow-haired Gannar had to walk quickly to keep up with her.

The others were left to tend the horses and eat fruit and nuts for lunch. Conan gratefully accepted a bowl from Fennick.

"You said you fought in my army," Conan said.

"Yes, for three years." Fennick crouched by Conan, never quite meeting his eye. He was squat and stocky like most Bossonians, and this close Conan could see scars across his face and exposed neck. "I served in the war against Nemedia, and picked up enough injuries to see me discharged and out of work."

"I'm sorry."

"I'm not. I dodged death a dozen times." He touched scars that were visible and many that were not, at least ten healed wounds on his neck, face, shoulder, and across his torso. "Now I serve music, not war. I used to be a crafter, making bows and arrows, but now I make musical instruments such as my fitar. It's what I was meant to be."

"You're a Bossonian archer," Conan said. "That is your calling."

"War and violence impose such callings," Fennick said. "The men and women who gave me these wounds each failed to kill me, and the more that happened, the more I realized I was only dodging death and that soon my luck would run out. I was meant for more, as much as any of us is meant for anything. As for fate..." He shrugged.

"You make your own, or leave it to your gods," Conan said.

"I have no gods, King Conan," Fennick said, and laughed. He seemed a cheerful soul.

Conan shrugged. "People are free to praise whichever god they will, or none at all."

"That's very open-minded for a king of Aquilonia."

"My mind is laid open by all I've seen and done," Conan said.

Fennick smiled and nodded slowly, and he met Conan's eyes firmly for the first time. "You'd be good with the Last Song."

"I'm hardly a singer," Conan said with a chuckle. "I leave music to those who can, and do what I'm good at."

"War. Killing."

Conan glowered at Fennick, but the Bossonian averted his gaze, stood, and walked away, and Conan did not call after him. Let him believe whatever he chose, be whatever he wanted to be. Conan's mind and drive was his own, and he never expected others to fall into his way of thinking. *Even though he is a true warrior*, he thought.

Fennick reached the wagon and plucked up an instrument. He unfurled a leather roll, and Conan wondered what this one would sound like. But Fennick sat and started working at the wood-and-metal object in his hands, slicing fine slivers of hardwood from the handle and turning tiny screws where the metallic parts merged seamlessly with the wooden frame, and Conan realized that he was still building and creating this instrument. The Bossonian's scarred face became as smooth and graceful as the instrument he worked on as he found peace in the process.

Conan rested his wrists on his knees and tilted his head back, closing his eyes and letting his other senses take in their surroundings. He could smell dust rising from the road as people made their way past and headed toward the town. From there, he could smell the heady aromas of street food—frying meats, rich spices, cooking vegetables. Faint music drifted from the town. They had halted away from the road, but he could hear the murmur of voices from those passing them by, mostly speaking in the Kothian tongue but also several other languages. This place felt safe, but he still kept his senses alert and alive for any threat.

A little while later, eyes still closed, Conan heard Jemi and Gannar return. Jemi swung herself on her crutches, a backpack slung over her shoulder. Gannar carried a heavy bag in each hand. He packed everything into the wagon and they continued on their way, aiming to skirt around the town on its northern road.

Conan spent a moment thinking about swallowing his pride and climbing up into the wagon. His wound was stiff and sore, his legs felt weak, and the thought of dozing while they made their way eastward was enticing, but in the end he decided to continue walking.

It was a decision that saved his life.

14

Forked Tongues of Truth

Conan smelled them before he saw them—a stale, mossy, green scent like pondwater and mold. It came from the north, carried on a gentle breeze that whispered down out of the mountain range in that direction, and the odor inspired old memories of deep, dank places untouched by the sun where no good thing dwelled. He became alert, senses heightened. He looked around at the others, but none of them seemed to have noticed anything amiss.

They were several hours beyond the market town, heading across countryside and following a rough trail that had not been traveled for some time. The mountains to the north showed no signs of being inhabited, and though the lowlands they traversed had once been farmed, they had been given back to the wild long ago. Undulations in the land hid much of the surrounding countryside from view. Rocky outcroppings and tumbled stone walls provided potential hiding places. It was the perfect setting for an ambush.

Conan slowed and fell back toward the wagon, and it was as

he turned to talk to Jemi that movement caught his eye to their left. Four shapes emerged from the rocky slope in that direction and streaked down the hillside toward the Last Song.

"Ambush!" Conan shouted. He drew his broadsword from its scabbard, relishing the soft *hushhhh* as it came, like a lover whispering into his ear.

The rest of the Last Song had drawn back around the wagon, but there was something strange about how they were acting. They seemed almost unconcerned.

Conan focused on the shapes moving quickly downhill. There were still four of them in sight, which meant there might easily be that many again hiding and attempting to encircle them. He hefted the broadsword and it felt good in his grip, a comforting weight that was a natural extension of his arms and muscles, senses and soul. The dank smell grew stronger, and then the figures charged with a guttural whooping cry and he saw why.

He had heard about the mythical snake people that lived in remote highlands across the central and southern lands, but he'd never seen one—and now here they were. They were tall and thin, with long limbs and narrow heads, and though dark skin showed through in places, at least half of their exposed bodies were clothed in pale-green scales. Their features were humanoid, with distinctive characteristics and hairstyles, but their battle cries were pure animal.

Conan ran forward and took the fight to them, and as the first figure closed on him he realized that he was alone.

The snake woman hissed and rolled, moving with a fluid grace he could not match or follow. She carried a segmented metallic whip which snapped out and caught him across the thigh, opening his skin. He pivoted on one foot and swung his blade, following the weight and letting it turn him further. Her whip cracked out again and he let gravity haul his heavy sword downward, lowering his head and shoulders and ducking beneath the strike. He slammed his shoulder into the woman as she darted in for another attack and sent her sprawling, then powered his lowered sword into her side. She screeched as parted scales scraped and whined along steel, and he twisted the sword and tugged it up and out through her stomach.

Blood and gore splashed across him, as red as his own.

Conan turned to the other attackers just as two of them came for him at once, running close together and flicking their metallic whips at his head. He raised his weapon and caught the whips, ducking his head down between his shoulders and feeling the sharp metal braids plucking at his hair. He heaved at the sword and his great strength tugged the weapons from their hands, yet their momentum kept them coming so Conan brought up his right knee and slammed it into one of the snake men's chest. He heard bone crunch and the strange creature went down hissing, forked tongue flicking at the air, tasting him. The fallen thing shouted something in a strange throaty language, but they had not come here to talk. If he was begging, raving, or mocking, he was too late.

Conan swung his sword and parted the beast's head from his body. His tongue still flicked at the air as his head rolled away, silenced.

The other snake man ducked beneath a swipe from Conan's sword and rolled several times, moving quickly away from him. Conan pursued, then realized his mistake.

As he paused and turned, he saw the shadow of the last snake woman coming at him, spinning her metal whip in readiness to open his throat. He lifted his arm to block the whip, and something whisked past his head. He heard a dull thud, and when he completed his turn the snake woman was staggering backward, pinned to the air by an arrow directly through her throat. She croaked, gagged, spat blood, and fell lifeless to the ground.

He turned his attention back to the remaining attacker, who

was reaching to snatch up his fallen whip. Conan ran at him, striking his chest with his boot heel and sending him sprawling. He continued forward and kicked the fallen man in the side. Bones broke. He hissed.

Conan placed the tip of his sword on the injured man's chest and let its weight part scales and pierce the skin. A little encouragement, a gentle push down, and the sword would sever this beast's spine.

Panting, Conan glanced quickly around to ensure the threat was over. The members of the Last Song had retrieved their weapons, but they remained motionless on and around the wagon. Fennick stood on the driver's seat, bow nursed in his hands, another arrow nocked as he gazed around for any more attackers. The rest of them were watching Conan.

Gannar was even smiling.

Conan assessed his injuries. There was a gash across his thigh, but it wasn't too deep and it hadn't touched any major blood vessels. Other than that, he had escaped fresh injury, though when he put his hand to his side it came away bloody, and the dull ache from his gored stomach had changed to a fresh, sharp stab. It was no surprise that he'd opened the wound again.

But he was back. His heart rate had barely increased and his senses were aflame and alert. Furious and glorious, he felt the dormant barbarian within him awoken once again, thrilling and reveling from the fight.

Conan felt like roaring in delight. He was in control and no one could defeat him.

"Who sent you?" he demanded, kneeling next to the prone snake man, one hand holding the sword and ready to shove it down through his gut and spine. He examined the beast and realized he was even stranger than Conan had imagined. He'd thought perhaps these were people who clothed themselves in snakelike garments, or who affixed scales to their own skin

that they harvested from some of the giant marsh lizards of the Ophirean eastlands, but this man was truly as much snake as human. His eyes were slitted and covered with an extra translucent lid that flicked back and forth in pain. His tongue was forked and long, tasting Conan's blood and sweat on the air. The scales across much of his body looked grown and natural, and were a shade darker than those on the other three dead snake people.

And no one could fake the smell of the marshes, the peat, the pit.

"Who?" Conan demanded.

The snake man hissed and writhed. And then a crossbow bolt slammed into his head and brains spattered across Conan's feet.

He turned, and Kaz stood twenty feet away, still aiming a small metal crossbow.

"I was questioning him!" Conan growled.

"I guess snake people don't only have fangs in their mouths," Kaz said, and she nodded at the dead creature's foot. Conan looked. Spikes had extruded from his upper foot and shin, several inches long and dripping a clear fluid. He'd thought the man had been writhing in pain, but Kaz had seen that he was about to kick and perhaps kill him.

He nodded his thanks. And then he gathered his breath and roared at the Last Song—those who had saved him and helped him and come with him to Koth, and who had just stood by while he had fought off these beastly attackers.

"Cowards!" he shouted. "Useless weak-blooded cowards!"

"You're welcome," Fennick said. He jumped from the wagon and stalked off in the opposite direction, alert and with an arrow still nocked in his bow.

"Yes, welcome," Kaz said.

"You let me stand and fight these things. Where's your instinct? Where's your sense of survival?"

"Safe and sound," Jemi said.

"It wasn't us they were attacking," Gannar said with a smile. "And you seemed to do quite well."

Conan strode past Kaz and toward the rest of them, bloodied sword at the ready. He stopped before Gannar and lifted his sword, aimed at the old warrior's throat.

And everything changed.

The Last Song tensed, ready for action, swords and a pike and other weapons resting easy in the musicians' hands. Even Fennick, formerly a faithful soldier in King Conan's employ, turned and pulled his bow a little tighter. It was a stillness rather than anything else that Conan felt from them—the stillness of a coiled spring.

"I could kill you all," Conan growled, and he meant it. He believed it. "I should."

"Do you really want to try?" Jemi asked. "Ease down, Conan. You know we were watching. You know you only killed two of the four. And you know we're not warriors and killers anymore."

"No. Not warriors and killers. Cowards! Look at what you're missing!" Conan held his arms out wide, sword pointing up now rather than at Gannar. It was Jemi who laughed this time, and the others smiled.

"Yes, Conan. Just look!"

He was covered in blood and brains and gore from the snake woman he had gutted, his leg open and bleeding, his older wound now opened and burning again. Jemi snorted, then turned away and started to tend the horses as if nothing had happened.

"I suppose you want me to treat your wounds again?" Kaz muttered.

"I can help myself," Conan snapped. He frowned, confused at what had just happened. He was used to surrounding himself with warriors and soldiers, and these people had been both, yet behind his anger he found it hard to look down upon them. Fennick had helped him by shooting down one of the snake people with a perfectly aimed arrow. Kaz had killed another before Conan could be spiked and poisoned. Despite what he said, they had aided him when he'd needed it. But Jemi was right—whoever had sent these snake people to hunt and kill him had not ordered the deaths of these others.

This was not their fight.

"My thanks, Fennick," he said. The Bossonian raised one hand and continued away from the rest of them, walking cautiously and quietly as he scouted for any further attackers. Conan nodded at Kaz again, and then he stood motionless, sword propped on the ground before him, while the rest of the Last Song readied to move out.

Someone knows where I am, he thought. Someone knows I am coming.

Of course, Grake and those other slave traders holding Baht Tann's family might have guessed that Tann was still alive, and perhaps Tann had let slip somehow that he might come to Conan for help. But would they really believe that the king of Aquilonia would come to the aid of a jewel-hunting family so far from home? They surely could not understand the promise steering his actions.

Yet from what Tann had told him, Grake was a merely an ambitious brute. Conan had known witches and wizards, sorcerers and conjurors, and he was certain that the attacks against him were the work of one of these. Who or what, he did not know.

But none of that mattered. His sword protected him. If the skirmish with the snake people had taught him anything, it was that in a fight he must only ever rely on himself.

"We are two days from Khoraja," Conan said. The others paused in what they were doing to watch him. He knew that despite what had just happened and how they had reacted, he cut an imposing figure. His long plaited black hair had come loose and hung over his right shoulder. His body was sheened in sweat and blood, most of the latter not his own. The sword glimmered in the late-afternoon sunlight, his enemies' gore already drying on it. He was the center of this place, the sun around which the Last Song orbited, and he knew that well enough. He was sure they did too. "Are you still with me?"

"We have another verse for yer song, Conan!" Jemi said. "How ya fought snake people from the Kothian mountains, shruggin' off yer own wounds. How yer sword parted their scales and sliced off'n their heads. Of course we're still with ya."

The others nodded. Fennick was watching from a small rise, and he too dipped his head in agreement.

"Then you do what I say," Conan growled. "I might be old, my blade might be blunted by my time on the throne, I might be weakened by wounds, but I am Conan. I am no longer traveling with the Last Song. The Last Song is traveling with me."

"We follow no one," Tathar said. "Our road is our own, our trail our choice."

"Yet he needs our help," Jemi said. "S'true, Conan, that we left ya to fight yer own battle just now, but I'm sure yer not really too proud or stubborn to accept that yer fight was eased by Fennick's arrow and Kaz's crossbow. Part of why'n we've left behind the life ya seem to be findin' once more, and relishin' perhaps more'n you ever did before—" She gestured at him—the blood, the gore, the sweat, the post-fight glow that seemed to suffuse his body. "—is that we seek to honor what's left of our own lives by livin' them the best, most honest way we can."

"You remember the great warriors with your songs," Conan said.

"That we do. We place value on honor, which is why yer task remains our own. Yer a king, perhaps the most powerful person in all the lands we know and those we gotta yet to discover, but ya set that aside for a foolish promise to an old friend. We gotta respect that."

Conan nodded. He dipped his head in thanks. The matter was settled.

I am leader here now, he thought. Let them think what they will.

He packed his own wounds this time, and though limping from the gash to his thigh he led the way. Tathar walked with him again, but this time the two men did not talk.

Conan walked taller than he had before, and now he kept his broadsword sheathed and slung across his back. He untied his long black hair and let it swing free. He took off the jacket Ally had given him and let the sun touch his skin. Soon they would come to a river or stream and he would be able to bathe, but he was quite happy feeling the stiff crinkling of blood and gore as it dried and hardened across his arms and shoulders and chest.

Whoever he was destined to face, they knew he was coming.

Conan walked into the future as himself.

15

Three Become One

Mylera rose up from dark dreams slowly, too slow for it to be normal sleep. Pain accompanied her waking, rooted deep in her bones and muscles and scouring through her veins as if a million fire ants had found their way inside her, stinging, stinging. She screamed as she woke and her throat was raw, making her wonder if she had also been screaming in her dreams—and what dreams they had been.

She sees Conan ahead of her at the base of a slope, standing slightly apart from a band of people gathered around a wagon. She runs toward him and he comes at her, and at the last minute she ducks and rolls past him, standing and turning with a brutal grace as she flicks a whip. It slices across his leg and he comes at her again, swinging his heavy sword and ducking his head. He slams into her and sends her sprawling, and before she can recover he drives his sword into her gut.

Her vision stutters and fades just as he rips open her stomach…

Conan again, blood on him now and the snake woman dead on the ground behind him, and she's running at him again with another like her by her side. They spin their whips and Conan catches them both around his sword, muscles straining and flexing as he heaves the weapons from their hands. Her momentum is too great and she runs at him, but he brings his knee up and slams it into her chest.

She goes down, struggling to right herself. Conan steps close and swings his sword. Her vision spins and twists, sky and ground, sky and ground, and she catches sight of her own decapitated body a dozen feet away as her vision fades again…

Mylera tried to sit up but the agonies across her body kept her down. Her muscles were knotted in cramps that twisted and bent her so much that she was afraid her spine would break, her limbs contort and snap. She concentrated on breathing because that was all that mattered, and at the same time she searched her dreams and memories for any clue that she might have been successful. If Conan was dead, she could die in horrible wretched pain, yet happy.

She searched and searched and…

She sees Conan knock down the man and slice off his head. The other snake man rolls several times to get away from him and comes up in a crouch, reaching for a fallen whip.

She is behind Conan and he does not see her. Now is her chance, now she can kill him and please the voice that has been gnawing away at her mind for the past few hours: Kill Conan, kill Conan, kill Conan...

She raises her whip and advances on him and—

A thump in her throat, shoving her back several steps. An arrow protrudes. She goes down.

She sees Conan from another angle, looking back over his shoulder at the figure with an arrow in its throat. She goes for him but he moves like the wind, such a big man shifting with the grace and guile of a panther. He kicks her down and presses his sword to her chest, ready to kill her.

He shouts a question down at her but she cannot hear.

Kill Conan, kill Conan...

He says something else, blood and fury distorting his face.

Kill Conan...

With a blink, she extrudes the poisonous barbs down the length of both shins and feet and readies herself to kick up at the gore-covered brute gazing down at her, and then—

They did not kill him. By luck and strength and with the help of the group he was with, Conan had killed the snake people she had sent to take his life.

"Nooo!" Mylera shouted, screaming again. The pain no longer mattered. She rode it out, letting it slice through her, writhing and twisting on the ground, fouling herself and kicking rocks and rolling through the soft-scented loam of the forest floor. At last, minutes or hours later, the pains began to recede a little and she came to a stop lying against a fallen tree. Twenty feet away was her sleeping mat beside the fire, where she had laid herself down to connect once more with the snake people, watch their attack, and see Conan die. Above the fire was the scorched head of the woman she had murdered just a few hours ago, skull cracked open, brains boiled away. Her stolen horse stood close to the mat, head down, somehow having slept through her screams and thrashing around. She had been riding it hard. Soon the time would come to ride it even harder.

Conan lives. The thought was poison in her mind, shit in her heart, and it made her want to vomit again. Conan lives, and the people he's with are helping him.

Belindra Zarn had told her, The first will scorch you with an agony you've never even imagined. The second will cripple you. The third will likely kill you. She was in pain but not crippled, yet again silently defying that sorceress of Set who had taken her beneath her dark wing to teach her darker magic.

"Zarn does not understand the strength of my commitment," she whispered to the forest. Insects buzzed back. Birds sang. Undergrowth rustled as creatures went about their day, eating or mating or following old trails. The ancient woodland swallowed her words and gave nothing back, because she meant nothing here. Her quest for revenge did not touch moss or leaf, twig or flower, because nature was impartial—yet it watched. She felt that, as dispassionate as the presence that had observed her when she dipped beneath the veil of reality, riding on the drop of creore and traveling across the land like a forgotten breath that never ends.

"I will kill Conan," she said, "if I have to do it myself or..."

Or with others who wish him dead.

She hoped that Krow Danaz had received her message. She did not know for sure, as sending mind bats was a much more passive engagement than a creore trip, and it gave so much less back. If he had heard her words, she hoped that he would be as keen as she was to find the vengeance he had spoken of all those years ago in that Shemite tavern.

There was no way of knowing. In her, time had solidified and strengthened her craving for revenge, but in others it might dull such a feeling.

Mylera tested her limbs, stretching them and bringing them back in. They seemed to shift and bend and work as they should. Her back hurt from where her body had distorted in agony. The pain was still there, burning and simmering, but she had control over it now, observing and engaging with it rather than being burned and swallowed. It gave her energy rather than stealing it away.

She sat up and her horse woke, turning its head and staring at her.

"Soon," she said. "You have a moment's more rest, and then we leave."

The horse snorted and lowered its head again.

Mylera stood on shaky legs and felt the vial around her neck. There was one dose of creore left inside, a single precious drop, and she was confident that she could use it without becoming crippled or dead. She hurt, but she was evidently stronger than Zarn had believed.

Now was not the time to try again. She was closing on Khoraja, and one day's hard ride would get her there. Then she would search the range of clifftops until she found Grake and his band of slavers. There, united in their cause, she would consider one last creore trip beneath the surface of the world.

Her spells had been cast toward weaker minds. The first time, she had passed over the three trained soldiers spying on Conan and settled on the ragtag group of bandits. This second time, she had sensed the group he traveled with, but they were strong-willed and she had feared her glamors might founder in their minds, and she had been delighted to discover those weird snake creatures nearby.

If Zarn was right, her next use of creore might very well kill her. And if that were to be the case, perhaps she would push hard to possess at least one of the minds of those closest to Conan.

Mylera rode fast. The horse was lazy and hesitant to begin with, but she used a shallow hex to seed a shadow of fear in its mind, and it ran faster to flee a terror that it perceived to be always on its tail. She held on tight, gritting her teeth against the discomfort as she bounced in the saddle, taking fuel from the pain.

I am stronger than you think, Belindra Zarn.

She passed scattered settlements, keeping her distance and trying to stay to the small valleys cut into the land by rivers flowing from the distant hills to the east. Several times she saw groups of travelers and farmers working in their fields, but she kept to herself and so did they. She understood that a lone traveler was vulnerable, but she had a destiny to fulfill. She could not die until Conan was dead. She rode with caution, and a few times she steered the horse from the rough roads and trails into the cover of woodland or behind small hills, hiding from larger traveling groups or diverting around farmsteads.

Soon the Kothian plains gave way to a rolling rise of hills, and as she headed up toward one of the lower passes the air grew cooler. The highest of these hills held the remnants of winter snows, and she knew that beyond and down the other side was Khoraja. That mountainous place ended where its sheer cliffs dropped away to the endless plains of the great deserts.

The afternoon wore on, and she followed her lengthening shadow higher and higher. When she reached the first pass into Khoraja, she passed the ruins of an old keep that had once spanned the trail from slope to slope. It had long fallen into dilapidation, but some of the structures remained, and behind a few of the glassless windows she thought she perceived the flicker of firelight.

Merely the setting sun, she decided, and rode on, passing the ruins without incident. Yet the sight had kindled a suspicion in her mind.

I am being watched.

She recalled the feeling of traveling with creore, lifting the veil of reality and skimming the routes beneath, the trails of truth and horror where great inhuman minds dwelled and cast their baleful glare on her intrusion. This sense of being observed was nothing like that, but still it set her nerves on edge.

She passed more ruins, remnants of ancient wars, and as the hills rose around her and the sun set at her rear, the flickering lights behind fallen doors and hollow windows became more obvious at last.

Yet Mylera sensed no human inhabitants here. There was nothing alive. She felt eyes upon her, but not the gaze of the living. So many had died here so long ago, and they had left some of themselves behind.

Tired, desperate for food and drink, and with her horse foaming at the mouth and slowly sweating itself to death, still Mylera did not dare stop. She carried some of the tricks of a sorceress with her, but for the first time since leaving Belindra Zarn she felt unprepared for her journey into the wild.

She rode through the mountainous valleys of ghosts, and when she reached a high ridge that looked out over the vast sunset-tinged landscape of Khoraja, her horse staggered, snorted, and dropped lifeless to the rocky ground. Mylera fell off and rolled aside just in time to prevent being trapped beneath the beast's dead weight.

A cold breeze blew down out of the higher mountains to the north, banishing the last heat of the setting sun, and Mylera knew that she could not remain here. Perhaps she might survive the night huddled in the fading body heat from the dead horse, and maybe she would succeed in lighting a fire in the strengthening breeze, but moving onward under her own steam would provide her greatest chance of survival.

But as she gathered her meager belongings and prepared to

continue east on foot, the shadow of something monstrous skittered toward her along the rocky ridge, and Mylera began to fear that she would not fulfill her destiny after all.

Krow Danaz was hungry. He was used to having meals provided regularly by the most loyal of his slaves, but even they had become Spidderel food before leaving his subterranean lair beneath Kerrodan Xen. Since then he had spent three nights riding on the beast's back and two days hidden away in deep forests. The creature had rested but not slept, and a couple of times when he'd woken from an uneasy slumber Danaz had looked around and found Spidderel missing. It had never gone far, though, seeming to sense when he was awake and returning to him. He could understand its curiosity; it had only ever known dark depths and basements and caves lit by fire.

Danaz was glad that the spells and hexes he had cast within his birthing vats had included a deep affectation of loyalty. Spidderel regarded him as its creator, its owner, its father. Even so, it still gave him only chewy remnants of the meat it hunted down while he slept—a finger, a toe, a gristly knee joint.

Danaz did not mind. Hunger did not concern him unduly, and he knew that this creature that was so important to him must eat to survive. So when he saw the small, weak figure further along the slope and Spidderel started stalking, Danaz resigned himself to eating the wretched scraps of its meal once again.

Spidderel's ten limbs were long, segmented, lined with thick spines, yet their pads were soft and delicate, giving it the ability to move incredibly quickly and quietly. Its large body atop these legs and the armored head protruding in front were also spiked with spines, though where Krow Danaz sat upon a leather saddle on its back there was a smoother surface, lined with a thick carapace as hard as metal. As it moved down the ridge toward its next meal, the breeze shushing and whistling past its spines made as much noise as its footfalls.

He did not need to steer Spidderel, did not need to instruct it, but that strange link he had with the beast whispered at the back of his mind, in deep dark places where his worst secrets hid.

WARM WET BLOOD AND FLESH, CRUNCH AND GULP...

They closed on the victim and Spidderel's excitement grew.

WET WET! WARM WARM! ARRRGHHHH...

It opened its mouth, mandibles clack-clacking at the air, and the shocked and terrified victim heard its approach and turned, wielding a blade that would not even nick the creature's skin.

Brave, Danaz thought—and then he realized who he was looking at.

"Hold!" he said. Spidderel skidded, its pounding limbs freezing, padded feet digging into the ground as it slid toward the woman facing it with knife raised and eyes wide.

She backed away and stumbled over the corpse of a horse that lay behind her. Danaz could smell the creature's sweat, feel its heat, and hear Spidderel's desperate urge to slice and cut, eat and gulp.

"Mylera," Krow Danaz said. "You should probably put down the blade."

The moonlight was weak behind soft clouds, but he still saw her terror, and he could hardly blame her. A dozen people had laid eyes on Spidderel since they had left his ruined castle, and all of them were now being slowly digested in one of its five stomachs.

"What... what is that?"

"Meet Spidderel. Spidderel, meet Mylera, invader of dreams."

"You came," she said.

"You didn't expect me to?"

"I wasn't sure you would."

Krow Danaz looked around at the inhospitable landscape, breathed in the aromas of dead horse and the wild, and let out a croaky laugh. It felt strange. He wasn't used to emitting such a sound.

"I'm not familiar with the world," he said. "My domain is below things, beneath. Being here feels... good. And if your mind bats speak the truth, good might become great."

"You heard me. I wasn't sure. I hoped, but—"

"Usually if someone invades my dreams and steers my thoughts, I send a hex along the uninvited connection to boil their brains in their skulls." The words hung heavy, and there was truth behind them. Danaz had been mind-touched by two other sorcerers before. The first had been seeking to steal his place in Kerrodan Xen, attempting to confuse his thoughts and drive him mad, and Danaz had sent a brief but powerful spell and exploded his brain. The second was a witch who had come seeking revenge for some dark deeds in his past. Danaz could not even recall which deeds these were, as he had performed so many. Maybe he had killed and eaten her husband, or fed her child to one of the creatures stewing and growing in his vats. Her skills had been more powerful and had resulted in the wasting sickness that took away the use of his legs—yet his skills were more powerful still. Back in his shady rooms beneath the castle, her ruptured skull sat on his great stone desk, a forever candle still burning within its fractured embrace.

"Usually," Mylera said.

"I have made exceptions," Danaz said. Though Spidderel is still hungry, and she is weak and tired. Perhaps she'd be more useful to me in death than in life.

Mylera stood up straight, brushing herself down. "I have become powerful, but never as powerful as you. Together we can rain vengeance down on Conan and those who help him."

Her humility pleased him. He smiled again. "You've tried," he said. "That vial around your neck. It contains something magical."

Spidderel moved a little, settling itself lower to the ground as its tensed legs eased. It sensed that this would not be its next meal. Its link with its master's mind told it there was discourse here and no real threat.

Of course, Danaz could change his mind in a moment and tell his creation to rip Mylera to shreds. Often this power was what drove him, but sometimes the ability to hold back felt like an even greater power.

He held her life in his hands. He enjoyed that.

"I tried," she said.

"You tried to kill Conan even after invading my dreams and inviting me to do so."

She went from fear to anger in an instant. "I want him dead. I don't care how. But I want him destroyed without honor, without grandiosity. Conan, dead in a pit of shit. Conan, slashed by filthy blades and growing mad from infection and disease. Conan, murdered in his sleep and buried in an unmarked grave, his myth dying and vanishing with him. That's all I want. I don't care how."

Danaz nodded. "I admire your candor. And your passion. He yet lives?"

"He lives," she said, averting her eyes.

"How far until we meet the third in our triptych of revenge?" he asked.

"The clifftops bordering the great deserts," she said, nodding past him at the inhospitable landscape beyond. She eyed his monstrous mount.

"Oh, it's still hungry," Danaz said.

"Grake will have slaves," she said, a little too quickly. "Plenty of slaves! Food for your creature of the night."

"Then I'm sure Spidderel will bear your weight to get there faster."

WARM WET BLOOD FLESH, he heard, and in his mind he said, Not yet, my friend, not yet. But soon there will be the muscle and bone and flesh of a great warrior for you to feast upon.

Mylera seemed to debate for a brief moment, soon realizing that if she did not accept Danaz's invitation, she would be left behind. Or eaten. She approached and Spidderel lowered itself onto its belly.

"Beware the spines on its legs," Krow Danaz said. "Some of them bear poison."

Mylera approached with caution, arms lifted, and he saw just how thin and twisted she was, the muscles in her neck and shoulders knotted with pain, her teeth in a permanent grimace. Her hair was thin and falling out in clumps. Whatever magic she used was draining her. He eyed the vial on a chain around her neck as she climbed up onto Spidderel's back.

"Sit in front of me," he said, "your legs either side of its neck."

"With you behind me?"

"If I wished you ill, you would be dead ten times over, and Spidderel would be digesting your flesh. Myself... I prefer a healthier cut of meat."

She settled herself carefully in front of him, easing her feet down the slope of the beast's back.

"Now find something to hold on to," Danaz said.

"What? Where? What can I hold if the spines are—"

And now we move, he thought, and Spidderel rose on its ten legs, pausing for a moment to rip several meaty chunks from the still-warm horse with its huge mandibles, shoving them into its maw and chewing noisily. Then it powered down the steep slope on the other side of the ridge. Mylera clasped on, leaning forward and hugging the smooth carapace around the thing's neck.

With the sun setting behind them, the darkness of Khoraja welcomed them in.

They rode hard through the night. Several times, Mylera looked close to slipping from Spidderel's back and Danaz reached for her, his fingers closing around the wasted muscles in her upper arms. He pulled her upright and she jerked awake, glancing back over her shoulder into his face – and recoiled in fear. He saw her looking at the tattoos across his bare scalp and trying to translate what she saw.

She never would. He had spent long, long hours staring into ancient mirrors in the depths of Kerrodan Xen, and he had never been able to make much sense of them himself. The markings upon his scalp reflected the trials of his subconscious, thoughts and schemes of his deeper mind given voice in ever-changing and flowing imagery and words, often in languages he did not recognize or understand. Some of these obscure tongues he could identify as belonging to civilizations from long ago or far away; some he could not comprehend at all. Danaz thought perhaps his subconscious had traveled further, perhaps deep down beneath his ruined castle where old things turned and grumbled in their endless slumber.

He was happy that he scared Mylera, because that way he could keep her under control. Yet she believes herself a powerful witch, a seasoned sorcerer. She does not see the damage her attempts at advanced magic is having on her. And that misplaced belief also makes her dangerous.

When dawn peeked above the eastern horizon, Spidderel's hunger came to the fore again. Its quiet thoughts turned noisy— FLESH, BLOOD, CHEW AND RIP AND SWALLOW!—and its attention kept twitching back to the second passenger upon its back.

Not yet, Danaz thought. *She and I have business. It will end with you satiated, but not with her, not yet. Perhaps—*

He saw movement up ahead, two human figures casting silhouettes atop a low ridge a mile distant.

There, Danaz said to his steed. *Breakfast. Perhaps you can leave me a meaty thigh this time.*

Spidderel accelerated, its mind loose and free and reveling in speed and movement. Danaz held on to Mylera's arm to keep her steady, and this time she did not look over her shoulder at him, sitting stiff and upright. He could feel her fear. He could also sense that she believed the end of their journey might soon be at hand.

They descended into a deep ravine that contained a foaming river. Crossing an ancient stone bridge guarded by long-fallen towers, several large, winged creatures sprang at them from beneath the bridge, scaled bodies borne on leathery wings, cruel beaks seeking meat. Spidderel did not even slow its pace as it lashed out with its long legs, spines piercing and taking down all but one attacking animal. The last it let come close before reaching up with a segmented foreleg and snatching it from the air, shoving the shrieking creature into its mouth without breaking pace. The crunch of bones silenced its cry.

Still chewing, Spidderel scampered from the end of the bridge and headed straight up the steepest wall of the ravine, leading directly to the ridge-line above. It grabbed trees, hauling itself upward, fast and almost silent. It was on a hunt.

Danaz leaned forward on its back, pressed against Mylera where she held tight to their mount's neck. He could feel a foul heat emanating from her, a sick fever that boiled at her insides. *She is not long for this world.*

Her determination and focus impressed him more and more. Krow Danaz hated Conan for what he had done to his master, Tsotha-lanti, but his hatred paled into insignificance compared to Mylera's. Her life was dedicated to Conan's death. Danaz could understand hate, but hers spoke of pure madness.

Soon they emerged from the trees and Spidderel slowed, picking its way across a slate-and-shale landscape as it closed on the ridge-line. Dawn had broken while they were in the ravine, and as they hit the ridge they found themselves facing the sun. Ahead of them to the east, the land dropped suddenly toward an endless desert. Heat danced above the sands, blurring distance and making what those far-off places might contain ambiguous at best.

"We're here," Mylera said.

An arrow struck Spidderel's head and ricocheted away. Another snicked Danaz's cloak sleeve. Before he had a chance to send a mental order to Spidderel, his ride turned left and sprinted along the ridge toward a spread of rocks.

More arrows flew, and Danaz pushed Mylera down and pressed himself beside her. He could feel Spidderel's power through its back as it ran, smell its exertion, and he heard its eagerness and excitement. It expressed no fear. Arrows might hurt it, if they struck in just the right place, but that was unlikely.

MEAT FLESH BLOOD, CHEW RIP TEAR!

The two figures they had spied from across the ravine stood atop the rocks, nocking arrows and letting them fly, again and again. One sliced down Mylera's arm. Another hit Danaz's hip, and he winced at the hot-and-cold feeling of skin opening, blood flowing.

BLOOD BLOOD BLOOD! Spidderel thought, and Danaz steered it ahead, distracting it from the scent of his own.

As it closed on the two figures—a man and a woman, Danaz saw, both dressed in armor and wearing swords, blades, and quivers still full of arrows—they turned and ran. The man barely had time to jump from the rocks before Spidderel leaped.

"Hold… on!" Danaz said, but there was no need. Mylera was gripping on for dear life.

Spidderel took the man mid-leap and landed on him, crushing him down into the rocks. Blood exploded from his ruptured head and splashed back across Mylera and Danaz. And then Spidderel started eating, mandibles ripping leather-and-metal armor and flesh aside, its head jerking back as it gulped them all down. Mylera was jarred up and down by these movements, and she released her grip and slid down the side of its neck. Landing on rocks, she twisted away between its spiked legs and stumbled down onto a stony surface.

The woman warrior who had fled now returned, a fresh arrow nocked in her bow. She aimed at Mylera, eyes wide and mouth open in shock and terror at what had come upon them. But Danaz also saw a hardness to her eyes. This warrior would not let that shock and terror affect her aim.

Without thinking, he commanded Spidderel to rear up on its hind legs and jump, and the loosed arrow skimmed against its underside and broke apart on the rocks beneath it. The beast was already running when it dropped back down, and with a powerful leap it mounted the rocky pile and lashed out with one forelimb. It knocked the woman to one side, and then the beast straddled her and convulsed, sending a spined knee into the woman's chest.

She gasped, her limbs went stiff and straight, and the *crick-cruck* sound coming from her hanging mouth on the otherwise suddenly silent hillside sounded like crickets. Paralyzed, she could only watch as Spidderel plunged its mandibles through her tunic and into her stomach, its jaws working as it sucked out her soft insides.

Crick-cruck-crock, the woman said, and Spidderel ate.

Krow Danaz twisted around on his saddle. Mylera was crouched down a dozen feet from them, nodding her thanks. Then her eyes opened wide as she looked past him.

"No, no!" she said, hands held out. "Grake, it's me!"

Spidderel shuddered beneath Danaz, and he felt its muscles tensing in readiness for another fight.

𝔹𝕃𝕆𝕆𝔻 𝔽𝕃𝔼𝕊ℍ 𝔹𝕃𝕆𝕆𝔻 𝔾𝕌𝕋𝕊 𝔹ℝ𝔸𝕀ℕ𝕊!

"Hold," Danaz said softly, realizing perhaps the beginning of his journey may have come to an end.

Before them stood four scruffy warriors, all of them knotted with muscle, all carrying heavy weapons, most of them staring in shock at the monstrous Spidderel who had appeared among them.

Most, but not all. The largest among them—the one with widest shoulders, the heaviest muscles, the most notches on his giant sword, and an array of scars that spoke of battles fought and won—stared past Krow Danaz and Spidderel at the pathetic Mylera, now slowly advancing and giving his ride and shivering meal a wide berth.

"You came," Grake said.

"I came," Mylera said. "And I brought help."

I'm not sure we need help from a creature of the pit, Grake thought. "You killed two of my followers," he said.

"They fired arrows at us," the man sitting on the monster's back said. The creature was like nothing he had ever seen before, a many-limbed freak with a forbidding array of spines, too many eyes, and a gaping maw of a mouth speckled with the blood and flesh of two of his warriors he'd sent on patrol just before dawn. The man upon its back was shriveled and gnarled, huddled within a large black cloak whose hood failed to cover completely the strange, fluid markings across his scalp. He exuded control. Power. Danger.

"Are you surprised, old man?" Grake asked, and he saw a flicker of anger in the man's eyes. He's not old, Grake thought.

My age, if that. He has the fire of middle age about him, and though he looks worn and wasted, I should be cautious.

"Besides, Spidderel was hungry," the man said. "What it wants, it takes." The thing he had called Spidderel worked its mandibles, slicking them into and out of its mouth to suck off the remnants of its most recent meal. Every one of its multifarious eyes seemed to be looking at Grake.

"This is the sorcerer Krow Danaz," Mylera said. "He can help us. He has cause."

Grake felt a flicker of recognition at that name. "A score to settle with Conan?" He laughed. "Show me someone in this world who doesn't!"

"I'd see him dead," Danaz said. He did something with his legs and the thing beneath him reared up on its back four legs, waving at the air with its other limbs as if to slice reality.

Grake stood his ground, though he sensed and heard his warriors taking a couple of steps back. There, beneath its mandibles, where its neck joins its body, he thought, looking at where he might plunge his sword to defeat this monster. Or its mouth. Or maybe through its eye-mounds, into whatever it has for a brain.

"Oh, you can't kill it," Danaz said as if knowing his thoughts. Maybe he did.

I have to be careful, guarded, Grake thought.

"But if our cause is common and you do as I say, you'll have nothing to fear," Danaz said.

"Do as you say?" Grake asked.

Danaz looked to Grake's left and right at the three warriors standing behind him. His expression displayed no fear. Grake felt that aura of control coming from the shriveled sorcerer again, and for the first time he felt a frisson of unease. He wasn't used to that. Grake wasn't afraid of anything.

"Please, let the three of us talk," Mylera said. "Grake, I came

to your summons after many years, because you sought my help. And I in turn brought Krow Danaz because he can help both of us."

"Help us how?" Grake drew his broadsword, slowly, his other hand held palm out to show he meant no violence. "This will defeat Conan. My sword, stained forever with the blood of the world's second-greatest warrior. Whatever help either of you can offer, it is I who will take Conan's head."

Danaz looked like he was smiling. It was difficult to tell on such a face. Mylera glanced aside, as if thinking something different.

"Grake, what by Macha is that thing?" a woman whispered from just behind him. "We can't ally with such a beast. Look what it did to—"

"Spidderel does as I say," Danaz said, interrupting her. "And it can help us all. What if Conan brings an army?"

"He has no army," Mylera said.

"Not yet. How many are you?" the sorcerer asked Grake.

Grake didn't like to reveal such information.

"Enough to take on an army behind Conan?" Danaz pushed.

"He has no army!" Mylera said again, louder. "He travels with a few people, a wagon, horses. He's hiding rather than marching. His mission is his own, not that of his country or kingship. And I can reach out and find where he is."

"Very well," Danaz said. "You do that, Mylera, and then I will use my own skills to ensure he's brought to us. And then Grake can kill him and become a big mighty warrior."

He's laughing at me, Grake thought. He reached for the leather pouch of quesh around his neck, stroking the material.

Krow Danaz stiffened in his saddle. Beneath him, Spidderel tensed and became utterly still, its legs stiffening so quickly that Grake heard joints clicking and snapping. It was coiled and wound, ready to attack.

Grake ran his fingers away from the pouch and across the muscles lining his stomach, tracing each one. He smiled. "You can bring Conan to me?"

"I can," Danaz said. "But first you must take us to your camp where you are working your slaves."

"And why do we need to do that?"

"Because your old friend Mylera needs food, drink, and rest. And I need one of your slaves in order to cast my spell."

On their way back along the clifftop escarpment to their camp, his warriors huddled close to express their doubts and fears, but Grake shrugged them off. He was without fear and any doubts he felt were balanced by the presence of that great, unnatural beast the sorcerer rode upon. He had heard of Krow Danaz in his travels, and knew him to be a pupil of the long-dead dark sorcerer Tsotha-lanti. Most rumors said that Danaz had been dead for many years, yet here he was. Grake was destined to be the greatest warrior of the ages, but if Danaz and his many-limbed beast had come to help, so be it.

Grake was still in charge. So long as everyone knew that, things would go to plan.

The slaves screamed when Spidderel emerged from the trees and entered the clifftop camp. Grake's warriors beat and pushed them back into their bamboo cage, shutting and locking the door behind them. They should at least have been grateful for a couple of hours' more rest before being lowered down onto the cliffs once again to search for more heartgems.

Grake stood watching them, trying to decide which slave to

give to Krow Danaz. He looked at Baht Tann's wife and two sons, considered, and then passed them by. He might need all of them alive when Conan arrived. Instead, he chose an older man whose left arm was almost useless after a slip on the cliff a day before.

Danaz climbed down from his creature, hobbled a few steps on wasted legs, then went to his knees with a groan. As he built a fire near the cliff edge, Spidderel crouched down close beside him. The fire caught quickly and leaped upward with unnatural green colors, smokeless but bright. When the protesting slave was dragged to him, Danaz looked him up and down and nodded. He ordered that the man's arms and legs should be cut off.

Grake's warriors looked to him and he nodded. The man screamed as they obeyed the order. He continued screaming when Danaz indicated that his writhing, bleeding torso should be dropped into the fire.

The flames surged around the dying slave and entered his orifices like questing fingers. He started to glow from within, and then his final screams were scorched from him as Krow Danaz pushed his own hands into the green fire. He turned them this way and that, with no apparent ill effect.

Grake watched from a distance. His warriors also watched, stationed around the camp's extremes, ever alert for dangers from without. *It's danger from within we need to worry about,* Grake thought, as Danaz bathed in green fire and muttered words in unknown, horrible languages. The tattoos on his head squirmed and twisted, and Grake was not sure whether some of those quiet words came from their own inked mouths.

After a short time the flames died down, leaving a charred mess that did not even smoke. At a muttered word from Danaz, Spidderel snapped up the dead man's limbs and swallowed them almost without chewing.

"Conan will be brought to us tomorrow by some new friends

of mine," Krow Danaz said, "and all those riding with him will be dead."

"Then I'll prepare," Grake said.

"You do that," Danaz said. "But first, bring me some wine. If we are to form an alliance against Conan, perhaps the three of us should sit and share our stories."

16

Between The Living And The Dead

Conan felt better than he had since leaving Tarantia, and Zenobia and Conn behind. In fact, he felt better than he had for months, maybe even years. His blood flowed strong in his veins, his muscles were tested and had found memories of their old strength, and he had fought off and bettered those sent against him, with a little help. His stomach wound ached and the new cut in his leg hurt, but they were badges of experience, proof of life.

As they headed east across Koth and toward Khoraja, he walked among the Last Song and talked to each of them. He thanked them for accompanying him, tried to prepare them for what was to come, and spoke of the loyalty of friends that had brought him this way. He did not mention the fight against the snake people they had held back from, because Jemi was right—they had fought when they needed to. If it weren't for Fennick's bow or Kaz's crossbow, he might have been more badly injured, or even dead.

Conan had no right to berate them for not joining in the

fight. Still, he found it difficult to understand their move from being warriors to musicians. Ironically, it was Jemi who'd tried to explain the similarities—though he suspected she had never been in a fight in her life. She'd told him that digging deep into one's heart to find a tune or the words to go with it was a struggle with yourself, and that sometimes it left them feeling beaten and tired. Conan had scoffed and said that thinking up words or tunes to pluck on some twisted gut did not leave scars.

Jemi had raised an eyebrow. She had not graced his comment with a reply.

Conan knew what he was doing. He was acting like a general now rather than a king, ensuring that his troops were happy and ready and safe, even though these troops were not marching with a willingness to fight. He was confident that they would, if their lives depended on it.

He also knew that he was in charge of his own safety, his own life. He liked it that way. He trusted no one more than himself.

Finally, he dropped back from the wagon and the rest of the Last Song to walk with Gannar, who as usual took up the rear. The sellsword didn't seem to welcome Conan's presence, veering from the path the wagon had taken to climb a small slope, standing on top of a rocky outcropping and looking around. Conan followed, not standing too close but still stopping when Gannar stopped.

"Something I can do for you?" Gannar asked.

"I have heard the others' stories," Conan said.

"Why does that mean I should tell you mine?"

"It doesn't."

Gannar started walking again, heading for the edge of the rocks and the steep drop back to the trail. The rest of the Last Song had moved ahead, and Conan saw Fennick glance back and then continue. None of them seemed concerned that the two men had fallen behind. Gannar was often not with the rest of them, and at first Conan had believed he was keeping watch on their tail, but maybe it was more complex than that.

Gannar started down the almost sheer drop, moving smoothly and quickly. Conan followed. Where Gannar gained advantage in being sleek and wiry, Conan was strong. Though he was likely twice Gannar's weight, his big hands gripped firmly around handholds and he moved down the small cliff almost without pause.

They reached the ground together. Gannar walked on without looking back at Conan.

"You have ghosts," Conan said. "You're alone in a group of friends."

"You should know, the things you've done," Gannar replied.

Conan said nothing.

"I know stories about you, Conan—the good ones, the bad ones, the wretched—so you'll understand why I like to be on my own."

"Because of your ghosts."

"Why are you so keen to know?" Gannar was growing angry.

"The Last Song are becoming friends," Conan said. "The fewer secrets between friends, the better."

"I haven't even told some of them my story," Gannar said, nodding ahead at the wagon.

"If you've told one or two of them, I'm sure the others know."

"If so, that's good. I don't like telling it. Doing so is living it again, and only a fool wants to relive their nightmares."

Conan grunted. He could understand. If he replayed his experiences in those dungeons beneath the Scarlet Citadel, he often did not sleep that night. They were always there with him, but telling the tales seemed to give them life once again. Even so, he sensed that Gannar wanted to talk, so Conan walked silently with him and, after a little while, he did.

"I'm sure you've fought with my kind before," he said.

"And fought against us too, most likely. I'm Aesir, and from an early age I became a sellsword. I never had any real desire to raid and pillage for my own gain, and my interest in history and storytelling set me aside from most of those around me. I was unusual in my clan. They saw me as freakish and they were all very willing to let me know that, with words and fists. So one day, when we attacked a caravan traveling into the border kingdoms from Brythinia, I slipped away and followed the survivors. Not to hunt them down and kill them, but to join them, because I knew they were also sellswords—rogues, true, and bad at their employment, because they'd failed to protect the family groups they were hired to guard, but I'd been thinking about my life and in them I saw potential.

"When I caught up with them, they didn't believe my intentions and three of them came at me. I killed them in a fair fight, and then told the others—there were a dozen left by then—that I could train them to fight properly. It was a bluff, of course. There were warriors there from Shem and Stygia, Ophir and Corinthia, and one mute woman from Zembabwei who was more scars than skin. Most of them knew more about fighting, killing, and dying than I would ever know, but I had more brain than all of them put together. I didn't set out to be their leader, and though that remained the case, it was often me steering our actions and commissions.

"So they accepted me into their squadron. I trained them and traveled with them, and heading south we picked up some work on the Road of Kings in Corinthia, guarding rich merchants when they headed east into Zamora to trade with the desert tribes. We became very good at what we did. There are a thousand unmarked graves back and forth along those trade routes that can be attributed to the Wild Boars. That's what we called ourselves; I've never been quite sure where the name came from. Our payments increased, and my dream was to gain enough luna to buy myself a small farm in Nemedia."

He trailed off, looking down at his boots as he kicked stones ahead of them.

"Dreams never come true," Conan said.

"Of course not. One day we were guarding a rich trader out of Kamalla. She traveled with her two husbands and seventeen children, and it seems she did not apprise us of her true situation. She had made some enemies, and it was on our watch that they came calling for revenge.

"By then, the Wild Boars numbered almost twenty seasoned warriors, but we were no match for the troop that attacked. They set a perfect ambush in a wooded ravine, raining arrows down into the horses pulling our caravan's three wagons, then rolling burning oil barrels down the steep slopes. The conflagration was instant and violent. The troop had some dark powers on their side, because they commanded a flight of sin-ravens from the deep Kambujan jungles, and these gruesome beasts swept down and attacked the Wild Boars.

"They wiped us out. Horribly injured, pecked, and lashed by ravens, I survived buried beneath the bodies of my friends, and I smeared their gore across my throat, face, and chest to add to my own. There was more insides covering me than skin. I lay there and watched as the attackers came down the steep ravine sides, and I saw them bring out the trader and her husbands and feed them to the ravens. Then they brought out the children.

"I struggled, Conan. I writhed beneath the weight of the dead, reached for my sword, but I was trapped there. Death stalked and teased me, and I invited it to take me, yet death eluded me. I believe that Ymir placed a curse on me that day, denying me Valhalla—to live, witness, and survive. But I did not allow myself the peace of sightlessness. I watched every sinful, brutal act, and I marked the faces of those who committed them. They took their time. When they departed that ravine of decadent death and horror later that day, I was the only living thing left behind, but for the flies and carrion creatures taking their fill. The heat took me, and the blood, and the terror of what I had witnessed and allowed to happen. It put a madness in me, and… I don't remember much of the next year. It is a dark spot in my memory. I cannot recall how I escaped that terrible place, how I survived my injuries, where I went, or what I did.

"The next thing I remember is seeing one of those mercenaries' faces staring up at me as I sliced his throat from ear to ear. And that was my life for the next few years. I sought them out, hunted them down, using my intellect to seek them in dark woodlands, golden cities, open plains, shady taverns. I always made sure they knew who I was, and though I had never learned their names, I ensured they had the faces of dead children on their minds when I killed them.

"I was creative in my methods. I became inured to death. In fact, I started to enjoy the killing more than I ever had before. I would spend days or weeks tracking down one particular member of their troop, plotting and planning how I would end their life. You've seen the cord around my neck, Conan. It's full now, and finished, because I caught the last one in Shadizar and poured boiling oil into her mouth. She screamed blue flames. It was beautiful. I wear their ears in the hope that they can hear the music we play, because since that last killing I have dropped my swords, renounced violence, and discovered happiness with the Last Song. Valhalla can wait."

"It's strange to hear a follower of Ymir speak of Valhalla so," Conan said.

Gannar shrugged. "I still feel purpose. At first I believed I had been spared from death to bring death upon those brutal heathen murdering scum. Yet I still live. Maybe you're my purpose, Conan." He turned and smiled as he said this, and Conan was about to reply when they heard Kaz calling from up ahead.

"Come and see!"

The wagon had stopped by the banks of a wide, slow river. There was an old stone bridge spanning the water, in poor repair but still standing. As ever they were following a less-traveled route across southeastern Koth, trying to avoid running into too many people on the road, and that meant the trail was often rough and sometimes washed away by heavy rains, and bridges and other route infrastructure was rarely well maintained.

Across the river from them, a flood plain spread across the floor of a valley, beyond which a range of hills rose toward the high border between Koth and Khoraja. Nestled in the foothills was the remains of a once-grand castle, its walls breached, its towers burned, roofs open to the elements like the scorched ribs of a fallen giant. Its lower walls were crumbled into grass-covered piles, and though the inner keep appeared mostly whole, several great trees grew inside. Their branches pierced walls, their roots questing down to undermine foundations. Flocks of bright-yellow birds roosted in these high canopies, singing sweet songs as they lifted off together, swept across the plains almost as far as the river, then swooped back to rest again.

The first fallen wall was maybe five hundred feet from the river, and on the flood plain there were several bulky ruins smothered in creeping vines. Rusted metallic skeletons protruded above these wrecks as if reaching forever for the skies, stanchions trailing thick chains.

"Siege engines," Tathar said. "Old."

"History has swallowed this battle," Jemi said from atop the wagon seat. The horses whinnied.

"I feel the ghosts watching us," Ally said from where she stood beyond the horses. She shivered.

"A battlefield always holds echoes," Conan said. "They aren't concerned with us."

"Up there, see that valley ta the right of the fallen keep?"

Jemi pointed. "That leads up inta the hills, and eventually the Ymak Pass. Beyond is Khoraja. We'll likely see more people on that side, but if we're careful an' travel through the night, we'll reach the Khorajan cliffs by dawn tomorrow."

"Then keep moving," Conan said.

"If the bridge takes our weight," Kaz said.

"Would you like me to go and test?" he asked, eyebrow raised.

"Well, you do weigh as much as all of us combined."

"Easy living," Conan muttered.

Laughter flitted among the Last Song as they moved onto the stone bridge, and Conan felt an unusual inner peace. They were strong together, and stronger still with him. His expedition was almost at an end. Soon he would fulfill his promise to Baht Tann, rescue his family, and then…

Then return home. To his beautiful Zenobia and Conn, yes, but also to the throne, its duties and rules, and all the pressures they brought. He breathed in deeply, smelling the cool waters passing by below, the drifting scent of wild flowers, and the whiff of histories known and unknown marking time in this wild place.

Maybe home doesn't mean only one thing, he thought.

The bridge crunched and cracked beneath the wagon's wheels, but the horses plodded on unconcerned. Conan had learned to trust an animal's instincts, so he was confident that the old structure would hold. Halfway across, he looked down at the water flowing slowly by and he caught sight of his own reflection.

Something niggled at him. An itch in his mind, worrying his thoughts. He paused and leaned over further, questioning himself.

"Something's off," Kaz said.

"The bridge is fine," Gannar said.

"It's not that."

They continued onward, and as they reached the opposite bank Conan's nervousness grew. We are all looking ahead, he thought, so he turned and looked back across the bridge at the bank they had just left. His blood ran cold.

"Necromancy," he said. Jemi halted the wagon on dry land, the others also turned to look, and both horses let out troubled whinnies.

Three figures were shambling onto the bridge after them. They looked like blurred shapes upon a sharp world, their features smudged by the filth of the grave, the passage of time, and death.

"We woke them?" Fennick asked.

"No," Conan said, because he felt the truth, and had sensed it looking at his reflection in the slow river. There was a deep, dark history to this place, yet it was also smeared with a shadowy magic that was far more recent.

Kaz dashed to the wagon and climbed inside, then leaped down with her crossbow. In one fluid movement she primed it, nocked a bolt, and sent it flying.

One of the shapes staggered a little but kept coming. Conan could not even see where the bolt had struck it. The figures were dead warriors from whatever battle had happened here long ago, their corpses fallen into the soft ground beside the river and preserved by its peaty embrace. Two of them were tall and thin, garbed in wet leather, hair long and knotted, their features indistinct. The third was short and squat, and this one wore metal armor. They all clung on to the weapons they had fallen with—the tall remnants dragged swords across the stone bridge, points drawing up sparks; the armored knight heaved a heavy battle-ax behind him or her.

Fennick nocked an arrow and let it fly, and it took one of the tall shapes in the head. Its skull exploded into shards, and the wet stuff inside spattered on the bridge behind it. The corpse paused for a moment, the remains of its head jerking back and forth on its neck, before staggering sideways and splashing into the river.

"The head, then," Kaz said, and she loosed another bolt. The squat knight's head flipped back as the bolt sheared off the top of its skull. The contents of its broken skull slicked down its shoulders. It continued forward for a few steps and then fell onto its front.

The third shape had almost reached their end of the bridge. Conan moved forward, drawing his sword from the sheath across his back. The corpse warrior glared at him with dead, hollow eyes. Conan squinted, certain that he could see the glimmer of some unnatural intelligence in those empty eye sockets. Then he lifted the sword and swung—

—and the dead warrior parried his blow.

"Huh," Conan said. He stepped to the left, waiting for a counterattack that did not come. So he heaved his broadsword again, smashed his opponent's blade into shards, and cleaved the body in two. Both parts fell to the ground, spilling moist and crumbling insides. They twitched for a moment and then were still.

He looked across the bridge to see if there were others rising from the ground to come after them. There was nothing. Yet something was still wrong.

It was too quiet. The yellow birds roosting in the ruined castle had stopped singing.

The horses whinnied and stomped their hooves.

Conan turned around just as Jemi shouted, "There. There! This isn't over yet."

"It's only just begun," Conan said. Across the plain between them and the castle, the ground was starting to move. It looked unreal to begin with, as if his eyes were watery and unsure, but deep down he knew what he was seeing. The ground broke here;

bushes shuddered there. A mass of trailing vines lifted as something pushed them from below. Rough grass turf parted and dark, wet soil was exposed to the sun.

As Conan and the Last Song watched with growing dread, the sad remnants of a forgotten battle pulled themselves up out of their graves.

Conan glanced behind them, already knowing what he would see. Their retreat across the bridge was about to be blocked by two-score corpses dragging themselves out of the ground and riverbank over there. Rusted metal scraped stone as they began to advance.

With the stink of the grave wafting across to them and the wet muttering of the dead filling the air, Conan said, "Friends of the Last Song, perhaps now is the time for you to take up your weapons once again."

17

All But Conan

Conan was aware that the Last Song had fallen in behind him, allowing him to take the lead. It was not because he was a king; it was because he was Conan, and these musicians and songwriters, these old warriors that had moved on, all knew the man he was and the one he had been. His myth went before him, and his song—its ending as yet unwritten—sang out across the land.

"Kaz, do you have anything to counter this?" he asked.

"This is the work of a powerful necromancer," she said. "I've received a glancing touch from a lowly shaman's skills, Conan. I'm no sorcerer."

Conan had known necromancers in the past, Tsotha-lanti being one of the worst. Is this him? he thought. Can he be back for revenge, after so long? He'd cut the evil wizard's head from his neck and seen it still alive, eyes burning with a terrible fire, before it was snatched up and carried away by a monstrous and unnatural hawk with the voice of the sorcerer Pelias. Tsotha's headless body had staggered into the hazy distance, and every shred of Conan believed the evil bastard to be dead, but with such sorcerers there was never certainty.

No matter who was responsible, they had a fight before them.

"Fennick, Kaz, make sure you have all your ammunition. Tathar, Ally, Gannar, grab your weapons. Jemi, stay on the wagon. You have any weapons at all?"

"Imma mean shot with a sling," she said.

"Then protect the horses," Conan said.

"And if they're spooked and they run with the wagon?"

"Control them," he said. "Or prepare to cut the harnesses."

Fennick and Kaz were in the back of the wagon, handing weapons down to the others—a heavy mace on a chain to Tathar, a pirate's cutlass to Ally, and a pike and shortsword to Gannar. They had already shrugged on quivers of bows and bolts, and now they remained on the wagon to maintain height advantage over the advancing hordes. They both wore swords on leather belts. When their ammunition ran out, they would join the fight at close quarters.

"They're dead," Conan said. "They have no brains. Use your guile. Be mindful, not mindless. But do not underestimate their determination. That zombie I just put down countered my sword stroke, and someone or something is driving them."

"And it'll be you they're after," Kaz said. "Remember that, everyone. Conan is bait."

"Fine," Conan said, and he took a few steps ahead of the horses. Surveying the plains, he saw scores of zombie dead now risen. Some of them were already lumbering toward him and the Last Song while others seemed to be shaking themselves off, looking around, as if coming to terms with sunlight again.

"We should head for th'valley past the ruined keep," Jemi said. "Fight our way through to there and we'll be away from them."

"But keep the wagon at our pace, Jemi," Conan said. "Don't roll ahead."

"Just the matter of cutting through a hundred walking dead mindless monsters trying to kill us first," Ally said.

"Well, put it like that and it sounds easy," Gannar said.

Conan walked ahead, glancing back over his shoulder at the bridge. At least forty zombies were crossing, packed tight between the low walls. One of them tripped and fell, rolling over the wall and into the river. None of the others seemed to notice or care. He knew that with the bridge packed, Jemi's plan to make for the valley was their best option, so he wielded his sword and took the fight to the advancing dead.

He cut down the first zombie with a sword through the head. It fell and spilled moist, rotten brains across his boot. He kicked it aside and approached two more. One of them raised a rusty sword, the other a pike with a rotten wooden handle. He knocked the weapons aside—the sword bent and broke apart while the pike smashed into wet shards—and then swept his broadsword left to right and cut them in half. They dropped to the ground, old musty things that still twitched and squirmed, and emitted a strange keening sound as if upset at being brought out of their graves.

Wagon wheels squeaked as Jemi urged the horses on, sitting on the seat with a slingshot in one hand. She twirled the sling and let fly, and a shuffling figure went down with its head shattered into pieces. She grinned at Conan.

Fennick had lowered the wagon's canvas cover and he stood in its rear, nocking, aiming, and firing arrows. Every shot found home. Though the Bossonian was more used to nursing the fitar on his shoulder, he had forgotten nothing about archery. His arrows blasted apart rotten heads and severed crooked spines, and the dead fell once again. Standing just behind Jemi, Kaz primed her crossbow, loaded it, and fired in a graceful fluid motion that looked almost like a dance. She moved around to switch aim in different directions, and she flowed, her body never still, her arms lifting the weapon and firing as if it were part of her. Conan knew Picts to be brutish and unrefined even in battle, but Kaz was a revelation. Her every movement sang graceful songs of violence.

Tathar trotted just ahead of the horses, swinging his mace in constant readiness. As Conan watched, the old Stygian knight claimed his first kills as three zombies darted toward the horses from a low ditch beside the trail. The mace barely slowed as it swung through their heads, shattering them one after the other. Tathar turned with the swing and used the momentum to bring the weapon back under his control, always moving, always ready.

Ally and Gannar ran along either side of the wagon, weapons at the ready. Soon they would need them.

Conan went on ahead, clearing the way across the old battlefield with his mighty sword. Soon he was splashed with remains of the dead—blood, thick and black and stinking of rot; bone shards that nicked at his skin; flesh that was rank and stinking, the smell invading his nostrils and staying there. However long ago this old battle had been fought, the dead had been preserved in the peaty ground, their skin wrinkled and hardened like old leather. In some of the shambling figures he saw shriveled eyes in empty sockets, and in all of those eyes he recognized the faint purplish glow of whatever dark necromancy had drawn these warriors up for one last fight.

Conan put them back down.

He glanced back again and saw that Ally and Gannar were now fighting off zombies probing the wagon's defenses from the side. That troubled Conan, because it implied more intelligence that he had attributed to these things. Two stumbled at the wagon and Ally sliced them apart with her fine pirate's sword, and a third took advantage of her distraction and ducked beneath the blade. It hacked at her midriff with a rusted ax and she flinched back, cutting the thing in half with her return swing.

Behind the wagon, Gannar used his pike in one strong hand to prod at those who approached, going for their head and neck to drop them. When a zombie ducked beneath his pike, Gannar gutted it with his shortsword. It paused, looked down at the stinking mess spilling from the wound, and rushed him.

Fennick's arrow pierced its head and saved Gannar's life.

Conan fought on, scything his way through lines of the dead, swinging his broadsword, feeling strong and confident. He was cautious of his stomach wound, but even that felt tight and secure. Every muscle sang, every joint swiveled and turned, and though he did feel the creak of age between his bones, he welcomed the pain and let it set his senses aflame.

This is easy, he thought. They had already worked their way halfway to the side valley rising slowly away from the battlefield and the ruined castle. As he sliced another zombie clean in two from scalp to groin, he thought, This is too easy.

None of the resurrected warriors were coming at him. They came close, true, but they did not try to stab, slice, or rend him. Some of them almost gave pause as they approached, and one or two backed away, lowering their weapons before he sent them back to the afterlife.

No, this was not easy. It was different.

"Fight me!" Conan shouted, dashing forward and skipping to the left to take down a huge revenant who carried two battle-axes. The man must have been seven feet tall, and alive he might have proved a worthy opponent for Conan. Dead, reanimated, he barely lifted his weapons before Conan cut him down.

The person who had encouraged the first two attacks on Conan had meant him dead. Whoever was behind this one—and he had no doubt it was a dark sorcerer, a great necromancer—intended something different.

"Fight me!" he shouted again, running at a line of seven zombies still shrugging off mud and grass as they stumbled toward him and the Last Song. He cut down one but the others parted around him... and then continued on their way.

They rushed the wagon and the warriors of Last Storm, and as one they fell on one of the horses. Rusted weapons rose and fell, the horse neighed and then screamed, and it dropped beneath the weight of the dead. More ran at it, jumping and falling into the attack as the other horse struggled in its harness to pull away from the horrific slaughter.

Jemi loosed her sling, Fennick and Kaz shot arrows and bolts, and the zombies began to fall away, but the fallen horse was now little more than butchered meat. The wagon was at a standstill now, and the attacking hordes took that as a sign to swarm in and attack.

Conan swung his broadsword and took some of them down, moist body parts striking the ground all around him, shriveled heads rolling, torsos quivering and twitching as whatever unnatural animation had been bestowed upon them flitted away once more.

"Tathar, hold them off," Conan said, and the big Stygian's mace continued to swoosh and swish through the air as it smashed bone and stripped old flesh.

Conan went with the flow of resurrected fighters, approaching the fallen horse and jumping across its open, tattered body to free the one that still lived. He slashed at the restraining harness and the horse bolted, hooves thundering across the plain as it knocked zombies aside and ran toward the valley.

Jemi cried out as three zombie warriors clambered up onto the wagon and tripped her. Her crutch fell and clattered to the boards beside her, and the sling was useless at close quarters. Kaz took one in the face with her crossbow, but then she was attacked by a zombie crawling up the wagon's side. She slipped in gore and went down, battering at the beast with her crossbow.

Conan stood on the horse's corpse and leaped, landing

on the wagon's seat, broadsword already swinging. Jemi was trapped beneath two zombies, fending off their short stabbing blades, teeth clenched, and he judged his strike perfectly, slicing through their skulls and missing Jemi's face by a hand's width. He grabbed her with his spare hand and pulled her upright.

"Stay with me!" he said.

"I can fight, just let me find—"

"Jemi, they're not attacking me," Conan said. "I don't know why, but stay by my side. Your crutch has gone. And you're no warrior."

Kaz cried out and pushed at the zombie attacking her with both feet, lifting it up so that Conan could hack off its head. She heaved it over the side with a grunt of disgust, and then she was on her feet again, loading and firing her last crossbow bolt before dropping it and drawing her sword. The fight was now at close quarters.

The zombies from the bridge were on them now, moving faster than their companions. They seemed in better condition, too, running at Ally and Gannar and taking them on with their wet, rusted weapons. Maybe they were the remnants of a more recent battle, or perhaps the peat of the riverside had preserved them better. None of that mattered to Conan. There was a threat and they had to fight. He concentrated on that.

Ally parried blows and her steel sang against the rusted iron blades of the old soldiers. She ducked and flowed, sliced and stabbed, and bodies fell around her. Gannar tripped the first attackers with his pike, stomped and crushed one head, cut off another. More came at both of them and they drew together, back to back so they could cover a killing arc in every direction. They fought without talking, and Conan saw their instinctive warriors' experience in every move they made.

Wood splintered, and a dozen zombies were battering against one side of the wagon. Fennick lost his footing and fell, striking the wagon's side and dropping his bow. He reached for it but a zombie grabbed it, tugging it hard until it slipped through Fennick's fingers. He drew the last arrow from his quiver and stabbed the zombie through the face, withdrawing it and stabbing again at the revenant that took its place at the wagon's side. He pulled but the arrow was lost, so he knelt up and drew his shortsword, slicing back and forth along the wagon's raised side. Fingers, arms, and a head flew.

Kaz stood beside him, hacking at the attackers with her own sword.

Conan turned a quick circle to assess their situation, kicking a rotten warrior that was climbing up onto the driver's seat in the process. Beside him, Jemi spun and loosed her slingshot, smashing the skull of another.

They were surrounded. Across the old battlefield, more ground was moving, more graves opening, and old rotten things were rising from where they had fallen or been buried in mass graves twenty years ago, or fifty, or maybe more. It did not matter to Conan what armor or uniforms they wore and what weapons they bore. All that mattered was survival.

I have faced worse, he thought.

He decided to test a theory that he had already verbalized. "Stay here, into the back of the wagon with Kaz and Fennick," he said to Jemi, and before she could protest Conan leaped down beside the dead horse in front of the wagon. He was already swinging his sword when he landed, and two zombies went down with limbs dangling, torsos split open. Their mouths opened and closed as they squirmed in an attempt to stand again, but Conan stomped on their heads as he stepped toward a line of attackers.

They slowed, stopped, and then circled around him so that they could assault the wagon.

Maybe they fear me, he thought, but it was not that. These

things were mindless and feared nothing. They were animated under instruction from someone or something, and their orders included not to kill him.

A scream rose behind him, quickly smothered. He spun around to see the horde that had circled around him now attacking Ally, pushing her down to the ground and falling on her. Metal clashed, sparks flew, and Conan saw her blade dishing new death to the monsters. But her voice was covered in their attacking mass, and however much Gannar stabbed and slashed he could not uncover her. The Aesir sellsword looked up and caught Conan's eye with a plea.

Conan jumped over the dead horse one more time, and as he landed he knew that the mystery of the zombies not trying to kill him gave him a huge advantage. He waded in, holding his heavy sword in one hand and using the other to grab at the zombies. His fingers sank through rotten tunics and leather and closed in wet, weak flesh, and when he gripped bone he pulled. An arm and half a shoulder was ripped off. He slashed his sword, grabbed again, and threw a shriveled woman aside, her rusted armor falling through the air as her body disintegrated. Her voiceless head screamed in silent rage.

Gannar was with him, prodding and stabbing, and Conan beat off two monsters going at the sellsword, smashing their heads together and crushing their skulls. He dove into the heaving mass on the ground, questing with his strong spare hand and clasping warm flesh at last. He grabbed and pulled, and as he braced his feet against the ground and tensed, he tugged Ally's arm from beneath the pile of zombies. He swept his sword again, hacking at them as if cutting his way through living-dead undergrowth, and with one more stab from Gannar the last creature fell away.

Conan hauled harder, and Allymaro the pirate rose once again. Conan could already see that he was too late. Her animal skin mask had been ripped off, revealing that her mask of old scars was now given new ones. One eye was missing, stabbed out by a zombie's weapon or bony finger. Her cheek was ripped back, teeth horribly exposed. Her throat was holed, and blood bubbled and spat as the last of her breath left her.

Still he pulled, hugging her to his side. Her head tilted back, opening her neck wound even more and gushing blood, and Ally's remaining eye rolled in its socket. She focused on Conan, and it was as if she had been grasping onto life for this moment, because as they looked at each other he saw the light of life leave her.

Conan lifted the pirate woman with one hand and offered her up to Fennick on the back of the wagon. The Bossonian took her and said, "Jemi, to me! Ally's hurt!" and Conan turned back to the fight rather than tell him the truth or see him realize it for himself.

He saw Gannar fighting off more zombies from the direction of the bridge and went to him, attacking those who were assaulting the sellsword, cutting and slicing and hacking with impunity. Rather than giving him the freedom to act it should have, their reluctance to attack Conan enraged him, and he roared as he swung his heavy blade, hewing down three zombies, stamping on their heads to still their pathetic mewling mouths, kicking at a figure clinging to Gannar's back and stabbing at him with a rusted knife, punching another in the head so hard that his hand smashed through its rotten skull and splashed moist brains across the ground, raging, shouting, roaring. Conan became a berserker, swinging his sword here, kicking there. His skin was stiff and thick with the spilled insides of dead things. He tasted them in his mouth and spat, inhaling their rancid scent, hearing the wet tearing sound of fragile bones parting from sockets, old skin ripping like damp paper.

Something grabbed his arm. He cut the thing's arm off but

the fingers still held on tight. Others held his ankles, his legs, and tangled their fingers in his clothing, and they started to pull him away from the wagon. It was easy for him to cut the corpses away and disable them, but still others came and took their place. Grabbing. Tugging. Trying to steal him away.

He cut them to pieces and gave them back to rot.

When Conan heard a cry and a groan from the wagon, he knew that the others were aware of Ally's death. He ran at several more zombies coming at them, chopping them down without fear, screaming blood-frenzy in their stinking faces when they refused to attack him with their degraded weapons. When they hit the ground, he kept swinging his sword, breaking them into pieces which he kicked this way and that. Some pieces he stomped into the mud; others he hacked up some more.

"Conan," Gannar said from behind him. He turned and the sellsword stood with a pile of dead around him. Some of them still moved, twitching as if in response to his voice. A hand rose here, clasping nothing. A head turned there, crushed, eye sockets glimmering and then fading with unnatural light. "They've gone."

Conan looked around. The dead made dead once more lay everywhere. The horse they had butchered steamed in the afternoon light, its stomach torn open, insides out. Fennick stood beside the wagon now, pacing here and there, gathering his arrows where they protruded from heads and chests. Conan saw tears on his cheeks and he looked away, back to the wagon, where Jemi stood propped on her regained crutch, looking down onto the wagon's bed. Kaz was there, sitting with Ally's head in her lap. Tathar was on the wagon's other side, slamming his mace down into a zombie still crawling toward it. He stood up, panting, and wiped disgusting fluids from his face. He caught Conan's eye, then moved toward the wagon.

Conan turned his back and left them for a while. He heard

heavy breathing, a growl of rage from someone, tears from someone else. Ally was not his friend to mourn—he had known her for mere days, not years like the rest of the Last Song—and so he left them alone to their grief. Instead he performed slow, widening circles around the wagon, finishing off several dead that still twitched and shifted across the disturbed ground. His muscles were warm and strong, his senses alive, and he remained alert for more threats.

As he went, he assessed himself for injuries. The stomach wound was aching and bleeding again—he would have to give it a chance to heal soon—and elsewhere he had cuts and scrapes, dealt by dead hands from old weapons. He knew from experience that such wounds would require thorough cleaning and treating with mauve-bloom pods, otherwise an infecting rash would set in and send poison surging through his blood.

He knew that Jemi had a store of mauve. He would ask her soon.

The birds started to sing again. A couple of hundred feet away, at the foot of the hills, a bright yellow flock took flight from the ruined castle, circled the battlefield a few times, and then sang a sweet song as they settled once again. A breeze picked up from the south and swept across the plain, carrying away some of the foul stink of the grave. Conan circled outward, guarding the Last Song and their battered wagon, and he wondered who or what Grake had recruited to send these hordes against them.

He hoped he would meet them soon.

Conan left the Last Song for a few minutes, but soon a sense of urgency started to prick at him again. The fight had held them up, and Ally's valiant death would delay them some more. Perhaps now was the time for him to part ways with the Last Song.

As he was considering this, movement in the distance toward the castle caught his attention. He shielded his eyes and made out the escaped horse slowly trotting back toward them. It veered around holes in the ground from where the dead had risen to enter into battle, and soon it closed on Conan and came to a halt. It was sweating, foaming around the mouth, and its eyes were wide.

"Shh, shhhhh," Conan said, reaching out his hand. The horse snorted, and though it smelled the stench of the dead all over him, it also knew that he was alive. Maybe it even recognized him. It let him approach and take hold of the trailing leather harness still affixed around its head, and he turned and led it back the rest of the way.

"Ally's dead," Jemi said as Conan approached.

"I know."

"I've known her a long time. She was… not a daughter but a friend who appreciated my advice."

"I'm sorry. We need to continue."

"Can you at least not let us bury our dead?" Jemi asked, and he saw anger in her eyes. It was the first time he'd heard her voice raised.

"Not here," Tathar said. "I wouldn't bury my worst enemy in this ground."

"Ally's a pirate, she's not for the dirt and worms," Kaz said. She was still in the wagon with Ally's head resting in her lap.

"Wherever we give her final rest, we can finish her song," Fennick said. Conan noticed that the Bossonian had put down his bow and the arrows he'd retrieved and picked up his fitar.

"You're getting ready to sing?" he asked in disbelief.

The Last Song all looked at him, standing there with their one remaining horse, but none of them spoke. It went without saying that they would sing their friend Ally into the afterlife and whatever might await her there. Valhalla, perhaps, or maybe nothing. Conan had always been one to let people believe whatever they wished to believe. He offered a small smile as apology, then turned away and patted the horse's neck.

I still don't understand them, he thought. They'd fought for their lives, and now they would sing for a life lost. Weren't they filled with rage? Didn't they realize that this had not been an accident?

Maybe they blamed him. He felt bad about Ally's death, but she had died valiantly. It was a risk that any warrior accepted. And somewhere deep down or in their past, these people were still warriors.

While the Last Song talked softly among themselves and tended to Ally—stripping her filthy, bloody clothes, washing her, dressing her in a simple robe, and laying a long, thin flute across her chest for her to bear into the afterlife, an instrument rather than a weapon—Conan readied the wagon for their onward journey. He was still wondering whether he would be best to leave them now or whether they were talking about making that decision on their own. He quickly decided that he hoped not. He felt strong and mighty, but his wounds still weakened him and his age clung on in every joint and bone and old injury that protested at his recent exertions. Besides that, he enjoyed their company and welcomed their expertise in battle. They had consigned war to their past, but today they had all fought like great warriors.

Maybe it would be different if those they came up against next were still alive.

Grake and whoever else holds Baht Tann's family are my problem, Conan thought. But getting there alive will be much more likely with the Last Song at my side.

If he had attempted to cross this old battlefield on his own, he could not guess at how his fate might have changed when the dead awoke and came for him. They had wanted to drag him away, not kill him. To where and to whom, he would discover quite soon, but on his own terms.

A lesser man might have turned tail and fled. Conan was no lesser man.

The butchered horse was still strapped to the wagon's harness and wooden shaft, so Conan went about cutting away the harness, trying not to become too embroiled in its spilled insides. When the wagon was free, he sheathed his sword and lifted the shaft, hauling it to the left on its pivot.

Gannar appeared beside him and helped, and then Tathar as well. They said nothing, but with their help Conan pulled the wagon a few feet away from the dead horse. Tathar led the surviving horse into position, muttering softly all the while, and Conan noted that the horse did not once glance at its dead companion. Perhaps like him, this beast knew that its best chance of survival was with the Last Song.

"Conan," Jemi said while Tathar strapped up the horse. "Come."

He went closer.

"Ally's ready for her onward journey," Jemi said. "Burial at sea—well, that ain't happenin' here, but Kaz says we c'n float her down the river. Mebbe she'll reach the great Styx, mebbe not, but if she sinks or's taken by a river beast, at least some of her will flow on."

"Seems fitting," he said. He leaned on the side, looking up and over onto the wagon bed.

"You wanna say some words?" Jemi asked.

Conan looked at the dead woman, who had been looking into his eyes the moment she'd passed. He shook his head.

"Then we'll do it now," Jemi said. "Been watching. You're welcome to join us, y'know. We're all friends here."

"You don't all blame me?" he asked.

Jemi snorted a soft laugh. "S'much as we blame fate for

anything. We made a choice ta come with you, Conan. Ally, too. An' now we get to sing her final song."

Despite Jemi's invitation, Conan held back as they said their goodbyes to Allymaro, pirate and musician. He stayed with the wagon and the horse, keeping the beast calm and assessing the vehicle for any more damage the living-dead assault might have caused. One iron-ringed wheel was fractured by an ax blow, but he thought it would hold. The wagon bed was a mess, with several of the Last Song's instruments broken and blood staining the floor. Otherwise, he thought they were ready to go.

The Last Song carried their dead member back toward the bridge, dodging around the scattered remains of withered corpses. Kaz, Tathar, and Gannar carried her while Jemi led the way, her crutch propped firmly beneath her arm, and Fennick strummed his fitar and sang a mournful song in an old Bossonian tongue. His voice carried across the landscape, low and deep, and his fitar strums gave a calming theme to the sad spectacle.

Conan stood beside the horse and watched. He was impatient to move, but he also understood their need to bid their friend a proper goodbye. He did not quite hear the words, because they sang a song just for themselves, but Ally's final tune brought tears from them all.

Once her song was sung, they let Ally float away down the river in silence. When they returned to the wagon, they stood together, silent and mournful.

"I wouldn't blame you if you left me," Conan said.

"Not likely," Jemi said. "Ally's passing's left a price that needs paying."

"Revenge?" Conan asked. "Isn't that the domain of warriors?"

"Justice," Gannar said. "And that is the domain of friends."

"But we need to know who or what we're up against," Kaz said. The short Pict looked around at the rotten bodies surrounding the wagon and shivered. The others seemed to know her intentions, but none of them communicated them to Conan. He watched, until she pointed to a corpse that seemed mostly whole. A slash from a blade—maybe Ally's curved pirate's sword—had opened its chest and severed the spine. Its eyes still held a glimmer of filthy light.

"That one," she said, and shivered again. "Bring it to the wagon. Lean it against—"

"We ain't touching that thing," Jemi said. "Those eyes are still glimmerin'."

"I'll do it here, then," Kaz said, and she knelt on the damp ground beside the corpse.

Conan shifted his stance a little, gripping his broadsword and readying to swing it, but then he saw that the rest of the Last Song were also ready to act. Tathar rested his mace on his shoulder ready to slam it down onto the thing's head, Gannar's pike was set in the ground beside its head, and Fennick had an arrow nocked and aimed. They had already lost one member of their troupe. They would not let another fall into peril.

Kaz moved her hands slowly above the corpse, shifting them back and forth, up and down, never touching its corrupt flesh or rotten clothing but tracing the shape it made in the world. She closed her eyes and moved her lips, telling a silent story, an unheard spell. After a few moments, she drew in a sharp breath and opened her eyes.

"Sing for me," she said. "It's dark, it's horrible, so sing for me and keep me fixed to this world and close."

They started to sing, all of them drifting easily into the same song. No instruments were played, and after a few moments Conan recognized it as the tune that had drifted to him from the riverbank a short time ago. They were singing Ally's song once more, and when Kaz closed her eyes again her brow was uncreased, her face more relaxed.

Conan watched as she performed her shamanistic task. Her moving hands hovered over the dead thing's face, and a pale light glowed there. He wasn't sure whether it came from Kaz's hands or was perhaps the reflected sick glimmer of false life still present in the broken thing's sockets. Her eyes rolled behind their lids and her face tensed again, teeth clenched and brow furrowed, and her jaw fell open as she muttered words in a strange language. Perhaps it was some form of Pictish, or maybe it was from farther away, longer ago. He respected what she was doing, but he did not like it.

Though maybe it will reveal who is set against me, and us, he thought. He had not for a moment considered ending his expedition and returning home, but knowing what he would face once they reached the Khorajan cliffs could only help. It was evidently someone with magic far stronger than Kaz's, and that worried him. He had encountered sorcerers and wizards and witches during his long life, and they had all harbored strange powers and arcane abilities.

"Please come back," he muttered, not really meaning to say the words out loud. No one heard him. They were singing, and whatever calming influence their combined song had over Kaz seemed to work.

Her eyes opened and she fell back, reaching out her hands to support herself, and then she leaned to the side and vomited.

Tathar dropped his mace and went to her, and Jemi also crouched by her side. Kaz held up her hands.

"I'm fine, I'm fine. It's just…" She puked again, one hand clutching her stomach as she retched.

"Finish that thing," Jemi said, and Conan stepped forward and sliced the corpse's head in two. He saw a brief flicker of light in its hollowed eye sockets, then nothing.

"What did you sense?" Gannar asked. "Who is doing this? Who killed Ally?"

Kaz wiped her mouth and shook her head. "I have no name, no sense of who or where he is, but…"

"But?" Conan prompted.

"I felt his mind in there. And I saw his face." She looked into some imagined distance, her gaze haunted and horrified. "He's withered but not weak, wrinkled and faded but not old." She paused for a while and her eyes went even wider, pale scars across both cheeks crinkling into deep red lines. "His head is covered with demons."

Conan heard gasps from some of the others. He glanced around at them, then back at Kaz. "Yet you see his face?"

"His bald scalp writhes and twists," she said. She blinked, as if bringing herself back to reality, and looked at Tathar. "Tattoos, but not like yours. His… They move. They're never still. And they speak."

"I recognize this man," Jemi said, and they all turned to face her where she sat up on the wagon's side.

"You've met him?" Gannar asked.

"Na, but I've heard tales told. Drunken whispers, dark taverns, mutterin's on the road—ya know how it is. Story has it he goes by the name Krow Danaz, and he's no man anyone's met, but there're a few who know of him, and he's supposed ta be a sorcerer, driven mad cos his master wuz killed. His master by tha name…" She frowned, scratching her cheek.

"Tsotha-lanti," Conan said.

"You know him?" Fennick asked.

Conan did not answer. He stared at Kaz, as if he might seek confirmation through her haunted gaze.

"Accourse he does," Jemi said. "He's the one that done him in."

Conan nodded, then sheathed his broadsword across his back. His fears about the old dead wizard's involvement had not been confirmed, yet in a way he was still involved, guiding or influencing vengeance from beyond the grave.

Where did that unnatural hawk take the bastard's head? Conan wondered. It did not matter. His path was set.

"So if he can raise a dead army against us..." Gannar began, trailing off, though his implication was clear: What next?

"A dead army that we defeated," Conan said. He turned and started leading the horse away. Wheels ground over the bodies of the dead, and soon they were heading across a battlefield both old and new toward the ruins of the fallen keep and the valley that led beyond.

18

The Devious Dead

Conan remained with the horse, holding its reins and leading it away from the dead and toward the side valley past the castle. Beyond the valley and the hills leading up from it lay Khoraja. Soon, not that day but probably the next, they would reach the giant cliffs overlooking the great deserts, and Conan would be able to make his way toward where Baht Tann said his family was being held. On his journey, he had made no plans about how to tackle whatever he might find there. Tann had told him about the group of bandits and slavers led by the brutal Grake, and now they knew there was a dark magician in league with him. Grake might also have reinforced his gang of bandits, they might have slaughtered their prisoners and thrown them from the cliff, or perhaps they had picked the cliffs clean of heartgems and taken the prisoners to trade as slaves in Shadizar or beyond. Conan had been driven purely by his promise to his friend and the loyalty that powered his soul, but now was the time to think deeply about what they might soon have to face.

The darker aspects made things even more dangerous. The

bandits and sellswords who had launched attacks against him along the road were promised payment for his head, and he could only connect it to his mission. No one else, other than Baht Tann and his beautiful Zenobia, had known where he was going and why. Now this aggrieved student of a dead wizard had sent the dead to drag Conan to him.

It was a strange alliance, for sure. Grake was a barbarian and slave trader. Conan had met and fought enough like him to know that he likely did not embrace the dark arts. Indeed, Conan was a man similar to Grake in some ways, and in his early life he had always turned his back on offers to indulge in or learn matters of sorcery or witchcraft. His power was in his fist and his heart, not in those haunted landscapes that lay beneath and around the truth of the world.

Time would reveal the cold fact about who was helping Grake, and this mysterious sorcerer who had allied against Conan.

They set a good pace. The ruined keep passed by to their left, and Conan was pleased to be leaving the battlefield. The smell of death hung around him, and he craved a stream to wash in. He had considered bathing in the river, but they had given Ally to those waters and he didn't want to pollute it with the remnants that clung and stuck to his skin and tunic, his boots and legs. Heading into the hills, he would find somewhere soon. It was late afternoon now, and he was also looking forward to a rest and some food. The fight had been short but sharp, and though Conan had flowed with fury and his muscles had recalled their warrior's sense, it had made him tired.

Growing old was the one truth he would not be able to fight. Time took no prisoners and gave no quarter. Zenobia always laughed when he mentioned such thoughts, and told him that she was looking forward to growing old with him. And truly, Conan, she would say, did you ever consider that you might make old bones?

A noise came from his left. The flock of yellow birds took flight again from the ruins, but this time they were not singing. They were saving their breath to fly high and fast.

"Oh, Conan," Jemi said. "It ain't over yet."

Conan sighed as the slow sound of stone upon stone ground across the valley. The beginnings of the fallen keep were two hundred feet to their left, splayed across the foot of a hill and climbing some way up the slope. Walls were tumbled, roof structures were smashed and burned and open to the sky, doors were rotted away, and a shallow moat around the castle's outer walls was home now to a lush forest of reeds and a small species of thorny tree. The edifice might once have been grand and a blot on the landscape, but now nature had taken control once again and subsumed what once had been great. Deep history hung heavy across the battlefield and castle—history that should have remained in the past.

"We can run," Fennick said. "Conan, gee the horse up and—"

"If we had two horses, mebbe," Jemi said.

Conan let go of the horse and went back to the wagon. While Jemi urged it onward, Conan climbed into the wagon beside Kaz and Fennick and looked toward the castle.

The sound of shifting stones was louder now, like heavy slabs being moved to one side.

"This is something different," Conan said. "Something worse."

"Worse than that?" Tathar said from behind the wagon. He held his mace by the long handle, its spiked ball and chain spinning behind his back. His tattoos pulled in together as he frowned. The fear on his face was of those unearthly monsters he had seen, the ones he felt he was destined to meet again.

Conan thought, Not this time.

"Smell," he said, and he took in another long breath. The stink of rich, thick oil was obvious, catching at the back of his throat.

"Smells like the oil marshes of eastern Vanaheim," Gannar said.

There was movement in the castle, and as several vague shapes crawled up and over the tumbled walls of the keep, Conan heard a couple of indrawn breaths. He'd been hoping the smell did not mean what he feared, but the things he saw brought home the fact that they were in terrible danger. I should have gone on ahead, he thought. I should have let them go! The image of Ally floating away down the river to eternal rest replayed again and again in his mind, and he did not wish to be the cause of the rest of the Last Song following her.

He did not know enough of their stories. He could not write their songs.

"Marsh drogs from Khitai," Tathar said, and his voice was low, breaking with fear.

"You know them?" Conan asked. "I hoped I was wrong."

"I fought them once on the coast of the Vilayet Sea," Tathar said. "They were ferocious, brutal, merciless, mesmerized giants from the darkest jungles of eastern Khitai. They knew no fear, felt no pain."

"Yet ya lived to tell the tale," Jemi said.

"I was one of a few survivors from a squad of twenty Stygian knights. And there were only two drogs."

Conan counted three, five, ten of the huge shapes shouldering and clawing themselves up from wherever they had been buried, for however long. The ground vibrated beneath his feet as yet more stirred deeper down. Though their scent was horribly familiar, they were also coated in something slick and black, a compound they had been buried in, perhaps, or maybe a fluid their bodies released in death. Their thick limbs caught the late-afternoon sun, throwing oily rainbows. Their movements were slow and deliberate.

Conan felt their unnatural focus aimed entirely at him.

"The ones you fought were living, Tathar," he said.

"By all the minions of Set," Tathar whispered.

"If those monstrosities were dead, then something killed them," Kaz said. "We can do that again."

Conan's mind whirled, not in fear for himself but for the Last Song. That ancient risen army that perhaps in the distant past had battled these marsh drogs had not targeted him, so perhaps these living-dead beasts would also follow instructions not to harm Conan. The mysterious sorcerer Kaz had seen in her vision had invested a lot of effort and the darkest of sorceries to ensure he was brought to them, no matter who or what stood in their way. Just an hour ago, that had been Ally, falling to the brutal blades of dead soldiers. This time, he feared that the rest of the Last Song were doomed.

Conan had once fought an adolescent marsh drog in the deep jungles of northern Brythinia when he was a younger, stronger man. It had almost killed him. He had been fearless at that age, but the years had brought him wisdom and knowledge. He still had no place for the crippling effects of fear, but realism was often the difference between losing in a fight and living to see another dawn.

Every shred of his muscles and tendons told him that he would not triumph against so many drogs, even if he marshalled the talents and strength of the Last Song behind him, yet it had never been in Conan's temperament to surrender. Especially to powers he did not yet know or understand.

"I'll fight, you go," he said.

"What? No!" Jemi said.

"Don't die for me."

"I don't intend to, ya stinkin' oaf, but we're not about ta let you die, either."

"They won't kill me," Conan said. He turned to look at the

others and saw not fear in their eyes but dawning understanding. They were old and experienced enough to share in his wisdom. "But you... They'll stomp you all into the mud, and I'll carry that with me."

"We're not about to—" Fennick began, and Conan interrupted him with a song.

There once was an archer called Fennick
Who said he'd fight, and meant it.

Fennick's eyes opened wide and his jaw hung open. Conan held in a laugh and continued.

He nocked a last arrow
Brave to the marrow,
And...

Conan trailed off. The others all stared at him as if he were mad.

"You see?" he said. "You hear? You want such a voice to sing your final songs?" He turned back to the drogs. They were coming now, big lumbering dead things each twice his size and three times as heavy. Humanoid in build, their limbs were thick as gnarly tree trunks and ended in long-clawed hands and feet, and their stocky bodies were clothed in mud-covered, wrinkled hide. Their heads were a warty afterthought with cratered scalps, deep-set eyes, and gashed mouths filled with long, yellow teeth. Their hands still clasped the jagged metal sheets they favored in battle. They could crush, hack, slash, and these dead-but-risen drogs would barely know the meaning of tired.

"As for my song... here's another verse for you, my friends." Conan leaped from the wagon and ran toward the drogs. He thought the monsters might have paused in surprise, but only for a moment. Then they raised their metal weapons and opened their oily maws to emit high, horrible screeches. It sounded as if death had lain within them for countless years, seeking this escape, and the combined howls sent a violent shiver down Conan's spine.

Without another word, he entered into battle once again.

Closing on the first drog, Conan noticed that the thick, heavy oils used to bury and preserve it also now slowed its movements. It swung its metal hacker at him and he ducked, hearing the sheet whisk by over his head. He slid across loose shale and slashed out at one of its thick legs. His sword sliced in and stuck, and he held on and used his momentum to turn. The drog also turned to look back and down at him, and its hacker swung up and down, ready to take off his arm.

Conan let go of his jammed sword to dodge the drog's weapon. It rammed into the ground and Conan used it as a footrest to launch himself up onto the drog's back, where he drew his knife from his boot and slammed it down into the top of the drog's head. The stench was horrific, the dank, warm feel of the thick oil on his legs and stomach sickening, but Conan held down his bile and plunged the knife in again and again, ruining whatever was left of the drog's brain. It shrugged its huge shoulder and flipped its battered head back, connecting with Conan's guts and winding him, sending him falling from its shoulders. He landed hard on his injured side and grunted, rolling three times to avoid the thing when it slapped a big hand down close by. It raked the ground with stumpy, blunt fingers, searching for him by touch because his blade had ruined its eye sockets. It should be dead! he thought, then remembered that it already was.

He sneaked forward within its reach, dodging its embrace, clasping his sword with both hands and pulling hard. It came free with a wet crunch, and he drove the blade up through the thing's neck and into its head. Spine severed, it slumped to its knees. Whatever facsimile of life had lifted it from its eternal oily grave left it again and the drog was a corpse once more.

Conan tugged his sword and dagger free from the dead thing, using the movement to spin on his foot and cut another advancing drog across the stomach. Its thick leathery hide pouted open and coils of rotten green guts spilled out, hanging down its front and splashing across its feet. It looked down at itself and let out a loud, wet grunt, and Conan jumped to cleave its head in two, but the drog swung a heavy arm and batted him to one side. He landed hard, keeping hold of his sword and swallowing a mouthful of mud, and pushed up onto his hands and knees, spitting muck and blood. Then he heard the drog coming for him, dragging its spilled guts, and tried to stand, but the drog grabbed his right leg beneath the knee, squeezing hard as it lifted him up with no apparent effort. It held him up like that, and Conan saw its upside-down face thrust forward as it examined him.

He slammed his broadsword point first into its face, pushing hard and twisting the blade.

The drog made a strange, high sound more akin to a fragile bird than a monstrous revenant. It released him and stumbled back, and as he fell he jerked the sword to one side and shattered its jaw. A shower of rancid insides splashed down across him as he struck the ground head first. Stunned, he still kept his head, rolling away as the drog dropped to its knees so hard that the ground shuddered, ending up in coils of putrid guts. As the drog tipped forward he jumped to his feet and leaped to one side so that he was not trapped beneath it. His stomach churned and lurched with the smell and taste of whatever had splashed across his face and lips, but he swallowed it down. Vomiting was weakness, and he needed all his strength.

Conan glanced back at the Last Song, fearing what he would

see, but they remained by their wagon, watching his efforts and ready to defend. Fennick stood on the wagon's back with an arrow nocked, Kaz held her crossbow ready, Tathar rested his mace across his shoulders, and Gannar gripped his pike and Ally's curved cutlass in his other hand. Jemi held the horse's reins, slingshot hanging ready from one hand.

"Go!" Conan shouted, but they either did not hear him or pretended not to.

A shadow fell across him and moved away, and he saw a drog to his right break into a lumbering run as it went for the Last Song.

Conan sprinted after it, quickly overtaking it and circling around to stand in its path. I have to make sure, he thought, and he raised his broadsword in both hands. The drog slowed, hesitated, then switched direction to pass around him.

Conan swung in a full circle and hacked down at the back of the thing's left leg. His sword passed most of the way through and the drog fell, its severed leg hanging on by a thick flap of skin. It tumbled and rolled, the slick oil smothering its hide, bubbling and popping as gases it had been holding inside since death erupted.

This time Conan did vomit. He was familiar with the stench of corruption, but a drog corpse's death-fart offended all the gods that ever were and those yet to come.

Still spitting puke, he fell on the fallen drog and hacked its head from its neck with three hard strikes. Thick black fluid that once had been blood dribbled out in a sad splurge, splashing across the ground and turning green grass brown.

He stepped away and turned his back on the Last Song, looking toward the castle and the other drogs that had risen from its depths. He saw eight of them between him and the ruins of the castle walls, and two more crawling out over the fallen structure like fat black slugs. The scrape of metal on stone filled the air, and the drogs acted in sickening unity as they all paused and watched him watching them, swinging their jagged metal weapons back and forth. As the oil had filled and smothered and preserved their dead bodies, so had it also kept rot from their deadly metal sheets.

Conan was strong, but these unnatural things wanted him alive, and that made him stronger. He could fight the drogs one on one and defeat them, though they died even harder than when they were alive. But they all had him in their sights now, and before attacking and killing them all, he had to draw their attention from the Last Song. He could do that by making them think he was running away.

Conan broke right and ran between the nearest two drogs, heading toward the fallen castle where it had once guarded the mouth of the valley. He saw them turning from the corner of his eye.

Good, he thought. Follow me.

He ran on, his breathing easy, muscles flowing, the heavy sword in one hand balancing him as if it were a part of him. Other drogs watched his movements and started after him, and when he reached the eastern extreme of the ruined castle he turned and faced them. He stood on fallen stones, giving himself the higher ground, passing the sword from right hand to left, left to right, catching it without looking. It dripped with grim ichor, and soon there would be plenty more. Soon, he would be surrounded by the stinking bodies of the dead made dead again.

There were eight drogs before him, all turned to look only at him now. A couple of hundred feet behind them were the Last Song, still watching Conan, waiting on and around their wagon. If the drogs attacked them as one, they would be subsumed beneath their evil dead weight.

"Come and take me, if you can," Conan growled, and he readied himself against the drogs' attempt to drag him away.

He heard a sound to his right. Small rocks tumbled, then larger ones. Metal scraped against stone, and he scrambled up the rocky slope to the top of the castle's fallen outer wall. From there he looked down into the guts of the wrecked castle, where nature had taken hold once again. Trees and bushes were shaking, small creatures scampering away, and between the green canopy and the tangle of undergrowth, he saw oily dark shapes pulling themselves up from ancient subterranean spaces—six of them, then ten, then a dozen, living-dead drogs obeying some arcane instruction to reanimate and rise.

Conan surveyed the dreadful scene for a few heartbeats before turning back to the plain beyond the castle and the Last Song. Flee! he was about to yell, but he saw that it was already too late. As if knowing more of their cousins were even now rising from oily graves, the drogs out there had turned their backs on Conan and were converging on the troupe.

Fennick released an arrow, Kaz fired a bolt, the horse reared up in fright, the wagon tilted, and Jemi fell from the seat.

Conan took a step to run and help them, and the rocks beneath him surged up and away from even more drogs trapped beneath. He went at them, slashing and hacking, punching and stabbing, driving them back down to the dark pits of death from whence they came, but every time he destroyed one drog, two more took its place. They glared with decayed eyes given a sickly gleam, and the dark sorcery at work here reminded him again of Tsotha-lanti. They did not fight him, but their weight was enough to drive him close to exhaustion. He caught quick glimpses of the Last Song between their hulking shadows, and he could barely see them or the wagon beneath the oily mass of the living-dead monsters attacking them. He made out a few fleeting shapes—the flashing of swords, the sparking and frantic impact of blades against heavy metal sheets, the horse lifted and torn and pulled apart. He saw the splashing of fresh red blood arcing through the air. The drogs attacked like ravening beasts, and though they fought valiantly and without surrender, Conan witnessed the terrible sight of the Last Song singing their last.

Furious, vengeful, his rage endless and deep and burning bright as the sun, Conan fought on though his muscles ached and protested and pain stabbed and scraped at his body, until his sword arm was gripped and squeezed by a giant hand. His rage gave him new strength, but he feared it could never be strong enough.

They fell upon him then. And while his fury blazed, his heart became heavy with grief when he realized what he had done. He gave one last mighty shrug, roaring and heaving his sword hand free, smashing rotten bones, butting his head against cold dank flesh, but their numbers were too many, their weight too great. When he opened his mouth once more to curse every drog back to the pit, a heavy wet fist pummeled his head against stone.

He heard his own voice raised in defiance. He saw blackness all around him.

Conan's senses faded to nothing.

19

The Triptych Awaits

Shadows move and twist and writhe, lumbering and heavy. Mindless, yet of a mind to obey. Thoughtless, yet thinking all the time of him, and his orders, and what he might yet do to them if they disobeyed. Their empty brains seem to provide a wretched echo of what they had been when alive, and the grim impersonation of living they now continue to project. Their basic thoughts are awash in the scent of hopelessness. Their memories are of darkness and rot, crawling things coming to consume but melting in the slick fluid surrounding them, and long, long time. He feels every moment of that time passing. The feeling is sick and forlorn, the abject sense of eternity offering only insanity as an escape.

Krow Danaz wallows in these feelings. He finds them quite beautiful. He moves from creature to dead creature, and in the hazy gaze of those drogs he sees Conan supported between four of them, each grasping one of his limbs as they bear him onward, closer, closer. With every step he feels Conan's death drawing near. Perhaps he will burn him with the scorching green fires of his sorcery, and in doing so send harbingers of death to also hunt and kill his family. Maybe he will tease Spidderel with the aged barbarian and king, until the beast can hold back no longer and rips him limb from limb, shredding flesh from bones. Or he might simply let the muscled oaf Grake take on Conan and kill him. Danaz might find a use for such a man whose intelligence is contained in his outsized biceps.

However it happens, Conan will be dead before the setting sun casts their shadows out across the great desert.

Bring him, he tells his shambling dead. Bring him to me.

Krow Danaz brought his mind back, riding waves of dark light beneath the veil of what most called reality, and he found himself in his weak and shriveled body once again. He slumped a little, then hauled himself upright next to the fire. Opening his eyes, he saw the final green flames flickering out in the torso of another slave he'd had thrown onto his fire. There were now two scorched bodies before him in the firepit, and Spidderel stood behind him still chewing the limbs of his newest victim.

Danaz thought of his old master, dead for years but still casting a shadow over his life. "Soon your death will be avenged," he whispered, and from somewhere far away, in a place even Krow Danaz could not reach, he thought he heard the echo of an evil voice saying, Soon... soon... soon... He sometimes heard Tsotha-lanti in his mind, and though Danaz had become a great sorcerer in his own right—informed by Tsotha's early guiding hand, yet having bloomed into his own dark world—he could never tell whether this voice was real or imagined.

Grake stood close by, watching Danaz's sorcery with a raised eyebrow. He feigned fearlessness, but Danaz knew that the big man was troubled by his dark arts. It did not matter. Though they were as different as could be, for now their aims were the same.

"Conan draws near," he said.

"And those riding with him?" Grake asked.

"Dead."

Grake nodded, stretching and flexing his heavily muscled body in a pitiful show of strength. Beyond him, away from the cliff face and across the vast deserts toward Kuthchemes and Zamboula, the sun blazed its way up out of the sands to welcome in a new, fine day. The day when King Conan would meet his end.

Danaz giggled, and he felt the shapes and creatures cast into his scalp and skull squirming with delight. He giggled again when Grake turned away and stared out from the clifftop, affecting a powerful, thoughtful stance rather than display his fear at Danaz's bald scalp.

Mylera stumbled into view from behind him, and she did not turn away.

"How close?" she asked. She fingered the small vial hanging around her neck, rolling it between her thumb and forefinger. Danaz could sense the power in its contents, brewed and nurtured by a witch other than Mylera from a combination of living things made dead. He knew that if Mylera used it one more time to cast her mind, thoughts, and intentions toward Conan or someone else, it would be the last of her. Even now she was a shadow of what she had been, walking and cackling through the previous night and out into this new, glorious day. He felt no duty toward her, but he did not want her attempting something that might fail and give Conan a chance at escape. The stricken king was powerless right now, but Danaz more than anyone knew that he should not be underestimated. His dead master was testament to that.

"You are weak," Danaz said. "You should eat and drink and get some rest before—"

"How close?" she asked, dropping to her knees across the firepit from him. The sight and stink of the limbless dead did not trouble her. Madness chased away fear as she stared into Krow Danaz's eyes. Her body was withered within her loose clothing, the skin on her face sloughing like a person twice her age, but there was still strength in her eyes, and a power fueled by rage. Danaz felt a prickle of respect for this fading woman. He knew that she had tried killing Conan already. Her frustration at failing was obvious.

"He'll be here by midday," he said. "Even now he is borne through valleys and up the hillsides toward these clifftops."

Mylera blinked, absorbing the information. "I told you where he was," she said, "so that you could…" She waved at the burned remains before them. "You could have just had him killed."

"Like you tried?" Danaz asked. "No, no. Conan is not so easy to kill. Here, before me, unprotected and unarmed, he'll be powerless. Then you can watch him die. Because that's all you want, right? To know he is dead?"

"Conan dead," she said, and he saw a sparkle of something approaching delight in her mad eyes. She cackled out loud. "Conan dead, in a ditch! Conan dead, in your monster Spidderel's guts!" She staggered to her feet and commenced a dance, feet kicking up dust and hands waving as if to ward off attacking wasps. "Conan dead, today for sure!" She scampered away across camp, laughing at the slaves contained within their cage, skirting around Grake's warriors, who watched her nervously as if her madness might be contagious.

"She used to be a sight to behold," Grake said, watching her go.

"Love?" Danaz asked.

"Huh!" Grake scoffed. "I have no room for love."

"Not in that big broad muscled chest of yours?" Danaz asked. He giggled again. Grake glanced away. *Good, good. Stay afeared of me, warrior.*

"If I had feelings, she destroyed them when she ruined herself."

"Such a shame," Danaz said. "Bringing her so that she could watch you kill Conan and be so, so impressed that she'd fall in love with you."

"I'll kill him nonetheless." Grake took a few steps closer. From behind, Danaz heard Spidderel's carapace click and clack as it tensed, coiled and ready to pounce. To Grake's credit, his eyes did not even flick up toward the beast. "We all have the same desires, my sorcerer friend, no matter our reasons. Now, do you need anything?"

"Another slave."

"To perform more dark magic?" Grake asked.

"Breakfast for myself and my dear Spidderel. This time, make it a young one."

They carried him through the night, and Conan let them. He was not a man prone to submission or surrender, and he did not view his current situation as either. This was grim acceptance that he had led his new friends from the Last Song into confrontation, conflict, and then a most horrible death. This was a chill understanding that if he did not confront those who wished him ill, they had the power to pursue and find him wherever he went. If he abandoned his quest as impossible, if the draw of Zenobia and Conn became too strong and he escaped to make the long journey back to Aquilonia, then the danger would surely follow him. Out here in the wild, that danger was now his alone to confront. He was sad about the Last Song, but now he was on his own, and his fate was only what he made it. Deep down in his heart and gut, that was how Conan always preferred things. He would never turn away from a threat, no matter how harsh or insurmountable it might seem. When there was a chance of that danger being leveled against the ones he loved, his sole aim was to vanquish it and drive it into darkness.

And so, this was also preparation. As the drogs carried him, he rested, recuperating and gathering his strength for the fight to come. He bore his promise to Baht Tann. He also nursed the flame of vengeance, simmering in his heart right now but ready to explode into fire and fury. He would compose his friends' last song in rage and sing it with the flash of steel and the spilling of blood.

His best estimate was that there were seven drogs carrying him. To begin with, four of them had taken a limb each, suspending him between them so that his joints were jarred and sprained and his head and back were impacted by rocks or fallen trees whenever they crossed rough ground. But soon they had found an easier way, taking turns to sling him across their shoulders to transport him away from that valley of death and into the mountains bordering Khoraja and the great deserts beyond. At first, during those moments when they slowed to transfer him from one beast to another, Conan had prepared to escape. He had already identified the drog carrying his broadsword in a decayed leather belt, and he knew that he could fight, grab the sword, and be at them before they reacted. Maybe with the element of surprise he could take down two or three drogs before leaving them behind. He was tired, but he knew he could run faster.

But these beasts were following orders, and they were taking him directly where he wanted to go. Without that advantage, he would reach the cliff edge and have to search back and forth until he found Grake and the sorcerer at the slave camp. This way, he was being carried directly to him and the foul sorcerer he had allied with.

So Conan rested. He remained slack and relaxed, not only

to give the drogs the impression that he was unconscious—he wasn't at all sure their limited walking-dead intelligence reached such levels of such understanding—but also because it made for a more comfortable ride. He was battered and bruised, cut and injured, and he focused all his strength on settling those wounds and injuries.

His mind also rested. His senses told him the sickening truth of where he was—the slick warm feel of the drogs' shoulders and backs and arms was horrible; the stench emanating from their drone bodies was worse than death; their hollow grunts and the tired creak of decayed joints as they negotiated the rough terrain was haunting. But he let his mind settle in a place of peace and solitude, where his son, Conn, grinned and played and laughed, and his love, Zenobia, smiled at him and saved his life again and again.

Darkness began to lift. They had been climbing through rugged forests since just past midnight, and now the trees were becoming sparse. Conan grew more alert, eyes open though he was still slung across a drog's shoulder. He viewed the world upside down, watching for any sight or sound that might indicate they were approaching their destination. He turned his head slightly and spied the drog still carrying his broadsword.

He was ready.

I need a head, she thought, twirling the vial on a cord around her neck. There was a single drop of creore left, and Mylera was starting to understand the implications of using it. She was also accepting that her mistress, Belindra Zarn, had been telling the truth and that Mylera's promise to return to her teachings was hollow.

Her flesh felt loose on her bones. Her hair was falling out in clumps. Her knee joints crackled as she walked, her elbows hurt, and she ached all over, as if her skeleton strove to leave her body. She had found two of her teeth lying beside her that morning when she'd woken in Grake's tent. He had not slept with her. Last night she'd believed this was because he was too wired and ready for Conan to arrive, but this morning when she'd caught her reflection in a water barrel, she had realized the truth. Her mind was still there, though, as focused and determined as ever.

"Today," she muttered, heading away from Grake and Krow Danaz and passing close to the strong cage containing the slaves. Every few steps she skipped, unable to hold back the dance she felt at the prospect of Conan's demise. She had never really cared how he died, or at whose hand, but now that Danaz had revealed he was close, the glorious idea of her killing him presented itself.

"Today," she said again, pausing by the cage and grinning at the wretched slaves contained within. There were a dozen of them, including the family that Conan was coming here to save— perhaps the woman with the two young boys, staring at her now as if she were mad.

I need a head. Maybe one of theirs.

"Today!" she squealed, breaking into a frantic dance that sent up a cloud of dust. "Today, today, today!"

One of Grake's warriors stood guarding the cage. She was a tall woman, heavily muscled, her limbs pierced with countless curved metal spikes that gave her a formidable appearance. Mylera nudged her arm and the warrior stepped away with a look of distaste.

"I need a head," Mylera said quietly, but not so quiet that the slaves did not hear. They had already witnessed two of their number taken away, chopped into pieces, and fed into Krow Danaz's unnatural flames. They stirred and huddled against the rear of their cage, trying not to catch Mylera's eye, trying to hunker down small, small.

The warrior's gaze flicked from Mylera across to Grake and back again. "The slaves are in my charge," she said. "Nothing to do with you and…" She nodded to Krow Danaz and the beast squatting beside him.

"He calls, you send," Mylera said. "Two for his fire and one for his gut already. So now I'm calling. I need a head."

"Use one from his fire," the warrior said.

"I need brains, not ash." Mylera moved toward the warrior, who, though she was scarred with the look of a hundred kills and armed to the teeth, took a surprised step back. She sees the real me, Mylera thought, deep in my eyes, into the very heart of what I could have been. There was a tinge of sadness there, because if she'd remained with Zarn and learned her witching ways for another three or four years, she might have been special. She might have been great.

But what she was doing now was more than special and great. Killing Conan was right.

The woman looked past her again, and Mylera saw something change in her eyes. Grake must have made some sort of gesture, and the woman drew her sword with one hand, the key with the other, and opened the cage's small gate.

It took her a moment to reach in and drag out one of the slaves. They fought and struggled for a while, but the warrior shrugged off their efforts, beat a couple of them to the ground, and grabbed one of them by the hair. It was a young man, one eye swollen closed from an older beating, right arm and right leg shriveled by some sort of wasting disease. His remaining eye settled on Mylera and she looked away.

"Just the head?" the warrior asked. Mylera nodded. A *schwick!* and the man's head bounced into view. She heard his body hit the ground, a gasp from the other slaves, and she snatched the head up by the hair and stared at it face to face. She thought she saw his one good eye still focused on her, filled with hate, but that was impossible. She laughed out loud.

"Today!" she said. She danced in a circle and caught sight of Grake watching her, a look of bemusement on his face. She smiled at him and he looked away.

Is my smile truly so monstrous now?

Perhaps so. She did not care. Today was the day.

Mylera made her own fire, away from the camp and in the shelter of trees. Once she'd spitted the man's head, she used her knife to crack and slice off the top of his skull. The fire lit, his brains starting to steam and then boil, and she took the precious vial from around her neck and pulled out the stopper. She held her breath and looked inside at the final drop of creore, and a jolt of uncertainty hit her.

I will be ending my own life, she thought, but it wasn't that which held her hand. It was the idea that this would not work quite as well as she hoped. She closed her eyes and smelled the flames, and for the first time since leaving she wished she might speak with Belindra Zarn one more time. Creore was a mind-strengthening concoction, allowing the user access to secret realms, arcane plains beneath the reality of things; it was not designed to bring strength to an ailing body. But the idea of dying before seeing Conan's demise was unbearable. She was not certain this would last for long, but she had to try.

She tipped the vial and watched the final drop of creore splash into the slowly bubbling skull. Using her knife, she sliced and stirred the mixture, blending creore with heated brain and fluid until larger, lazier bubbles formed.

"Today," Mylera said. This time, instead of breathing in the sweet fumes and casting whispered spells, she pursued a more basic route through darkest magic. With her blade, she started scooping up the hot fluid and pouring it into her mouth—one gulp, then another and another, not caring about her tongue being singed or her throat scorched and burned. She drank and drank, and when her knife started scraping the insides of the man's skull she tugged the head from its spit atop the fire and tipped it to her mouth, swallowing down the slick, thick, hot contents, her stomach roiling, her tongue blistering from the heat. When the final drops were gone, she grinned at the blackened head and threw it from her, then stood on shaking legs.

Let it work, she thought, if only for a while, only until I see that bastard king dead, let it—

She froze. Her heart hammered, strong and certain. Her senses sang with renewed vitality. It had been only days since she'd left Belindra Zarn and started taking the creore, but it seemed like forever since she'd felt this good.

"Yes," she said, and then she shouted, "Yes, yes!"

To add to her delight, she heard and saw something which made her feel even better. Down the slight slope through the woodlands that led away from Grake's clifftop escarpment camp, something was coming.

Mylera looked at the small knife in her hand and realized that she needed more. She discarded it and ran back through the trees, so strong and excited she was almost flying. She burst from the trees and sprinted into the camp, and as she headed for Grake she saw his look of shock.

"He's here," she shouted. "He's here. And it's going to be today!" She reached Grake and grabbed for one of the two swords in his belt, surprising him. But as she drew the blade, his hand closed around hers.

"Mylera, he's for me to kill in battle."

"I kill him," she growled, and the rage in her voice seemed to smother the whole camp. "I'm strong now, Grake. Feel me, feel me! I... kill... him." Everyone was looking at her—the guards, the encaged slaves, even Krow Danaz and his many-legged beast. She knew that she was wizened and haggard, but her physical form belied the amazing new creore power surging through her muscles and pulsing in her soul.

Grake squeezed her hand harder.

She tugged at the sword.

Conan arrived.

20

Killing Conan

Conan knew they had reached the slave camp because everything around him changed. The trees disappeared and gave way to scrubby grass and gravel, worn and eroded by many footfalls. Sunlight caught the shadows of the dead-but-walking drogs and cast them back the way they had come. The drogs themselves changed, their movements more jerky and excitable.

They are close to their sorcerer master, he thought.

He tried to look around, but he could not see very much. The drog carrying him had him slung across its shoulder, and his upper body and head were pressed against its slick, pustulating back. He saw its feet kicking up dust as the terrain changed from crawling plants to gravel, and he felt a cool breeze as they reached the clifftop. He could act now, but that impulse might put him at an advantage, because he still had no real idea what he faced.

Conan knew when to bide his time.

The drogs stopped at last, and with a heave he was dropped to the ground. He hit hard and held in a groan, affecting unconsciousness so that he could better assess the situation.

"I… kill… him!" he heard a woman's voice growl.

He opened his eyes a crack, glad to find that he'd landed with a clear view across the escarpment. Only a moment later, he wished he could unsee what he had seen.

Calm, calm, Conan thought as shock tried to force his eyes wide, his body to rise ready to defend. I still have the element of surprise, but…

But would surprise aid him against the forces he now saw arrayed against him?

Conan took everything in with a glance. Ahead of him, a huge barbarian and an old woman performed an angry dance. Further to the left, a large bamboo cage contained a group of slaves, their mistreatment apparent in their appearance and demeanor. It might have been fifty days since Tann had left, and he'd told Conan there were twenty or more captives. He saw a dozen now, maybe fewer. Other warriors stood scattered around, all facing him and the drogs that had brought him to this place. He could already tell that they were battle-hardened and brutal, and the one arguing with the woman was one of the biggest men he had ever seen.

Grake, then.

But Conan's attention was ripped away from these mere human enemies by the sight of what awaited him beside a blackened firepit close to the cliff's edge—a huge beast, the size of a horse but with many segmented spidery legs and shiny black body armor that reflected the morning sun. The thing seemed to sway left and right as if readying to launch itself toward him.

Before this monstrous abomination, crouched on the ground beside the dead fire, sat Tsotha-lanti.

It took all of Conan's control to remain motionless, studying his situation and preparing. As soon as he leaped up and grabbed his broadsword from the drog standing nearby, the fight would be joined. He was ready, his muscles itched and tingled, his mind was sharp, but he had to let the shock settle. He had to be ready to face…

He looked again through hooded eyes, and the man sitting before the monster came more into focus. No, he was not Tsotha-lanti after all. Smaller, thinner, his face narrower, his skull was covered with constantly moving tattoos which perhaps told his history, or maybe attempted to reveal the near future yet to come. Kaz had seen this sorcerer in her vision, and Jemi had named him Krow Danaz. He was an old student of the man-thing Conan had decapitated all those years ago, though if anything the sight of him now was even more shocking.

"Welcome, King Conan of Aquilonia," the man said, and his voice was like a metal file drawn down his spine. Conan remained still, silent.

"He's not welcome!" the old woman screamed. "My father died for him, and now he will die for me!"

"He dies by my sword!" Grake said.

"Stop squabbling," the sorcerer said, and the two became silent. "And as for you, you are no longer of use to me." Among the shouting and chaos, every one of the drogs started walking toward the cliffs. Including the one still wearing Conan's broadsword at its waist.

Conan took in a deep breath. His time had come.

"A thousand fathers and mothers have died for me," he said as he stood, and he felt the strength in his muscles, the power in his mighty hands. "And I have killed a thousand more." He dashed to the drog bearing his broadsword and pulled the weapon free, ducking a slow punch, slamming the blade up into its chest and mashing its rotten heart. The thing slumped and fell and Conan stood on it to withdraw his sword.

Danaz was laughing.

"Mine!" the old woman shouted. "Mine today, mine today!"

Conan stood away from the drog as others around it continued their mindless walk toward the cliffs. The first passed Danaz and his beast, reached the edge, and tipped over, disappearing from view. Conan stared at the sorcerer, a man diminished physically yet with an aura of great, dark power sitting around him like a shadowy mist.

"Today is not my day to die," Conan said. "Your mistake was bringing me here to kill you all." He held the broadsword across his body in both hands, gritting his teeth, bracing his feet, anticipating the fight to come.

The raving woman paused for a moment, backing away from Grake and letting go of the sword she'd been trying to draw.

Grake started stalking back and forth, displaying himself like a proud lion, tensing his muscles, parading, and never once taking his eyes from Conan. "Today is the day I take on King Conan in battle, slice his guts open, and chop off his head while he's still screaming for mercy. The day I best Conan the Barbarian, because even if he wasn't fat and old and rusty in the ways of combat, I would still best him!" The warriors around the camp shouted and waved their weapons in reply, and Conan eyed them, assessing and preparing. "Today is the day—"

"Grake," Conan said, and that single name silenced the camp. All eyes fell on him. "That is your name? Grake?"

Grake did not reply, but he puffed up his chest and swung his sword, swishing at the air and throwing up sparks as its point zinged across the ground.

"Sounds like fake," Conan growled, and he took his first step forward.

Danaz moved then, and the beast behind him tensed even more. The mad old woman snatched a sword from the distracted and angered Grake's belt and ran at Conan. And in that moment, Conan realized that though these three might have drawn together into a loose pact intent on his death, they had no real plan. They all wanted to be the one to take his life, for their own personal reasons.

Their chaos would give him an advantage.

"I am no fake!" Grake screamed, but Conan was watching the sorcerer now. The man's scalp tattoos danced and writhed faster than before as he held out both hands toward the firepit by his side. The dead fire burst into unnatural life, sickly green flames surging and pulsing and forming around his hands in a glowing ball the size of a human head.

Conan remembered facing Tsotha-lanti on that long-ago battlefield, piles of dead all around him, and how a bolt of cold fire from his hands had paralyzed Conan and dropped him to the ground. He tensed, glanced around, assessing where he might be able to hide, even as Krow Danaz rose on thin, shaky legs and molded the flame into a smaller, deadlier form.

Behind the unnatural glow, Conan saw the man's face split into a hideous grin.

Conan leaped to the right and fell behind the corpse of the drog he had just killed. The air sizzled and spat as if charged with lightning, and then he heard something whip at the air. He rolled as he struck the ground and came up into a crouch, just in time to see Danaz staggering backward with an arrow piercing his right shoulder. The ball of green flame erupted from his hands and streaked wildly across the escarpment, bouncing from the ground and striking one of the slavers. He burst into scorching fire, his body glowing, his flesh liquefying so that his skeleton became visible as he melted into a gelatinous puddle.

Conan looked back over his shoulder. Fennick grinned at him from the shadows beneath the trees. Kaz appeared close beside him, crossbow aimed. Tathar was there, swinging his mace, and Jemi spun her slingshot where she rode piggyback in a harness on his back. Gannar hefted his pike as he burst from shadows into morning light.

They were all bloodied and battered, but the Last Song were all there.

Conan felt a flood of relief and gratitude as he stood and charged. Where Grake and his slave-trading bandits might have perceived chaos in the sudden attack, Conan observed the opposite. This was a plan coming together—hastily drawn, for sure, but created and refined by five people who knew and loved each other so well. He sensed conflict and confusion in those who sought his death—the mad woman raving, accusing him of her father's death, and seemingly in the grip of some berserker drug or damaging magic; the huge barbarian Grake, too concerned with the myth of himself to be fully conscious of what was happening around him; and the sorcerer Krow Danaz, an obviously accomplished dark magician now with an arrow through the right shoulder—but the Last Song were at peace with each other, not conflict.

They acted and flowed like separate limbs of the same person, and though their minds were their own, each friend fought the same fight.

Tathar dashed along the tree-line with Jemi secured on his back. As he ran, her arm spun and a stone exited her slingshot and downed the warrior guarding the slave's cage. She fell hard with one hand pressed to her throat, rolled to regain her footing, and then Tathar's mace swung down and shattered her skull. He skidded in the bloody dust and used the movement to swing his mace again, catching another bandit across the stomach as he ran in to attack. The man grunted and flinched back, bare stomach open and bleeding, and the swords he carried in both hands swished in and tangled with the mace's chain. Tathar felt the tug as the weapon was almost pulled from his hands and he crouched as if in supplication, only for Jemi to loose another shot from her slingshot. It struck the man in the face, popping his eye and crunching his eye socket. He staggered back and

Tathar heaved the mace up, swinging the spiked ball into the underside of his chin. His jaw shattered, his neck snapped, and his lifeless corpse fell to the ground.

The slaves were hunkered down at the rear of their cage, but two of them took the initiative and started kicking at the cage door, shaking the thick bamboo bars. Tathar nodded to them to continue, turned with his back to the cage, and readied for another attack.

Tathar saw the monster then. *I knew I would meet them again,* he thought, and though he was terrified, in some ways it was a relief. *My time has come.* But this thing was not from elsewhere. He could see and sense that, however horrific and terrible the many-legged beast was, it was of earthly origins, not from beyond.

"What in the name of all the gods…" Jemi muttered on his back.

"The construct of dark power," Tathar said. "That's all." He sniffed. "I've seen worse."

An arrow streaked in from a scattering of tents back toward the tree-line, slicing the old Stygian's upper arm and ricocheting from the cage behind him. He grunted, cursed himself for becoming distracted, and crouched again, offering a smaller target, turning to face the trees and give Jemi some protection. A short bandit emerged from behind the tents with a new arrow already nocked and aimed. Tathar tensed, ready to drop left as soon as he saw the movement of the arrow leaving the man's fingers. Even then, he would have less than a heartbeat to avoid its path.

A crossbow bolt slammed into the man's head and powered straight through, splashing brains and gore across canvas. He dropped like a felled tree, taking the tent down with him.

"There's our Kaz," Jemi said as Tathar found his feet again.

Kaz nodded at him as she ran and ducked down beside a tent,

priming her crossbow and firing one more time. Her bolt came so close that Tathar felt it passing by his left ear, and he turned to take on the woman bandit bearing down on him. She had a bolt embedded in her chest, but she raged and screamed and came on with a heavy battle sword raised.

Tathar feinted left and stepped right, and the warrior stumbled against the slaves' cage as she swung her sword. She screamed a bloodcurdling war cry, and the two slaves trying to smash down the door reached through and clasped her throat. One of them grabbed the bolt with her other hand and twisted, grinding bone, mashing flesh.

As Tathar finished her off, Jemi said, "Now let's get this cage open."

Kaz turned away and loaded her crossbow again. She scanned the camp for dangers, threats, and new targets, and decided she was best placed covering Tathar's efforts to smash open the slaves' cage. As she crouched down beside a stack of equipment belonging to the slavers, movement to her left caught her attention and she saw a heavy shadow shifting beyond the slave cage. It moved closer, mostly hidden in the cover of trees, and at the last moment she saw the long, heavy spear held across its chest. She aimed past Tathar and Jemi, frustrated that the encaged slaves were huddled too close together, offering her no clear view of the target. Before she had a chance to shout a warning, the shadow lifted the spear and aimed it at the gathered slaves.

Kaz knew the way these bastards' minds turned. This attack meant their work here was done and they had no more use of those they had tortured and mistreated.

She took a deep breath and fired. The bolt flicked Jemi's hair as it passed, snapped bamboo splinters from the cage's door, ricocheted from a heavy upright at the rear, and slammed into the bandit center-mass. He or she stumbled back, but not before one of the startled woman in the cage grabbed the spear. She tugged it through the bars, turned it around, and thrust it into the staggering bandit.

And that shot will form part of my song, Kaz thought as she plucked another bolt from her belt. There was a great roar to her right and she saw Gannar taking on two bandits. She loaded her crossbow and waited for the opportunity to shoot.

Gannar parried a sword strike with his pike, countered with his own shortsword, ducked a sweeping blade from the second attacker. One of his attackers was a short, stocky man, covered in scars and stinking of hate; the other was a tall woman with razor blades braided into her long hair, the other side of her head shaved, tattoos across her throat and chest. Their eyes were dark and heartless. Gannar could tell that there was no music in their lives.

He gave them some now, humming as he fought, singing random lines from eulogies he had written with the Last Song. It enraged them more, and he liked that. Some of those slaves were children. His own rage burned deep and constant, but he controlled it rather than letting it control him.

He ranged and roamed, and never went home.

Gannar diverted a sword strike and stabbed with the pike, slashing the woman's shoulder. She barely seemed to notice.

She stood high and mighty, proud of her pain.

The man rushed him and Gannar slammed the pike down, tripping him, kneeling and slashing his sword low to the ground. It parted the flesh across the man's shoulders and he screamed. Gannar went for the killing blow, but the woman was on him, her sword blade raking along the pike and taking off two of his fingers.

He raged and swore, rode and roared, and—

Gannar's voice was strained through the pain, but his skills were not dampened or affected. His next movement drove the pike into the woman's hip, forcing her to half-turn and offering him the side of her neck for his next sword slash. He opened her to the spine. Her screech of agony and fury bubbled out through her lacerated throat, and he leaned on the pike and forced her to her knees.

And her soul took flight, alight and right,
And ever did she cry no more.

The man came at him again, and Gannar dropped onto his back. The man tripped over him and fell on the dying woman, and Gannar stood and pierced them both, their blood flowing together, death holding them close.

And they were both forgotten in death,
Because neither deserved to live.

That final line he made up on the spot, with blood pouring down his arm and pain singing in his mutilated hand. He drew out the pike and turned a slow circle to find another target.

The slaves were free. Tathar and Jemi were beside the broken cage door, and Kaz was there now too, scanning the escarpment and ready to protect the thin, malnourished people. Some of them took up weapons. Gannar caught Tathar's eye and nodded, then he saw two bandits breaking cover from behind a spread of rocks. One of them went down quickly, taken by an arrow from Fennick's faultless bow. The other sprinted at him.

Gannar went to meet the barbarian, his pike and sword composing another song of violence and death.

Fennick plucked one of two final arrows from his quiver and nocked it, looking for another target. There was the injured sorcerer, hunkered on the ground with the monstrous beast protecting him. There was the huge barbarian, bristling with muscles and weapons, standing close to the monster with eyes only for Conan.

And there was Conan, facing a little old woman as if she had something to say, or some unexpected violence to impart.

I will protect King Conan, Fennick thought. Alert for other dangers, the Bossonian archer retreated back into the shade of the trees and waited to pick out his next target.

Conan saw and heard the fighting all around, and he was about to join the fray when the old woman charging at him skidded to a halt in the dust. She held Grake's short blade in one hand, and the gleeful light of violence glimmered in her eyes. If looks could kill, Conan would not have survived her obvious wrath.

Grake stood back and watched, a strange smile on his lips. Behind him, closer to the edge of the cliff, the arrow-pierced sorcerer Krow Danaz hunkered beneath the armored protection of his gruesome beast. As Conan watched, the last of the walking-dead drogs reached the edge of the cliff and disappeared into space.

He believes he can defeat me without them, he thought, and he took caution from that. Krow Danaz was down, shivering in pain and sweating, but he was still powerful.

Conan had expected a direct attack from him or Grake, but instead this ragged-looking woman spat and cursed just a few feet from him. He was old and scarred enough to know never to trust an enemy by their appearances, especially when there was sorcery at hand. And the raving old witch stank of dark magic.

Perhaps it was she who sent those bandits and snake people, he thought, and he said, "I do not know your argument with me—"

The woman charged. She was faster than she looked, and as she closed on him he saw that she was not old at all but driven by whatever sorcery cursed her.

Conan turned his shoulder, thinking of knocking the woman to the ground with his massive weight advantage. But instead of striking him she twisted around, snaking herself behind his back, and slashing him across the shoulder with the shortsword. Conan winced and flinched forward, swinging a fisted hand around to meet her face.

She ducked beneath his arm, stabbing upward and piercing his forearm.

Conan growled and pulled back, holding his broadsword with both hands.

Laughter sang out across the escarpment, a strange sound amid the chaos of fighting and death. It was Grake. He likes the look of himself and the sound of himself too much, Conan thought.

The woman screamed as she came at him again, and Conan heaved his sword up from his side. He felt the parting of flesh, muscle, and bone, and the woman's left arm spun through the air, trailing bloody patterns. It struck the ground with a dull thud.

The woman froze and looked down at where her arm was severed above the elbow. Blood flowed freely, pulsing with her frantic heartbeat.

"Stand down and—" Conan began.

"I am Mylera," the woman growled, and if anything the terrible wound had made her more furious.

"I've never heard of you," Conan said.

"You never heard of my father, either. Ungrateful! He saved

you from pirates and their unearthly beasts in Zingara. High and mighty! Stood between you and their monsters, taken apart by them, eaten, and you do not honor his memory, do not know his name. Bastard!"

Conan looked the woman up and down. She was losing lots of blood, but that seemed to give her more strength. Her telling him her reason for hating him was a precursor to another attack. There would be no easy or peaceful end to this confrontation. He glanced past her to where Grake stood laughing and Krow Danaz glared at him from the shadows cast by his monstrous creation.

She darted at him again, so fast that he blinked in surprise, and an arrow whispered in and sliced across her neck. She coughed blood and laughed, jabbing inexpertly with the sword.

Conan parried and stabbed at her, turning his hips to add power to the sword stroke. She had already leaped aside and jumped on his arm, curling her good arm around and biting hard, taking a lump of flesh and skin from his already-wounded forearm.

Conan turned and caught sight of Fennick aiming another arrow, but the Bossonian was too far away. The woman was now attached to Conan like a leech and he shook his arm to free her, groaning at the pain of her teeth meeting in his flesh, then tossed his sword into his other hand. He was about to cleave the woman in two when he sensed Grake moving close, and he turned to defend himself against the charging barbarian.

Fennick's arrow bounced from the broadsword Grake held up before his body, breaking in two and spinning away, and Grake's grin was wide and confident and entertained no concept of defeat. As he reached Conan, his sword was already moving, swinging in to take his arm.

Conan heaved Mylera even higher, and Grake's sword sliced her open from the base of her skull to the small of her back. She cried out through teeth still clenched in his flesh, and then the cry turned into an impossible, insane laugh. Conan waved her back and forth, her blood splashing his legs and the ground and spurting into his face to blind him, and Grake was skidding low and fast past him, sword still moving and now sweeping around to slice Conan's legs.

Conan jumped, grunting as he carried Mylera's wretched weight as well as his own. He landed hard, just missing trapping Grake's sword beneath his feet.

"There's something on you!" Grake shouted. "A spider, perhaps! A fly! But no, no, a leech, supping on a little of your blood before I take it all."

"You can take this," Conan said. He laid his sword across his bicep and swept it down the length of his arm with all of his great strength.

Mylera's neck was sliced through. Her body dropped at his feet, and it was as if she still sought to tackle him and take him down because somehow her remaining hand reached out and grasped at one of his ankles. Conan took a step to shake her off and tripped, landing heavily on the arm still being bitten and ground between Mylera's teeth. Her screeching and laughter had stopped now, but her eyes rolled in her decapitated head and he could not recall ever seeing such frenzied, mad delight. Some dark sorcery indeed!

He rolled and tugged his leg, freeing himself from her death-grip. He kept his arm beneath his body, hoping that doing so would also loosen her clenched teeth. It did not, but he had no more time to think about that because Grake was stalking closer. The huge man circled as he came, but he did not attack Conan while he was on the ground.

"You want to kill me face to face," Conan said, "to make your legend greater."

Grake grinned like a madman.

"Face to face, then," Conan said, and as he stood he swung his arm. He growled out as the dead witch's head ripped away from his arm with a chunk of his flesh still trapped between her teeth, trailing blood and skin as it flew toward Grake.

The barbarian slammed his sword down and cut the head clean in two.

"Thus ends poor Mylera," Grake said, "and here begins—"

Conan saw Grake's eyes widen a little, and then he sensed movement as Fennick streaked past him, his bow abandoned and his sword raised.

"Fennick, don't—" Conan said, but it was too late. Grake offered a strange smile as he stepped back and Fennick attacked, swinging his sword this way and that, the sound of clashing steel ringing across the escarpment. The Bossonian was much smaller than Grake, but he appeared faster, ducking and slipping beneath the bigger man's sword and jabbing at his exposed belly. Grake flinched back several times, parrying more blows and stepping this way and that, and all the time he was grinning.

He's playing with him, Conan thought, and he dashed forward to join the fight.

Grake saw his movement and his smile grew even wider as he brought his sword down in a mighty two-handed blow, burying the blade deep in Fennick's shoulder and upper chest. Fennick coughed blood and dropped his sword, and the only reason he didn't fall was because Grake held him upright with his sword.

"As I was saying," Grake said, "here begins Grake's greatest triumph." He dipped his hand into a pouch around his neck, sniffing hard at the stuff stuck to his fingers. Then he tugged his sword free from Fennick's shoulder and hacked at him again, and again, butchering the corpse and bathing in his blood and gore.

Conan went for him.

The remaining members of the Last Song screamed in grief and fury as they charged.

And everything changed. The atmosphere across the clifftop started to tingle and buzz, sparks danced back and forth along metal weapons, and Conan felt his hair standing on end. Pulses fired along his arm from the sword handle, and it was only instinct that prevented him from dropping it.

Behind Grake, toward the cliff edge, Krow Danaz was rising to his feet in front of his monster. The arrow was still in his shoulder, but now a mesmerizing white fire burned and wavered along its length, singeing its feathery flight and sparking in the air around it. The tattoos across his head squirmed and moved and rose from his skin like strange hair, twisted entities given form and mass all their own. His hands were held up, fingers splayed. As Conan drew in breath to shout a warning, green sizzling specks of pure energy erupted from the sorcerer's fingertips.

Each speck grew in size as it powered through the air and impacted every member of the Last Song. Tathar fell to his knees and toppled forward onto his face, Jemi slumped on his back. Gannar froze as if pinned to the air, his pike buzzing with fiery power, eyes wide and desperate. Kaz fell onto her side, her crossbow skittering across the ground, and she quivered in frustration as she tried but failed to move.

The freed slaves ran, disappearing into the trees in a panic. Soon they were shadows, and then not even that. Conan wondered which ones were Larria Tann and their sons, and he hoped they might find their way away from this dreadful place and make it home.

Krow Danaz relaxed and dropped to his knees again, but he was still in control. He said, "Grake, I won't give you long."

Conan looked around at the strange, bloodied scene across the escarpment. His friends were frozen and still sparking with energy where they had been struck by Danaz's spell. Fennick was dead and mutilated at Grake's feet. Scattered around were the bodies of Grake's bandits, a couple of them still moaning and writhing as they bled their last into the ground.

Conan felt a flush of grief for Fennick, but he kept it constrained. It must feed him, not hamper his efforts. It must aid his vengeance.

"Your people are finished," Conan said.

"You're all I care about now, Conan," Grake growled. "You, on the end of my sword. And after I'm done with you—"

"I don't need drugs to be a man," Conan said and wielded his sword, given strength by his wounds. They were proof of life, the same as the scars that marked his body from head to foot. These were merely new scars that would form and blend in, becoming a part of him while Grake's name faded into obscurity.

Grake's smile slipped as he grew more serious. "Look at you, Conan. You're old, weak, slow. Once I kill you, all will know my name, and everything will belong to me. Grake, the greatest warrior who ever lived. Grake, the man who bested the mighty Conan in combat. Grake—"

"—the fake," Conan said, and Grake came at him. Which was just what Conan wanted.

Grake was taller than him by six inches and more heavily muscled, but Conan had fought and defeated larger warriors and less-than-human things before. He knew that not every conflict was about brawn, because the brain could be the strongest muscle.

He fell back beneath Grake's first assault, fending off three heavy sword strikes, five, seven, sparks flying as broadswords met and clanged and scraped each other aside. He stumbled back, pummeled beneath Grake's undeniable strength. There was no humor in the bigger barbarian's expression now, no bluff and bluster. His smile had fallen into a determined grimace. He was all fight.

Almost falling onto his back, Conan let the assault continue for a time until Grake showed the first signs of carelessness. He really does think I'm old and weak, Conan thought. That will be his downfall. When Grake's violent assault lessened and a look of dawning triumph chilled his expression, Conan went on the offensive.

He deflected the next sword strike, stomped Grake in the right knee, and jumped up to elbow him in the nose. Grake grunted as blood bloomed across his face and his eyes watered. Conan pushed the assault home, kneeing him in the stomach so hard that he crumpled to one side.

Conan swung his sword down but Grake was ready, parrying the blow and driving a fist down into Conan's shoulder. Pain bloomed all down his left arm and his hand went numb.

Conan caught sight of his Last Song friends still paralyzed by Krow Danaz's magic, and the sorcerer himself still watching this spectacle. His spider-beast had advanced a few steps now, readying to join the fight.

Grake came again, swinging his sword in both hands. Conan braced to deflect, but it was a ploy and he did not see Grake's pivot as his right foot kicked out into Conan's stomach. The breath whooshed out of Conan and he stumbled back, winded. Grake gave him no chance to catch his breath before leaping forward and punching, kicking, swinging his sword.

Conan ducked down and twisted away beneath the assault, elbowing the bigger man in the kidneys as he crouched behind him. As Grake grunted and turned, Conan slashed his sword upward for the killing blow.

Grake caught the sword in his left hand, before its point dug in beneath his ribs, and squeezed hard, blood pulsing from his lacerated palm and fingers. Conan pushed harder. Grake grimaced, sweating, and slowly he turned the sword away from him. He let go and flinched back, and the unexpected movement sent Conan falling into him. He could smell the bigger man's sweat, his unwashed stink, and the scent of fresh blood as Grake locked both arms around him, bringing Conan's face in close to his chest.

"There, there," Grake said as he lifted and squeezed.

Conan let out all his breath, then drew in and expanded his ribcage with all his might.

Grake lifted him higher, then slammed Conan's feet down onto the ground. And Conan punched him in the balls—a weak spot for any man, Conan knew, no matter how strong.

Grake let go and crouched down, glaring at Conan through clenched teeth.

Conan backed away to give himself enough space to swing his sword, then kicked out with his left leg, lifting his foot high and driving his heel into the taller man's chin. Taking advantage of Grake's stunned shock, he brought his foot down in a forward step and hacked at his opponent's tree-trunk leg.

Grake cried out and smashed at the embedded sword with his own, and the action shook both of their grips. The weapons clanged to the ground and bounced away.

Conan tried to grab a breath, but Grake had other ideas. He came at Conan punching and kicking and biting, a mountain of muscle and fists, feet, and teeth. Conan stood up to him, taking some blows and returning them. It had been a while since he'd been beaten with such strength and fury, but though it hurt, it also energized him. Conan had always been fight, never flight. He slammed his bloody-raw forearm into Grake's mouth, and perhaps it was surprise or maybe disgust at tasting where Mylera's determined head had been clasped on, but Grake's eyes went wide and he paused in his assault.

Conan continued his, and one well-placed punch crunched the big man's already-mashed nose and drove him down to his knees. Grake reached for his sword and grabbed the handle, just as Conan found his own. Steel clashed, sparks flew, swords sang—

And once again, something changed.

Conan sensed it, a pause around them ending, a stillness breaking. As he felt a strange vibration beneath his feet, he heard Danaz's voice.

"Boring. Spidderel, kill them both."

Grake's eyes went wide, and Conan turned to see the many-legged beast running at them across the escarpment. Motionless, it had been monstrous, a statue of something that should not be. Moving, it was death given form.

"Together, eh, Conan?"

I'll not please him with a reply, Conan thought, but he and Grake had time to bring their swords up before the thing reached them.

Conan had believed it spider-like, but up close he realized it was so much more, with ten limbs or more, each of them sprouting vicious barbed hooks. He slashed at the barbs and cut several away from the limb bearing down on him, stepped to one side, then swung at the thick limb itself. His sword bounced away from its tough carapace armor, black sparks dancing in the air for longer than they should. The thing stank of rotten flesh and dark depths, and Conan retched and spat as he ducked beneath another swinging limb. He darted forward toward the thing's gross body, not away, and jabbed upward. Again, the sword skimmed across hard armor and cut only the air.

Spidderel's body was the size of a big horse, four segments linked by thick, flexible leathery connections from which a steaming fluid slow-dripped and spattered through the air. One drop splashed Conan's lower leg and immediately started burning, searing skin and setting his flesh aflame. He wiped it away with his sword and continued the movement, aiming up at a spread of this apparently softer connective tissue. The creature shifted and his sword clanged harmlessly against its belly armor.

Its limbs slammed down and rose again and again as it

performed a frantic attacking dance. Dust and gravel showered Conan from these impacts, and he saw Grake also similarly coated in dust. The big barbarian was ducking and slinking, avoiding the deadly limbs and hacking at them when he could. He caught Conan's eye and grinned.

Conan crouched and scooped up a handful of dust, and as he rolled to avoid a scathing limb he rose into a crouch and flung the handful into Spidderel's monstrous face. Its mandibles clicked and clacked, its wet mouth gaped, and it let out a high-pitched roar that caused Conan to retch again at the stink of the thing. He hacked at a limb piercing the ground close to his feet, putting all of his mighty strength into three heavy sword blows. The limb's thick skin cracked at the first blow, shattered at the second, and his third strike severed the leg completely. Its bottom half, the size of his own leg, fell to the ground. Thick black blood spilled, steaming and hissing, and he was careful not to let any splash across his skin.

"First blood to Conan!" Grake shouted. He tried to copy Conan's move and scooped up a handful of dust, but Spidderel had become wise to that. It slammed Grake aside with a heavy impact from one of its legs, then went to stab him through the chest. Grake deflected the blow with his sword and rolled out of reach, standing and quickly entering the fray once again.

"The eyes!" Grake said. "The neck! The only weak points I can see."

Conan ducked around a swinging leg and looked up at the thing's horrible face. Above the gaping maw of a mouth and the slick mandibles set around it was a scattering of dark globes, which he'd first thought were pus-filled boils of some kind but he saw now were small eyes—scores of them, peppering the high head. Some were still coated in the dust he'd thrown, but Spidderel's mouth mandibles worked at them, brushing and stroking with a surprisingly delicate touch to clear its vision.

Conan left the eyes to Grake and jumped around and between the thing's legs, keeping watch on the body suspended above. The segments were well protected, but where its head section met the torso he saw loose flaps of leathery skin exuding that thick, noxious fluid. Maybe Grake was right.

Conan went for the neck, stabbing up and feeling his sword almost sucked in with a horrible wet sound.

Spidderel screeched again, and Conan thrust his sword harder and higher, ducking down and pushing forward beneath the monster's heavy body, feeling and hearing the sword crackling and slicing through its insides. He glanced to the right and saw Grake standing before the beast, his body sliced and bleeding from dozens of cuts from its leg spines. But his sword was buried high up in the thing's face, both hands raised above his head, legs braced, muscles knotting as he hauled the sword left and right to cause maximum damage.

He reminded Conan of a younger version of himself.

Spidderel's limbs started thrashing more violently than before. Conan clutched his sword's grip, and with a powerful shove from his legs he tugged the thick blade all the way through the thing's neck. Sickening blood splashed down around and on him, scorching his skin, and he sensed the body above him slumping down.

Making a momentary decision, Conan let go of his blade and jumped out from beneath the dying creature. He struck the ground and rolled, trying to wipe away as much of the burning blood as he could. He felt a heavy *thunk!* as Spidderel hit the ground, and its scream lessened into a sad mewling. He turned and saw that its head was mostly detached from its body, mandibles scratching at the air as if to hold on to its unnatural life. Its legs slammed down and up, down and up, in a vain attempt to lift itself up again. One of these limbs crashed across Conan's legs, pinning him to the ground.

Grake was at its head, and he rammed his sword down into its mass of eyes one more time.

With a final gurgle, Spidderel died.

Grake came for the trapped Conan without pause. He presented a fearsome sight—a mountain of a man, marked by scars both old and freshly made, coated in his own blood and the dark, smoking blood of the vanquished monster.

"What songs they'll sing about us, Conan!" he shouted as he raised his bloodied sword.

"Your song is a sad one," Conan said, and he grabbed Spidderel's severed leg and thrust upward.

The limb's tip pierced Grake's navel and Conan used all of his strength to sit upright, shoving hard. The leg drove in and up, parting Grake's skin and flesh, entering his stomach cavity and carving upward, shattering ribs and shredding organs.

Grake's eyes widened, his mouth gaped, and he died still holding his sword aloft in a killing blow.

"Noooooooooo!" Krow Danaz screamed. "Spidderel! Spidderel!"

Conan struggled beneath the dead monster's heavy limb, trying to writhe his way out. Grake tipped slowly sideways, and as he fell Conan grabbed his sword and plucked it from his dead grasp. He pulled free at last and stood, ignoring the pains of his injuries and the blood and the dizziness and the burning in his legs, because he knew that if he did not act he would have only moments left to live.

The Last Song remained paralyzed by the sorcerer's glamors, and a greenish glow had diffused all across the escarpment.

Conan edged around the bulk of the dead creature and looked toward the cliff edge. There stood Krow Danaz on shaky legs, a weak figure physically, yet now he was conjuring a green-tinged glow in both hands above his head, and his face was a rictus of rage.

"My Spidderel!" he spat, and his breath erupted into flame that shimmered in the air.

Conan started running. Grake's sword felt solid and powerful in his hand. His body was alight and alert from the fight, but he had a hundred feet to cover.

"My master…" Krow Danaz said, breath flaming even more.

Conan sprinted against time, because Danaz was heaving the ball of blazing energy back to fling it, and Conan knew he had only seconds left.

"…this is your vengeance."

Conan tried to run even faster. Eighty feet, sixty, fifty—

He saw a flicker of movement behind the sorcerer, and a woman and two boys mounted the escarpment from the cliff face. The woman ran one way, the boys the other, and seconds later they flipped a rope over and around the diminutive sorcerer, circling him and pulling tight.

He fell to the ground.

The flaming-green ball sputtered and faded, spattering to the ground around Danaz just as Conan reached him.

Krow Danaz was fighting against the rope, and even now the spilled green fire was eating away at his bindings. He grimaced and then grinned at Conan, because a man like this could not be beaten. A wizard, a witch, a sorcerer, a man of dark deeds and darker heart, he would never accept defeat.

And so Conan knew what he had to do.

With one sweep of his sword he sliced the man's head from his shoulders. He kicked the head over the edge of the cliff, then pushed the body with his feet. One final kick sent it too sailing into space, the climbing rope trailing behind it.

The violence ceased, and for a few heartbeats peace fell across the escarpment. Then the woman spoke.

"You must be Conan," she said.

"And you must be Larria."

Hearing groans and cries from behind him, Conan turned, ready to raise his sword again even though his muscles and soul were drained from the fight. But he saw his friends from the Last Song stirring from their fugue, released now from the sorcerer's binding spell. Tathar and Jemi sat against the cage's broken walls, Kaz held her head and rubbed at her temples, and Gannar was on his feet, advancing toward Fennick's sad corpse and ready to fight.

Conan held up one hand to them all, signaling that the fight was over.

"Thank the gods," Gannar said. "I've got a hangover from hell."

"Conan—" Larria said, but she got no further.

A growling, roaring sound echoed across the escarpment, shaking the cliffs and vibrating through the ground. Beyond, far from the cliff face, Krow Danaz's body and his decapitated head rose into view on flaming green wings, shimmering like heat haze against the vast deserts beyond as they were carried away to the east. The noise lessened as the sorcerer's body parts grew ever more distant, and soon they were lost to view.

"And so perhaps he lives to fight another day," Kaz said from beside Conan.

"That is always the way with the worst of them," Conan said.

Gannar looked him up and down. "You look like shit."

"I feel worse."

"You killed the big spider monster thing, though."

He shrugged. "I can't deny Grake's help with that."

"Then I suppose we sing that into his song," Jemi said. She was still on Tathar's back, and they joined them at the edge of the cliff.

"You'd sing a song for Grake?" Conan asked.

"It's a good story," Jemi said. There were tears on her cheeks, and Tathar also cried. Kaz and Gannar stood close to them, and the four remaining members of the Last Song held each other, unashamed of their shared grief.

"But first, a song for Fennick," Conan said. "Already a friend to me, I can't imagine what he was to you."

Conan led Larria and the two boys away from the Last Song, giving them space and peace.

"Baht is well?" Larria asked.

"When I left him, he was being cared for by my leech. I can't imagine Baht Tann would have let himself die before knowing you were all well."

"Thank you, King Conan. For me, and for Baht and our children. This is Davin, and this is Korum."

"You're as brave as your father," Conan said to the boys.

"We're cliff spiders…" Davin said.

"…and we didn't run away like the others," Korum said.

"I'm glad for that," Conan said. "You saved my life."

"Hear that, boys?" Larria said. "You saved the life of a king."

The boys frowned at Conan.

"Doesn't look like a king to me," Korum said.

Davin nodded his agreement. "Looks more like a barbarian."

21

A Song of Conan

"I thought you were all dead," Conan said.

He sat back against a tree while Kaz tended his wounds. The others of the Last Song also had injuries, and they were helping each other treat and bind them. Their real wounds were deeper, though. Conan could already sense them drawing together to heal, closer and stronger than before.

But Conan's physical damage was the most severe, and would leave the harshest scars. He did not mind. His life was imprinted upon his body, and this was simply another chapter.

"So did we, for a moment," Tathar said. "Then Fennick…"

"Fennick fought like a demon," Jemi said, "an' he said, 'Bollocks to this, Conan needs our help.' So we all fought with 'im."

"I cast a glamor," Kaz said. She pursed her lips and did not look up from treating Conan. The rest of the camp fell silent. Tann's family fed the fire and cooked a couple of rabbits they had caught while the Last Song hummed a little beneath their breaths as they worked. Conan was growing used to that, and was even starting to like it. They had all been through traumatic times, and they drew close through music, even if it was mostly tuneless and without direction for now. "Just a small one. It hurt as much as ever, but for a few seconds we were all dead already in the eyes of those stinking drogs. That gave them pause, and that afforded us a chance."

"I imagined myself covered in gore and protected from sin-ravens," Gannar said, touching the necklace of shriveled ears he still wore. "And instead of their mindless dead faces, I saw on the drogs the visages of each and every one of those mercenaries I've already hunted down and killed."

Conan looked to Tathar. The Stygian was silent, staring into the distance beyond the cliffs while tears streaked blood and dirt down his cheeks. After a while he felt Conan's gaze on him, and he glanced sidelong at the king.

"You know my story," he said. "I'm destined to die at the hands of unearthly beasts, not those filthy living-dead drogs. So I tried to fight as hard as Fennick."

"By Gullah, those things stank!" Kaz said.

"So'll you when yer a century dead," Jemi said.

"Thank you for coming after me," Conan said.

"Weren't about to leave you to them things," Jemi said.

Conan nodded his thanks to each of them. They accepted. That conversation was done.

"That thing." Gannar nodded across the escarpment at the remains of Spidderel.

"I made sure it's dead," Conan said.

"Right, sure. Like the wizard who lost his head and died, and then flew away in two parts."

"You want to push it off the cliff?" Tathar asked.

No one agreed to that. Spidderel was a dead, heavy mass, and they were all tired.

"I guess you'll be heading home to your kingdom now?" Kaz asked.

Conan grunted.

"Home to yer throne an' politics an' all that fun," Jemi said.

Conan winced as Kaz cleaned the burn on his leg where the monster's blood had splashed him. He wondered if she had prodded hard on purpose.

"You're... Are you thinking I'd rather come with you?" Conan asked.

"Ha! You can't hold a tune," Tathar said, and there was a flurry of mirth around the fire at that.

"You're a man of violence," Kaz said. "Our life wouldn't suit you."

"Am I so different from you all?" he asked.

"Are you a man seekin' a path of peace?" Jemi asked.

Conan did not answer.

"Cos that's my story," she said. "There's a long tale, which I ain't often told, an' I only tell to those who seek what I offer. But there's a shorter version, too. I lost my son and daughter to violence an' war. They chose that path, followin' their bastard father, thinkin' wealth and adventure is what makes a person. I told 'em it ain't like that. They didn't listen. And..." She shrugged, but she did not break eye contact with Conan. "They died. Don't matter where or how. Next thing, I was wanderin' the land, making music and singin' songs about my dead children, and I bumped into Kaz here. She was seekin' her own path, and our aims sorta... converged. Then the others joined us, in dribs and drabs, the ones you know and a few you never did. An' that became my new journey in life. Mother to two dead 'uns, now I sing an' steer others from the path that took them."

"I respect that," Conan said. "You've all more courage in your little fingers than most of those I know back in Aquilonian society. But like Tathar says... I cannot carry a tune."

"Yer always welcome with the Last Song, King Conan, should ya wish to learn."

Conan smiled and nodded at Jemi.

Kaz sat back from tending to Conan's wounds, looking him up and down. "There. All done. You'll be hurting and aching in the morning."

"What's new?" Conan said. "I carry these years, despite trying to believe otherwise."

The food was ready. They shared and ate. The Tanns' boys stayed close to Conan's side, gazing at him as if he were a wild animal, which he supposed in some ways he was. Their father had been like him a long while ago, but he'd found some route to change his life in a similar way to the Last Song.

Conan's life had twisted and turned over all these years, yet he had always maintained a course of barbarism. Sometimes that was obvious, sometimes more camouflaged beneath a veneer of civilization. Yet he knew from experience that the honesty of the life he chose held more value than the lie of denying one's true course.

The Last Song had showed him that. They were honestly in love with what their lives had become. Conan ate rare rabbit and listened to their humming turn to words, and as they slowly started to compose a song to another dead friend, he admitted to himself that he could see the allure in what they had.

But it was not a life for him.

"I'll head away in the morning," he said. "My dear queen Zenobia and my son await me, and it's them who draw me back. Not my throne. Not the kingdom I am steward of, for a while. And I have an old friend waiting for me. It will be good to see him reunited with the family he loves."

"You're a man of rare honor, Conan," Larria said.

"I just keep my promises," Conan said.

The Last Song sang into the evening, composing Fennick's tale and segueing seamlessly into that of Allymaro the pirate. Then more songs, moving from tune to tune, myth to myth.

Some of the names they sang about he recognized, others he did not. He absorbed it all, because Conan knew that a person who stopped learning was one who ceased living.

As he started to drift off, feeling safe and content for the first time in many days, he heard his name mentioned beneath Kaz's whistling and Tathar's loud humming.

"Enough of that!" Conan said without opening his eyes. With friendly laughter, the Last Song fell quiet for a while, and only the crackling fire and the cries of night animals sounded across the camp. As he fell into sleep, he thought, Only I am destined to write the end of the song of Conan.

ABOUT THE AUTHOR

Tim Lebbon is the *New York Times* bestselling author of *Eden*, *Coldbrook*, *The Silence*, and the Relics trilogy. He has also written many successful movie novelizations and tie-ins for *Alien* and *Firefly*. Tim has won a World Fantasy Award, four British Fantasy Awards, a Bram Stoker Award®, a Shocker, a Tombstone and been a finalist for the International Horror Guild and World Fantasy Awards. *The Silence* is now a gripping Netflix movie starring Stanley Tucci and Kiernan Shipka.

A NEW ERA OF BRAVERY AND HEROISM!

COMICS AND COLLECTIONS

CONAN THE BARBARIAN VOLUME 1 | CONAN THE BARBARIAN VOLUME 2 | CONAN THE BARBARIAN VOLUME 3 | CONAN THE BARBARIAN VOLUME 4 | CONAN THE BARBARIAN VOLUME 5

CONAN: BATTLE OF THE BLACK STONE | THE SAVAGE SWORD OF CONAN VOLUME 1 | THE SAVAGE SWORD OF CONAN VOLUME 2 | THE SAVAGE SWORD OF CONAN VOLUME 3

REMASTERED, OVERSIZED, OMNIBUS EDITIONS

CONAN THE BARBARIAN ORIGINAL COMICS OMNIBUS VOLUME 1 | CONAN THE BARBARIAN ORIGINAL COMICS OMNIBUS VOLUME 2 | CONAN THE BARBARIAN ORIGINAL COMICS OMNIBUS VOLUME 3 | CONAN THE BARBARIAN ORIGINAL COMICS OMNIBUS VOLUME 4 | CONAN THE BARBARIAN ORIGINAL COMICS OMNIBUS VOLUME 5

THE SAVAGE SWORD OF CONAN ORIGINAL COMICS OMNIBUS VOLUME 1 | THE SAVAGE SWORD OF CONAN ORIGINAL COMICS OMNIBUS VOLUME 2 | THE SAVAGE SWORD OF CONAN ORIGINAL COMICS OMNIBUS VOLUME 3 | THE SAVAGE SWORD OF CONAN ORIGINAL COMICS OMNIBUS VOLUME 4 | THE SAVAGE SWORD OF CONAN ORIGINAL COMICS OMNIBUS VOLUME 9

EXPLORE THE FULL RANGE ONLINE!
TITAN-COMICS.COM

CONAN (R) AND © CPI

CONAN: CITY OF THE DEAD

John C. Hocking

Two epics in one book!

The long-awaited follow-up to *Conan and the Emerald Lotus* brings John C. Hocking back to the sagas of the Cimmerian.

In *Conan and the Emerald Lotus*, the seeds of a deadly, addictive plant grant sorcerers immense power, but turn its users into inhuman killers.

In the exclusive, long-awaited sequel *Conan and the Living Plague*, a Shemite wizard seeks to create a serum to use as a lethal weapon. Instead he unleashes a hideous monster on the city of Dulcine. Hired to loot the city of its treasures, Conan and his fellows in the mercenary troop find themselves trapped in the depths of the city's keep. To escape, they must defeat the creature, its plague-wracked undead followers, then face Lovecraftian horrors beyond mortal comprehension.

TITANBOOKS.COM

For more fantastic fiction, author events,
exclusive excerpts, competitions, limited editions and more

VISIT OUR WEBSITE
titanbooks.com

LIKE US ON FACEBOOK
facebook.com/titanbooks

FOLLOW US ON TWITTER AND INSTAGRAM
@TitanBooks

EMAIL US
readerfeedback@titanemail.com

FOR EVERYTHING CONAN RELATED
CONAN.COM